JUDGE DREDD

WHIT

A massive pile-u sinister mystery fc troyed tanker truck turns c ily disguised transport, but the cc ave been stolen. Is there illegal weapons research going on in the city? Meanwhile, small-time criminal Wes Smyth has discovered the Skorpion, an artificially intelligent weapon that transforms him into an unstoppable killer, and he's using it to exact petty vengeance on his rivals.

As the body count begins to pile up, Dredd goes head-to-head with Smyth and a weapon that's programmed to anticipate his next actions!

It's an edge of your seat, futuristic battle to the death in the streets of the largest, most lawless city on earth.

Judge Dredd from Black Flame

DREDD VS DEATH
Gordon Rennie

BAD MOON RISING
David Bishop

BLACK ATLANTIC
Simon Jowett & Peter J Evans

ECLIPSE
James Swallow

KINGDOM OF THE BLIND
David Bishop

THE FINAL CUT
Matthew Smith

SWINE FEVER
Andrew Cartmel

More 2000 AD action from Black Flame

ABC Warriors

THE MEDUSA WAR
Pat Mills & Alan Mitchell

RAGE AGAINST THE MACHINES
Mike Wild

Durham Red

THE UNQUIET GRAVE
Peter J Evans

THE OMEGA SOLUTION
Peter J Evans

Rogue Trooper

CRUCIBLE
Gordon Rennie

BLOOD RELATIVE
James Swallow

Nikolai Dante

THE STRANGELOVE GAMBIT
David Bishop

IMPERIAL BLACK
David Bishop

Strontium Dog

BAD TIMING
Rebecca Levene

PROPHET MARGIN
Simon Spurrier

RUTHLESS
Jonathan Clements

DAY OF THE DOGS
Andrew Cartmel

Judge Dredd created by
John Wagner & Carlos Ezquerra.

Chief Judge Hershey created by
John Wagner & Brian Bolland.

JUDGE DREDD

WHITEOUT

James Swallow

With eternal thanks to:
Ashley Levy (Master of Elephants)
and Jane Saint (Queen of the Fairies).

A Black Flame Publication
www.blackflame.com
blackflame@games-workshop.co.uk

First published in 2005 by BL Publishing, Games Workshop Ltd., Willow Road, Nottingham NG7 2WS, UK.

Distributed in the US by Simon & Schuster, 1230 Avenue of the Americas, New York, NY 10020, USA.

10 9 8 7 6 5 4 3 2 1

Cover illustration by Clint Langley.

ISBN 13: 978 1 84416 219 2
ISBN 10: 1 84416 219 2

A CIP record for this book is available from the British Library.

Printed in the UK by Bookmarque, Surrey, UK.

THE CURSED EARTH, 2125

It had been hunting them for three days, non-stop, day and night. A ghost in the shadows of the twisted wasteland around them, appearing only in the moments before it struck out and killed. As one, the ragged cadre of Mutancheros who formed Happy Bruce's murderous band had decamped from the rubble-strewn ruins of the Boulder Pebbles and fled southwards, toward what they believed would be the relative safety of the Denver Death Zone. To be precise, that was what they had done after Happy's head had popped like a yellow-skinned balloon, there in the middle of his speech about how they'd find this invisible maggot and crush him like a munce bud.

Before Happy's messy death, right there in the middle of their camp, right there surrounded by eighteen of his hardest, most unpleasant banditios, the gang were in relatively upbeat spirits about killing the interloper. A couple of the newbies, the kids Happy had forcibly recruited from the ghetto settlement at Leadville, had been the first to go. Both of them died real quiet like, nothing but a hot hiss of molten flesh and steaming blood-vapour to announce their ends. Derek the Teeth saw the killer moving like liquid mercury across the stonework over their heads. His whistle had roused everyone, but in that few seconds the figure was gone.

Derek liked to think he knew something about everything, and he insisted that the wet-nosed boys had been murdered by Gila-Munja, the claw-handed tribe of malformed killers that terrorised the Western Ranges; Happy had, quite correctly, pointed out that Gila-Munja didn't use energy weapons because they lacked the opposable thumbs to even pick the damn things up, to which Derek had mouthed off, only to get Happy's fist in his mouth. While they were fighting, a third and then a fourth beam shot had taken the lives of High Hand Freddie and his buddy Lester. About that time, panic had set in.

So they ran and scattered for a while, finally regrouping in the usual place, the artificial cavern formed when the Boulder SupaMall had collapsed in on itself during the Atom War. In the hollowed-out chamber, the slagged remnants of high-fashion stores and food court franchises had melted into a post-nuclear frieze. There were arcane symbols and words across the walls that had no meaning to Happy's illiterate troupe, and dead norms still sealed under sheathes of molten plexi-plasteen, coated in floods of the see-through plastic in the seconds after Boulder had been air-burst by Sov MIRV warheads. Happy sat on the Fat Guy, the preserved corpse of a rotund fellow who had been on his hands and knees when the nuke strike came, reaching for a TasteeBurger that had dropped off his tray. The dead man's bulk formed a natural podium from which Happy could expound to his gang.

Happy got his name from his head; it was a bloated fleshy sphere in jaundice-yellow with black, beady eyes and a mouth that was far wider than it should have been. His mutation kept his lips in a permanent smirk of amusement, even in moments like this one, when he was angry and quite afraid. Happy brought himself up to his full height and started to rant about the unseen killer. Days earlier, the Mutancheros had swept down on a band of hapless Helltrekkers out of the Big Meg and killed everyone they could. It had been poor pickings and Happy was sure that some of the norms had got away. This, he reasoned, was who had killed Lester, Freddie and the others: the survivors coming after the mutants for revenge. Happy was an unsubtle person, and he lacked even the most basic understanding of anything beyond the coarsest emotions. If he had known the real reasons for the deaths, there would have been no comprehension behind those doll-like eyes of his. Happy Bruce's spitting and snarling reached a crescendo and that was when he died, just at the instant calculated to create the biggest reaction in his audience. Fragments of his skin and bone went everywhere, coating the Fat Guy in hot blood and brain matter. The gang tore the air with gunfire and shouts, firing as they ran from the ruined mall. Like ants from a smoke-filled nest, the Mutancheros poured out into the weak daylight and mounted their vehicles, fleeing something so invisible that it could walk right past them and into the very heart of their secret camp.

In a roar of combustion-fuelled engines they fled, leaving Happy's decapitated corpse to cool and decay among the shrink-wrapped bodies of dead shoppers.

Inside the operations room, the air was dry and thin, the moisture drawn from it by the faint ozone scent of the computers and monitoring systems that crowded the rectangular compartment. There was little direct lighting aside from soft tactical lanterns and the cold glow of the console displays. A low, distant rumble formed the background to the chorus of whispered commands and mournful beeps as the technicians worked their panels; once in a while a flutter of far away sound would accompany a slight twitch in the decking.

The senior scientist glanced up and blinked at the brief sliver of light from the corridor outside, the security hatch opening and closing like an iris. He tried to keep a thinning of his lips as the new arrival approached him.

"Status?" asked the mission commander, sipping on a synthi-caff.

The scientist indicated the master situation display with a jerk of his head. "Nominal. The fifth target has just been prosecuted."

The commander accepted this with a wary nod. "Dead?"

"Of course," the scientist retorted , a note of arrogance entering his tone. "As the mission briefing demanded, no survivors."

"Good." The other man leaned forward, his free hand reaching up to scratch absently at the white growth of beard across his chin. "They've moved on to vehicles now? Will it be able to keep pace with them over a sustained period?"

"If you want it to."

He considered the reply for a moment. "Yes," he said, "just let the unit proceed as it feels best. After all, if we keep micro-managing it, then we defeat the whole object of this exercise in the first place." When the scientist didn't reply, the mission commander turned his full attention on him. Reflected sheets of data codes and tactical plots painted his angular face with colour. "Doctor?" he prompted.

The words spilled out of the scientist's mouth with sudden intensity. "Once more, I feel myself obligated to question the intentions behind this field test! I have stated on several occasions that the project is not at a stage where it can accurately be supervised in an uncontrolled environment–"

"In your opinion," broke in the other man. "Many of your colleagues do not agree. They find your estimates to be overly conservative."

"This is not some crude firearm or explosive device!" he snapped back. "We are developing a weapons system of unparalleled sophistication and capacity. We cannot afford to make mistakes." He blew out a breath. "Frankly, I have my doubts about the continuing value of this endeavour as a whole."

The commander's jaw stiffened. "While I respect your knowledge, doctor, perhaps I might draw your attention to the length of the this project's development cycle to date? This unit's inception began in the ashes of a war that almost destroyed us as a people, and now, a decade later, we are still without a workable weapon!"

"A workable weapon," repeated the scientist, seizing on the words, "not an unpredictable hazard! This project should be shut down, pending a total re-evaluation."

"Please, doctor. Don't be so excitable! The device is functioning perfectly."

"Is it?" The other man brought up a series of data panels and tapped his screen with a stubby finger. "Twice since the commencement of this test scenario I have logged neural response spikes outside the standard parameters. And before... before the activation I noticed some unusual behaviour patterns."

"Explain."

The scientist blinked, eyes focussing on a distant point. "I... find it difficult to put it into words, but I got the impression the unit was... that it was hiding something."

The commander frowned, crushing the now-empty caff cap in his hand. "You spend too much time cooped up in the test labs, doctor. It's affecting your perceptions," he sneered. "You should be glad I gave you the opportunity for this little outing."

The other man opened his mouth to speak, but a duty technician interrupted. "Sir? Targets and unit are entering the periphery of the Denver Death Zone. Ambient radiation levels are increasing and we're having problems with the telemetry links."

The bearded man glanced up at the main screen; the multiple camera-eye views were becoming foggy with interference and static. He threw the technician a nod. "We can't afford to lose any data. Instruct the pilot to descend to a lower altitude where the signal is stronger."

The order was relayed and the deck shifted slightly beneath their feet, the frame of the big transport VTOL biting into the heavier Colorado winds. Ignoring the sour expression on the face of the scientist, the mission commander watched with interest as the test unit's primary optics broadcast the wavering image of a patched ground rover, skidding across hard-packed earthen craters.

Minx had been the last person to speak to Derek the Teeth before he died; as she was gunning the engine of the DuneRail, he skipped up on to the back runner and said something about oranges. It was hard to tell. Derek's mouth had so many teeth, in such odd profusions and shapes that his speech was mostly clatterings of blunt enamel and jets of spit. Minx twitched her whiskers and gave him the same nod of fake understanding she always did – but then there was a flash at the edge of her vision and, like all the others, Derek's skull went *pop*. One razor-sharp canine cut a gouge over her steel shoulder pad as it came away with the rest of his head. Reflexively, Minx slammed her foot on the accelerator and the DuneRail chugged away, his headless body flapping behind for a mile or so when his bootstrap caught around the axle. By the time he fell off they were on the glassy stone of the DDZ highway, and Minx's attention was firmly fixed on keeping up with the rest of the pack. She kept her eyes wide open all the time, not wanting to blink even for the briefest instant. Minx didn't see things like most muties or norms did; her supposed "gift" from the cocktail of Strontium 90 isotopes that had mutated her genome, were peepers that worked on frequencies way beyond those visible to typical human eyes. Minx could see in the dark by reading the wave of heat bloom from the ground and the air, and the sight of Derek's body going from warm orange-red to featureless blue made her feel sick. Oh sure, she'd seen it happen before, more times than she could remember; but Derek had been kind to her, and Minx didn't have any other friends among the Mutancheros.

She pressed her weight into the vehicle's steering yoke as the fleeing convoy bounced over the abandoned freeway interchange towards the gaping maw that had been Denver. The DuneRail felt wrong, sluggish; the rear wheels skidded and refused to hold fast. Reluctantly, Minx glanced over her shoulder, half-expecting to see a piece of the hapless Derek clogging the gears.

In the dark void between the twin trans-axles, there was a faint yellow shimmer that could have almost been the shape of a man. Minx blinked and felt the fur along her spine go taut.

It knew she saw it. The mutant girl stamped her foot on the brake and the DuneRail fishtailed wildly, yawing across the road and bumping into two other vehicles. The yellow shape flickered and flowed up over the back of the rover – and then vanished.

"Remarkable," commented the commander. "Did you see that? It modulated the temperature of the outer skin sheath to nullify the mutant's advantage."

The scientist shook his head. "That wasn't part of the program."

"Adaptation, improvisation. That is exactly what we want from the project."

On the screen, the cat-faced girl was gone, and the viewpoint quivered as the killer leapt from one moving vehicle to another.

It was past her in a black rush of noise, then Spooky's trike was upended with the impact of its landing. The thin, wispy bandit spun around with his neck bent in odd places, riding his makeshift cycle off the elevated road and into the abyss below. Some of the other Mutancheros were trying to extricate themselves from the logjam Minx's skid had created, and they burst like sacks of wet meat as the murderous silhouette sliced through them. Minx was rooted to the spot, trying to capture the ephemeral ghost in her vision, but all she saw was a dark blur, ice blue on ice blue, fast as death.

Gunfire crackled past her as Happy Bruce's former enforcer Bottleneck opened up with the twin .50 calibre machine guns mounted on his weather-beaten pickup truck. A rain of hard-jacketed slugs chewed through the other vehicles, hitting anything but the target they were meant for.

At last, cowering under the DuneRail's fender, Minx got a good look at the killer as it leapt from cover, bouncing off a bent concrete stanchion to dash over her head. It had skin that shimmered like black oil and trailing forests of cilia extending out of every inch of its limbs. It looked as if it might once have been human, but the coat of shifting matter all over it seemed more alive than the flesh beneath it. It was iridescent, like insect wings, and so dark it seemed like a hole in the air. Minx's heart froze when she saw the weapon growing out of its hand; a yawning black void like the tunnel into hell.

■ ■ ■

"You see how quickly it evaluates and determines targets? The large one represents the greater threat to it now."

"Then why did it not terminate him first, doctor?"

"I think... I think it's enjoying itself."

In mid-air the killer's gun spat death at Bottleneck and his crew, a storm of sun-hot plasmatic darts ripping apart the pickup. One instant the vehicle was rolling forward, guns chattering; the next it was a fireball filled with shrieking men and bullets. Minx was thrown to the tarmac by a wall of octane-tainted heat, her vestigial whiskers coiling back along her protruding snout. Time blurred around her for a moment and, when she tried to stand, a hard and inflexible hand clamped around her throat like an iron collar. Through blurry streams of colour she made out the smooth, featureless oval of the assassin's face. She tried to speak, but the muscles in her neck could not move air through her vocal cords.

Minx saw the gun again, and then the white of a killing heat.

The VTOL's engines threw dust and dead bodies aside in a ring of compacted air, extending spindly legs to settle on the Denver highway. On the monitor, the flyer seemed fat and docile under the targeting displays that ran through the mind of the killer.

"Deploy recovery team," ordered the commander. "I want the unit on ice and in standby mode until we complete debrief–"

On the screen, one of the commander's men nodded in a strange, spastic jerk, before bursting into flames. Except for one single display, all the tactical relays went dark; the remaining screen showed the other men ripped open and dying in strobe-speed murders, the VTOL looming larger as the killer loped toward it.

Explosions sounded through the hull like distant thunder.

"Abort!" the commander screamed across the room. "Do it now!"

"I warned you!" snapped the doctor, stabbing a termination sequence into his console. "Damn you, but you did not listen!"

Without warning, the killer's viewpoint flared brightly, a bright sodium glare washing over the dark room. Streams of information from the unit's internal systems went wild, readouts shredding into garbled confusion.

"Whiteout..." murmured the scientist. "Neural overload!"

"Stop it!" roared the commander, as the sound of tearing metal reached them. "Kill it!"

The deck trembled beneath their feet as the pilot attempted to lift off, but fuel was already streaming from scored wounds in the fuselage and winglets. The VTOL wobbled in the chill air and fell back to earth, trailing smoke and flames.

MEGA-CITY ONE, 2127

SHAKEDOWN

"How many is this? I've lost count." Keeble glanced at his partner in the dingy half-light of the corridor, his fist paused before the patched plasteen door of Apartment 435/G.

Lambert consulted the data pad in her hand with a morose look. "Forty-six."

"Feels like we've been at this forever," Keeble said in a low, fatigued tone. "Ah well, perhaps this one won't be a complete waste of effort." The dark-skinned Judge slammed his gloved hand on the door in textbook fashion, three hard knocks and then the declaration. "Justice Department, open up."

"You said that last time. And the time before that." Fresh information crawled across the pad's screen as the sound of shuffling feet approached the door. "Huh. Evans and Donner just made an arrest six floors down. That guy who was stealing nipples? They found two hundred of them in jars of synthi-vinegar."

Keeble nodded. "And what have we got to show for it? Couple of cases of peeping and an unlicensed crocodile. I'm sure Hershey will be pinning a medal on us for that one." The door opened and the manner of both Judges changed instantly, each law officer projecting an iron-hard, expressionless exterior.

"Yes?" Pallid eyes peered out at them through an inch of open doorway.

For the forty-sixth time that evening, Keeble repeated the words: "Good evening, citizen. Crime Blitz."

And once again, he got the same reply. "But I haven't done anything."

"We'll see," said Lambert, pushing open the door all the way. "Mega-City One Criminal Code, Section 59 (D). A Judge may enter a citizen's home to carry out routine intensive investigation. The citizen has no rights in this matter." She tried to keep the bored tone from her voice. Chet Hunklev Block was not her usual beat, but the directive handed down from Justice Central had meant that every Street Judge the city could spare was being poured into the rundown avenues of Sector 88, as part of a high visibility crackdown on crime. Double-Eight was the kind of sector that had its picture next to the word "slum" in the dictionary, a rat's nest of heavy industrial auto-factories and megway interchanges mingling with dilapidated citiblocks that dated back to the days of Chief Judge Fargo. Tonight, all across the sector, there were units of Judges kicking in doors and hauling perps away in pat-wagons for crimes that ranged up and down the statute books. The Judges were making an example of Sector 88, an object lesson to the rest of the city: you could be next.

The resident was a small, paunchy guy, with a waddle in his walk, and he matched the interior of Apartment 435/G as if he had been extruded out of the grimy walls. He made way for the two Judges, blending into the peeling, stripy wallpaper as they began a careful and exacting orbit of the small three-room hab module.

"Just you here?" Lambert demanded. "Any pets?"

The citizen shook his head slowly from side to side. "No Judge. Just me."

Keeble approached the kitchen alcove and his nose wrinkled. "What is that smell?" A pungent aroma that pitched itself somewhere between wet dog and stale gym socks seemed to concentrate itself in the far corner of the room, around the washer-dryer unit. Keeble opened the oval loading hatch and the stench reached out and swatted him.

Lambert caught a whiff and grimaced. "Ugh. Any worse and I'd need a respirator! What have you got in there, citizen?"

"Just my smalls, uh, sir. I, uh, like to jog." The little guy stared at the floor. "I have a glandular problem."

"No doubt," said Keeble, breathing through his mouth. The smell was everywhere. The Judge managed a closer look before his eyes began to water, spying the shapes of rotten underwear piled within the washer. "Do yourself a favour and use the industrial laundroteria on level fourteen. This is a borderline health hazard."

"Tried that, sir," said the man. "Got banned."

Lambert met Keeble's gaze and nodded to the exit. "That's an order. Other than that, you can consider yourself... clean."

In the thin, yellow light cast by the lamps in the corridor, a huge, angular figure became visible, filling the doorway. "I don't think so," he said.

Keeble blinked and looked at Lambert, who was shaking her head as if she'd just been given the worst news possible. "Dredd," murmured the other Judge. "Perfect."

Keeble had never seen him before in the flesh, just the odd glimpse on a monitor or when a newsflash painted his stone-cut aspect on a street-screen. It wasn't difficult to match that larger-than-life legend to the man who stalked into the apartment after them, hooded eyes peering into every shadowed corner of the room.

"Sloppy technique, Keeble," said the senior Judge, addressing him like a cadet on his first patrol. "You're missing something."

Lambert considered protesting, but from the corner of her eye she saw the citizen shift nervously, a tiny, almost invisible tell on his face, and she knew Dredd was right. The Judge let her handcuffs slip into her palm as Dredd went on.

"Smell that?" Dredd pointed a finger at the washer. "If that's just underwear in there, I'm Otto Sump."

"I..." began the resident, but he fell silent when Dredd shot him a leaden glare.

"Don't lie to me, creep, unless you want another three years on your ticket."

Gingerly, Keeble removed the largest pair of soiled u-fronts Lambert had ever seen from the washing machine – and from inside a packet of something greenish-white and gelid flopped on to the greasy flooring. "It... looks like–"

"Cheese," said Dredd, sounding out the word like a curse. "Limberger, maybe. Gorgonzola? A prescribed food product." He prodded the perp in the chest. "That's way too much for personal consumption, creep. You're dealing. That's ten years' cube time."

The sweaty little guy erupted into a flurry of motion, hands flapping and denials spilling out of his mouth. Lambert caught him by the wrist and cuffed him in one smooth action, propelling the criminal on to his knees.

"It's just cheese!" he shouted, eyes welling. "There's nothing wrong with it!"

"Just cheese?" Dredd repeated. "It's class two contraband, that's what it is." He glanced at Keeble. "Almost let that one slip by. Don't get complacent."

"Sorry, Dredd," the other Judge glowered from beneath his helmet. "Won't happen again."

"He's got customers on this floor, count on it. Why don't you encourage him to share that information with you?"

Keeble nodded and crouched next to the perp. Extending his daystick, he began a hushed but intensive interrogation of the man.

Lambert followed Dredd back out to the corridor. "I didn't think a senior officer like you would draw this kind of detail. Kicking in doors and busting small fry... Not exactly Angel Gang calibre."

"This bust is all about visibility," Dredd grunted. "Puttin' the fear of Grud into the cits."

The younger Judge's face soured. "Well, excuse me for speaking my mind, but if the Council of Five wanted to shake up this sector, then we ought to be kicking in Ruben Cortez's front door, not some cheese-loving spug."

"Cortez will get his." Dredd's words dripped with acid. Lambert was right: Cortez, the man they nicknamed "The Eye" on the streets, had fingers in every piece of Sector 88's illicit economy, but a network of corporate double-blinds and legal connections had kept the criminal from ever standing trial. He was adept at finding men to take the fall for his crimes, and more than a dozen undercover Wally Squad Judges had ended up dead trying to pin something on him. The continued existence of creeps like Cortez was an affront to Dredd, and it had been one of the reasons he wanted to be seen on the streets of Double-Eight tonight. He was serving notice; the law was not to be disrespected.

"Not soon enough," said Lambert, tapping in an arrest code on the data pad.

Six apartments away, Wesson closed the front door to his hab with shaking hands, terrified that the mag-lock would make too much noise as he did. He pressed the door shut with damp-palmed hands and stood there in the gloom, his chest heaving and his heart pounding. He had left it too late, typically for him, fretting and worrying and finally doing nothing until the thing he was afraid of was right on top of him. Judge Dredd, for sneck's sake! Not that it mattered which Judge it was, Wess's bad luck meant that whatever random algorithm the lawmen were using to choose which doors they knocked on, his would be one of them. Wess Smyth had learned very early on in his sorry little life that if something could go wrong, it would go wrong.

He wandered back into the bedsitting room, wringing his hands, calculating the scale of malfeasance in his apartment. Tobacco crumbs on the floor by the bed where he'd enjoyed a cherootie instead of smoking it at the Black Lung Smokatoria on 543rd Street; half a can of Boing®; a couple of back issues of the banned *Bite-Fighters* magazine; all those pens he'd taken from the post office; oh, and how could he forget, the sachet of zzip crystals he'd palmed from Bennie Freemish down on Floor 96. Wess felt a horrid pressure building in his bladder and he rocked back and forth in place, suddenly consumed by the fear that he'd be arrested in the toilet stall if he gave in to his bodily needs.

He had to get out, and get out now. But where was he going to go? Down on the ground level, there were roving Judge patrols at every exit, with X-ray booths and sweat-scanners ensuring that nobody got away from Chet Hunklev Block without submitting to a search. The decrepit building was sealed tighter than a drum, and even if he could get to the underground parking levels, Wess had left his ageing podcar at that shuggy place down in the skid district. He had to find an alternative exit.

Wess felt the curious mix of excitement and abject terror that came on him in moments like this. He might be barely stopping himself from soiling his underwear, but by Grud, he felt alive! All through his life, Smyth had got himself through by the skin of his teeth, and he knew that today would be no different. Wess took a deep breath and stuffed the Boing® can and the zzip pack in his pocket before dialling a string of numbers on his vu-phone. In apartment 427/T, down the hall from Smyth's squalid flat, another phone began to ring; it trilled twice before a reedy voice snarled out an aggressive "Yeah?" In the background, he could hear a musichip player pumping out a bleak, moan-filled dirge.

Wess's phone had long ago lost its camera, and the audio was so poor it made him sound like he was eating soy-chips while he spoke; he preferred it that way, keeping his identity hidden from outsiders. "Yeah?" repeated the voice.

"This is a friend," Wess told his neighbour, "with a warning. Judge Dredd is on his way to your apartment with a strike team. They know all about the plan. They know all about what you're doing." He hung up before they could ask any questions or guess at who he actually was. Smyth pressed his ear to the door and heard the faint sounds of disturbance from 427/T, mostly running feet and raised voices, followed by anguished shushing and more arguing. Wess didn't know the four teenagers who lived in 427/T very well, but he had crossed paths with them once or twice in the wee hours of the morning, usually when he was slinking back from Bendy's with empty pockets or after being thrown out by his girlfriend Jayni. Each time, he'd seen them shifting what were clearly industrial chemical containers into the tiny hab. They'd shaken him down for credits in the elevators, the four of them grinning and brandishing shivs, and to his eternal embarrassment he'd folded like a deck of cards.

Wess didn't have any idea what they were up to over there, but he had done enough illegal things to know the look of it on someone else. Hopefully, they were doing something dangerous enough to cause a distraction.

Inside apartment 427/T, the four members of the Global Anarchist Army were loading spit-guns and scribbling down their manifestos, arguing over which of them got to record their suicide message first and shifting the drums of crude napalm they had been making in the hab's bathtub. Theirs was not a large group of freedom fighters by any stretch of the imagination, and for the most part their list of anti-establishment "acts" had largely been restricted to the daubing of graffiti in the 'tweenblock plaza and the odd act of opportunistic vandalism; but membership of the GAA had given the four of them some sense of belonging, some camaraderie that had been forever denied to them by the bigger and less anaemic teens in the serious block gangs. For the most part, the GAA had spent their time listening to DedRok music and writing morose poetry with moody, repetitive imagery – that was until one of their members had found the keys to his mother's citi-def home militia locker, and looted the contents. Along with some hazardous chemicals stolen from the local tox-dump, they had finally reached a status that could be classed as dangerous; and so they had decided to write some more poetry about how everyone would be so upset when they were dead. Unfortunately for them, this rather inward-looking viewpoint had meant they were utterly unaware of the Justice Department's random crime sweep on their block. Unaware until now.

Dredd's head came around like a seeker scope tracking a target, and it took Lambert a second before she realised what the senior Judge had noticed. "Music's stopped." Dredd nodded, his hand slipping toward the Lawgiver pistol holstered in his boot. "It's probably nothing," Lambert added, drawing her own weapon.

"Probably," said Dredd, inching closer to apartment 427/T. His tone did little to convince Lambert that he agreed with her. Part of Lambert's mind wanted to sneer at the elder Judge's sudden change of behaviour. It seemed ridiculous that anything more dangerous than a go-ganger with a switchblade could be hiding in this shanty block. Another, deeper tactical sense told her that Dredd was on to something. It was undeniable; the man had been on the street for longer than Lambert had been alive, and even if Old Stony Face wasn't some kind of psyker, Dredd had an uncanny predictive ability that other lawmen could only dream of developing. Grud, thought the Judge, it's true what the Academy instructors used to say. Dredd can actually smell a crime happening.

He halted and drew a bead on the door of 427/T. "This is Judge Dredd! Come out with your hands in the air!"

At the sound of Dredd's voice, every member of the GAA panicked. All their tough talk, every promise to stick it to the Judges and their corrupt government, all of it crumbled into the mealy-mouthed bravado it had always been. Suddenly, they were all scared kids; and scared kids make mistakes. A finger too tight on a spit-gun trigger, a nervous twitch. Dredd's stern command was followed by a screech of accidental weapon fire as hot rounds tore though the plasteen door. There were ricochets too, the kind of factor that a real terrorist would have known about, and one of them sank into the jerry-rigged napalm buckets, with a catastrophic ignition. The blowback threw superheated air out of the apartment and blew doors off their hinges down the length of the corridor.

"Lambert, down!" Dredd tackled the other Judge to the floor as a sheet of orange combustion rolled overhead, clinging to the ceiling. Fire licked along the walls like grasping tendrils, and ripped into the open doorway of the hab where Keeble and the perp were standing.

Dredd caught the sound of burning, curdling flesh inside and heard a strangled yell of agony.

Smyth was punched to the floor by a hot fist of gas, rolling across the threadbare carpet as his front door sailed off its hinges and into the sofa bed. The primitive fight-or-flight reflex that had kept Wess alive for the past thirty-odd years kicked in with gusto, and suddenly the petty criminal was on his feet, running into the singed, still smouldering corridor. From the corner of his eye he saw a shrieking man-shape made of flames as it stumbled out of apartment 427/T. Wess threw himself into the smoke, bouncing off the walls, feeling his way toward the spinal shaft of the citiblock.

The burning citizen's screams were horrific; the improvised napalm, a recipe plucked from the pages of a dog-eared banned militia manual, had worked far better than the erstwhile members of the GAA had ever hoped. Dredd's jaw set in a grim line as he fired a single standard execution round into the skull of the unfortunate victim, cutting off the wailing in mid-cry.

Lambert rolled to her feet, pulling down her respirator. "Where's the damn extinguishers?" She punched an emergency switch on the wall, but the fire alert klaxons and the corroded retardant spray nozzles in the ceiling remained silent. "Drokk! Nothing works in this fleapit!"

"Control, Dredd. Fire on floor 177, Chet Hunklev," the senior Judge spoke quickly and carefully into his helmet microphone, his measured tone level and even. "Improvised incendiary device. We need fire-fighter droids, expedite immediate."

"Control, responding," said a voice in their ears. "Fire units inbound."

Behind them, Keeble staggered forward, clasping an extinguisher canister. The gold Eagle of Justice on his right shoulder pad was warped with heat damage. He emptied the fire foam on the flames, but it might have been spit for all it did. The napalm fire was taking hold, chewing eagerly into the structure of the 177th floor.

"The perp?" Lambert asked, jerking a thumb at the cheese-lover's apartment.

Keeble shook his head. "Took a backdraft in the face. One less grub smuggler."

Dredd rounded on them, the flames framing him like an orange halo. "Evacuation protocol, now! Get these cits out of here!"

Older blocks like Chet Hunklev were constructed around a tower of ferrocrete and steel that concentrated the elevator shafts, drop tubes and repair conduits in one location for ease of maintenance. Radial corridors extended out to the habitat floors from the core to allow quick movement for residents and service mechanoids, but they also gave freedom of movement to smoke and flames, and as Wess ran through the growing crowds of panicking Hunklev blockers, the fire came wandering after them.

Perhaps on some level, Wess understood that the unfolding disaster was his fault; but if he did, he wasn't allowing it to get in the way of his very finely honed sense of self-preservation.

At the elevator bank there was a group of people shouting and banging on the lift doors. Despite the fact that the fire retardants had failed to operate, the citiblock's so-called smart internal sensors knew enough to deactivate the elevators. The null-grav drop shafts that accompanied them had never worked in all the years that Smyth had lived in the squalid building; local legend had it that drunken gang members from neighbouring Daisy Steiner Block had sabotaged the tubes way back in the 2090s after mistaking Hunklev for their archrival, Tim Bisley Block. The tubes had never been fixed, just blocked off and left to accumulate trash and dirt. Wess shoved his way past the screamers and pushed open a panel. He squeezed into the dark access channel and smelled the sour gust of trapped air. There was a chemical bio-lume pack flickering feebly on the wall, warning him not to come closer for fear of stepping out into the open shaft, and he ripped it open, tearing out the light stick. Smyth let it drop, and watched the greenish dot fall away, growing smaller.

For one brief instant, the smarter part of Wess's brain reminded him of where he was and what he was thinking of doing, but encroaching panic smothered that rational thought, and Smyth produced the can of Boing®. He flicked off the cap with his thumb and began to spray himself, feeling the thick, gelatinous plastic expanding and enveloping his legs, then his torso and finally his face. The Boing® hardened into an egg-shaped sac around him in seconds, still porous enough to let him breathe, but rigid enough to resist all but the most severe impacts. Wess closed his eyes and tipped forward, letting gravity take hold of him. Like a pinball in a chute, the plastic-encased Smyth dropped down the inert shaft, bouncing from wall to wall, falling nearly two hundred storeys in as many seconds.

Wess had been a Boinger in the years when the craze had first hit the Big Meg. These days, Boing® was passé, the thrill sport crowd having migrated to sky surfing and rocket jumping, but in its heyday the miracle plastic-in-a-can was the craze of crazes in a city with millions of bored, unemployed people. Now, as then, Boinging anywhere except inside a regulated park like the Palais de Boing® was against the law – but Smyth suspected the Judges would have more to concern themselves with than him. He struck the basement parking level with a whoop of fearful excitement; but it took another ten minutes of bouncing and up and down, before at last he could roll sideways and out of the empty drop-shaft. By then, the plastic ball was already puckering from the heat snaking down the tube after him, and Wess clawed his way free, a beady-eyed newborn escaping from his protective shell.

He quickly found the sewer grate and dropped into the ankle-deep slurry below. Ignoring the screams and the noise of the alarm sirens as they finally kicked in, Wess left Chet Hunklev block behind and splashed away, a free man.

"Grud. What a mess." Keeble pulled his helmet from his head and ran a hand through his hair. His arm felt tight where the robo-doc's dermal knitter had sewn a patch of fresh plastiskin over his burns. "Maybe we should've just let it burn." He nodded at the citiblock towering over them, still wreathed in smoke like a stubby volcano. Four complete floors of Chet Hunklev had been gutted in the hour following the explosion in 427/T, and the death toll was still clocking up. Beyond the staging area for the Justice Department H-Wagons and drone tenders from the fire department, a crowd of smoke-blackened people shifted back and forth like a grey sea, quiet with shock and worry.

Lambert glanced at her partner and narrowed her eyes. "These people live here. Sure, it's a slum, but it's their slum."

Keeble's teeth flashed. "It's a breeding ground for crime, that's what it is. Drokk it, man, you were there, you saw it! What were they making up there? Bombs? I'll bet it was those Democrat spugs or some other terrorist kook crew!" He made an angry gesture. "Rat-holes like this one are infested with perps! Chief Judge oughta get 'em dozed–"

"I'll pass that along," Dredd's voice sliced into Keeble's tirade like a razor, silencing him as he approached. "Meantime, look sharp and keep an eye on the cits. Fire's got them spooked, and scared people turn into perps real easy."

"Right," Keeble replied in a sour voice. "Whatever you say, Dredd."

The senior Judge leaned closer and gave the other man a measuring stare. "Yeah. Whatever I say. Now get your gear on and start acting like you fit the uniform."

Lambert approached him as Keeble stalked away. "I'm not making excuses for him, but he's had a tough time recently, Dredd. The SJS picked him up for a random physical abuse test last month and this week Central turned him down for a transfer to MegWest. He's a little short on patience."

Dredd gave the smallest of sneers. "You are making excuses for him, Lambert. Don't turn it into a habit."

"It's just been, y'know, difficult days for him."

The senior Judge studied the huddled forms of the Hunklev blockers. "Those cits over there just lost everything they own – if they were lucky – so don't talk to me about 'difficult days'." Dredd took a breath. "Right now, what they need is order, and that's what we do. Order." He threw her a nod. "Get to work."

Lambert followed Keeble as Dredd took a moment to replace the filter in his respirator. In the ear-bead speaker of his helmet, the familiar voice of Justice Central's dispatch control issued another critical advisory, the ninth one since the sun had set on Sector 88. "Item. Nark tip-off indicates possible wrecker action planned for junction 846, Braga Skedway and trans-sector underzoom. Senior Judges respond."

Dredd tapped his throat mic and set off toward his Lawmaster, the bulky motorcycle parked in the lee of a pat-wagon. "Control, Dredd responding. Feed the intel to my bike computer. I'm on my way."

The Lawmaster's broad tyres bit into the road surface and launched the bike on to the highway, into the flashing streams of four hundred mile-per-hour traffic.

The only good thing about the skid district was that coming down here made you appreciate your own neighbourhood a hell of a lot more. Unless you were unlucky enough to be living in a rad-pit in one of the bombed-out sectors, it wasn't an exaggeration to say that there was little in Mega-City One to compare to the 88 Skids in terms of squalor and general noxiousness. It was almost as if the city proper had disgorged this part of itself and divorced it from the rest of the metropolis, shying away from this horrible piece of effluent, its back alleys and drinking pits. Wess had never seen a uniform in the skids, not a Judge, not a medic, nothing. He assumed that the government had probably decided to let sleeping dogs lie and just allow the area to slowly choke itself to death in its own filth; but like a colony of cancer cells, the no-go zone kept alive by eating itself, festering there in the shadows cast by fractionating towers and manufactory domes. Perhaps one day the Judges would drop a warhead on the place and torch it clean once and for all.

Wess emerged from the sewers and took the over-pipes route from Fissile Fuels Inc to the broad blockhouse of RubbaBaby BuggiBumper Baby Foods, then down the inert electricity pylons to street level. This was the floor of Mega-City One, the concrete plate of City Bottom that had been laid over the radioactive ruins of dead conurbations like New York, Washington, Boston and Philadelphia. The smell of the skids never failed to make him retch; it was like a ritual he went through every time he arrived here. Smyth snaked his way through the cardboard shantytown at the foot of the Braga road junction and into the skid proper. He'd been careful about his pod last night, not ready to risk driving it out of the area while there was a chance he was being looked for. Sure, he ran the risk of finding his vehicle gutted, but for the most part the locals in this part of the skids knew and liked him. Wess kept the hobos and the street people sweet by dropping off packs of GrotPot and InstaFuud every now and then. It was easy to be generous to folks who considered a single hot meal like a fortune in diamonds. Wess enjoyed playing the big man and laying a little on the derelicts, especially when Jayni was around. She told him that it made him seem sensitive, and while Wess wasn't exactly sure what she meant by that, anything that made her like him better couldn't be bad.

He rounded the corner and spied the oblate lump hidden underneath a camu-net, shaded from the dim lights of the rushing highway overhead. A smile crossed Wess's thin lips. The net was SovBlok army surplus from the Apocalypse War, a mimetic camouflage sheet that mimicked the urban environment around it. Wess kept it rolled up in the trunk of his podcar for times just like these. He checked the street and then approached. After the disastrous game of shuggy against Bob Toes and that alien guy he partnered with, Wess had finally topped out with a cold, hard five grand in creds owing – and naturally, he didn't have the money with him. Truth be told, Smyth hadn't ever had that kind of cash, but he'd been hoping that Toes would be a walkover. All that sweet dough was going to go straight up the line, to Cortez's loan sharks. Wess had owed them for quite a while now, and they'd already taken one of his kidneys as a "holding payment". His fingers strayed to the crude surgical scar on his belly. They had threatened to take an eyeball next time, although privately

Wess was more afraid Cortez's ripperdocs would go for a testicle.

What had made things worse was finding out that Bob Toes had set him up; Toes actually worked for Cortez, and now because Smyth had tried to get a little leverage on his debt, he was five thousand deeper in the hole for his cleverness. Bob's alien pal had tried to peel the clothes off him and that was when Wess has run, hiding the car and footslogging it. Now, he'd get the pod back and drive out nice and careful in the light of morning, right under Toes's nose, so to speak. He figured that the pod might be worth a couple of hundred and he knew a guy in Sector 87 who owed him a favour. Some cash - any cash - might just keep the goons off him until he could come up with a scheme.

Old Foley gave him a crack-toothed grin as he reached the car. The tramp threw him a shaky salute. "Kept an eye on 'er for ya. Just like ya wanted, Smythy."

Wess gave him a wan smile in return and flipped a pack of SoyBoy Crunchies into the hobo's hands. "Thanks, pal. You're an ace."

Foley nodded and tucked the packet in his pocket, which was odd, because normally the old geezer attacked food like it was going out of fashion. Wess suddenly became aware of the fact that a snowdrift of used snack cartons surrounded Foley's nearby cardboard hovel. Smyth looked him in the eyes and read the duplicity of the tramp like ten-foot tall neon letters. "Who fed you, Foley?" Ice formed in the pit of Wess's stomach.

The tramp turned away and wobbled toward his hide. Behind Smyth, the camu-net changed shape as the pod-car's gull wing door creaked open. A man, a very large man, one so big that it was difficult to imagine how he'd fitted his bulk inside the car, emerged from Wess's parked vehicle. Smyth darted an accusing, betrayed look at the tramp, but Foley was gone. He sighed. It wasn't as if he wouldn't have done the same thing if the roles were reversed.

"Uh," Wess managed. "Hey, uh, Flex." Other people were coming out of the shadows now, and among them were Toes and his alien guy.

Flex was like the contents of a meat locker stuffed into a tan suit; a face like a red fist on a body made from planes of muscle. He rolled his head around, and it made cracking sounds. "Little seats make me uncomfortable," Flex said, speaking to nobody in particular. "I get stiff."

Toes made a *tsk* noise and it was then that Wess knew he wouldn't escape without shedding blood.

"Got something for me?" Flex turned his gaze on Smyth. For such a large and threatening man, he had warm, cornflower blue eyes that utterly belied his character.

Wess just blinked. There was little point in denying it.

"No?" Flex asked, and Bob's alien buddy chugged with amusement. "Ah. The Eye, he's been lenient with you, Smythy. Because he likes you. We all do." Another crack of the neck. "But last night you misbehaved. Sets a bad example."

Wess suddenly found his voice. "I... I'll get some creds."

"Yeah, you will," Flex nodded his assent. A red blur flashed across Wess's vision and then the world spun around him, pain igniting in storms across his skull, the black asphalt flipping up to pin him against it. "By tomorrow."

They all came in and took a turn. Wess kept waiting to be knocked unconscious, but, as ever, he wasn't that lucky.

NO HIGHWAY

The city blurred past in a stream of neon and shadow, the endless urban sprawl reduced to a smear of sound and colour along the ferrocrete expanse of the megway.

Dredd rode the Lawmaster like the machine was an extension of himself, a union of law-man and law-machine prowling the ten-lane road like a sentinel. He could have put the bike on auto, simply snapped out the destination he wanted to the Lawmaster's central processor and let the computer handle the ride – there were some Judges who did it that way, taking the easy option – but Dredd preferred the feel of control in his own hands, sensing the texture of the road through the handlebars and the thrumming vibrations of the Notron V8 engine between his knees. The split-second difference between automatic and manual control could save a life when you were hurtling along at hundreds of kilometres per hour.

Of course, it was impossible for any human, even one as well trained as a Mega-City Judge, to know the layout of the entire city by heart. Human taxi drivers and truckers were very much in the minority in MC-1, the complex matrix of megways, underzooms, skeds and slips enough to drive an organic mind mad with their insane patterns. No vehicle could be considered roadworthy in the Big Meg unless it had a functioning automap – otherwise the unwitting driver might make the mother of all wrong turns, ending up in one of the

NoGo Slum Zones or worse, a rad-pit left over from the war.

A discreet indicator in the corner of Dredd's view blinked, showing him the upcoming turn-off on to Braga Skedway, and he gunned the motor, deftly slipping out of the lee of a Big Mo mobile service station and across two lanes of sparse, late evening traffic. There was no rush hour in the city, because there were hardly any commuters with jobs to rush to; the closest equivalent was the pick-up and drop-off jams that took place in the mornings and afternoons when citizens living in mopads docked with fuel bowsers or mobile utility rovers. In a city where having a three-room habitat was an achievement, there were millions of people who chose to live in mobile homes that never made port, circling the arterial highways in endless loops.

The itinerant populace of MC-1's city-in-a-city had their own infrastructure, with schools and shops and libraries, the static landscape of the "rooties" forever flashing past them. In a lot of ways, the mobiles – as Justice Department parlance labelled them – were a subculture of their own, with the attendant pros and cons that encompassed. Mobbie juves had their own gangs just like the teenagers in the citiblocks, and their parents had the same problems as their permanent neighbours, just at 650 KPH. And where there were people, there was crime. Snatchers, who used anti-grav snares to steal cars off the road, thrill-seekers in overcharged dragsters, mobi-bank robbers, even high-end perps like Cortez, rolling around Sector 88 in a casino the size of a cargo blimp. But wreckers were among the worst.

In ancient times, there were criminals who would set up fake lighthouses on treacherous stretches of coastline, enticing unwitting helmsmen to pilot ships into rocky shoals. The beached vessels would be swarmed, the crews killed, the cargo looted – and by the time the authorities had arrived, the booty would be gone and the locals would claim innocence. On Mega-City One's freeways the same crime had been reborn in the ashes of the Apocalypse War, when parts of the metropolis were still lawless and ungoverned. Unprotected stretches of highway became prime choke points for wreckers, causing traffic accidents and halting hundreds of vehicles, killing and robbing whoever was caught in their traps. As time passed, the smarter wrecker gangs prevailed, some of them building fake tollbooths or staging roadblocks in huge sting operations. These were no gentleman highwaymen; they were murderers, opportunist thieves and rapists.

Perversely, Sector 88 had a very low incidence of wrecker activity, something Dredd attributed largely to Ruben Cortez's fondness for the mobile life. Cortez had grown up as a mobbie punk and wrecking was something that the rooties did. There was a little of the law of the sea among mobile folk, a gypsy code about not picking on your own – although in Dredd's experience it was as elastic as any other variation on "honour among thieves". Cortez didn't like wreckers, especially if he wasn't getting a cut of their haul, and it was highly likely that the source of the snitch about tonight's crime had come on The Eye's orders. The thought brought a grim sneer to Dredd's face.

The Judge rode down across the slip road and headed westward, toward the forest of looming processor stacks in Double-Eight's industrial district. The indistinct glow of the RubbaBaby Company's holographic billboard hovered in the distance, a bloated cartoon infant with a single, protruding tooth in its goofy smile.

The glint of light off a lens suddenly drew Dredd's attention up from the highway to a grey stone half-arch above. It was a watch bay, one of thousands of elevated parking areas reserved for Judges dotted around the city. Officers on patrol would routinely check in and observe the traffic from the bays, watching for signs of trouble. In the handful of seconds it took Dredd to spot the figure standing up there he had already halved the distance to the arch. It was a Judge and a Lawmaster, the officer studying the highway through a pair of magnoculars. In itself that was nothing out of the ordinary, but the message from Justice Central had ordered all available officers in the area to converge on Junction 846; the Judge was deliberately ignoring that demand.

"Watch bay Bravo 63 Delta, this is Dredd," he growled into his radio. "We got a wrecker situation brewing up ahead, or haven't you heard?" He raced under the arch, glancing over his shoulder in time to see the Judge throw him a look. Whoever it was up there, they'd heard him. When no reply came, Dredd thumbed a control on the bike's console, pulling up the identity code for the silent Judge. All Lawmasters broadcast an encrypted transponder signal to other Justice Department units, and if the officer in the watch-bay wasn't going to answer him, Dredd would find out who the hell they were.

"Restricted data," said the Lawmaster's computer. "Access denied."

Dredd frowned and punched in his personal security clearance, glancing up as the sign for junction 846 rose up before him.

Reluctantly, the computer gave him a terse response. "Judge ident: Vedder, Thessaly. COE. Current assignment: classified."

The senior Judge began to slow, heading for the emergency lane where two other Lawmasters were parked, but his thoughts held fast to the three-letter abbreviation attached to Vedder's code. COE; the Covert Operations Establishment was the city's pro-active external intelligence arm, one of the most secret divisions of the Justice Department. Some street Judges called it the "spook squad", much to the amusement of Psi-Division's actual ghost-hunting department; but COE agents had their own term for the group. They called it "the Company", a throwback to the organisations that had been the progenitors of the group, with acronyms like NSA, CTU, SD-6 and CIA. Vedder – it wasn't a name that Dredd recognised, but the presence of a COE operative anywhere was a red flag. He rolled his bike to a halt and a waiting female Judge acknowledged him with a nod.

"Dredd." She saw the set of his chin and paused. "Problem?"

"We'll see, Leary." He put aside all thought of Vedder for the moment. "What's the situation?"

"Got word that a gang are gonna hit the junction. I've put an H-Wagon on overwatch," she jerked her thumb at the sky. "We got nothing yet."

"Could be a false alarm," said one of the other officers.

"Don't count on it." Dredd looked back along the highway, to where the arch of the watch-bay was barely visible.

Wess coughed into the sleeve of his coat, and it came away with a muddy red stain on it. He winced, jabs of needle-sharp pain stabbing into him along the lines of his bruised ribs and thighs. His skin down there was a mess of purpling blotches and shallow cuts. For the fourth time in as many minutes, he tried adjusting his posture in the driving seat, but nothing seemed to ease his discomfort. The pathetic suspension in the podcar rattled him each time the vehicle rolled over a seam in the highway slab, as if it were shoving him in the back like some harsh reminder of his own stupidity. He glanced up through the spider-webbed plasteen of the windscreen and saw a dozen little reflections of himself. Smyth's face, the skin tight and swollen, made him look like some kind of mutie, his nose puffed up to twice normal size and his right eye a bloodshot mess. He wanted to urinate, but Wess was petrified that he would pass out from the agony of pissing blood. Looking away, he saw the automapper blinking green and white as the car changed lanes and accelerated. It had been all he could do to crawl into the vehicle and mumble a destination to it. His lips were so thick that it had taken three attempts just to make himself understood by the voice recognition system.

Smyth took a painful breath, ghostly knives jabbing into him, and eyed the digi-map. Just over the junction and down the underzoom to Sector 87, and he'd be at Tricke's House O'Pods ("Pods! Pods!! Pods!!!" went the holo-sign) where he intended to use his poor state to elicit some sympathy from Tricke Yipple, former drinking partner and ex-gang buddy in the days when they had both been members of the Hunklev Hunka Boyz.

Tricke wasn't really a soft touch, but he had a blind spot where Wess was concerned, over a misunderstanding that make him think Smyth had saved his life as a youngster. In truth, it had been a civic-minded citizen who pulled an unconscious little Yipple from the overturned robo-bus, but even at that tender age Wess was smart enough to take credit for someone else's work – especially when that someone had been killed instants later when the bus had fallen on him. Originally, Smyth had intended to parlay his wretched car into some cash by off-loading it on Tricke, but now that Flex and his cronies had reduced the already pathetic value of the pod with baseball bats and rocks, he was hoping to play the "you're my last hope" ploy instead. Tricke Yipple's greatest achievement was getting out from under in Sector 88 and making himself into a businessman – but his greatest error was not getting far enough away from his old pal Wess before he did it. Smyth coughed out another globule of bloody spittle. In a way, Flex's beating might actually have been a good thing, because it was sure to make Yipple part with more creds than normal. Wess sniffed as something like self-respect threatened to rise up among his thoughts, and he quashed the emotion with force. He had no time for that stomm. This was about cold, hard, cash.

Smyth glanced out of the window and saw a handful of Judges parked in the shadow of a support stanchion. The automatic reaction that came over him whenever he spied the big gold eagle shoulder pads twisted in his gut, and he groaned. If any one of them saw the broken windscreen, they'd pull him over for a moving violation and then he'd have to explain his sorry state. With his Fight Club membership long-expired, Smyth would have no excuse. But they didn't come after him, even though Wess kept craning his neck to look out of the back window just in case the red, white and blue strobes lit the evening.

He was still looking backwards when the highway in front of the podcar became a lake of raging fire.

Tyler blinked and rocked back from the scanner hood, pinching the bridge of his nose. His head itched underneath the open-face helmet and he longed to take it off. It wasn't his size, but it was Mega-City regs so he had to wear it.

"You okay?" Tek-Judge Clark looked back at him through thick data-spex, lines of code scrolling down past his eyes.

Tyler gave a wan smile. "Just tired. I'm havin' trouble sleeping down here. Must be the gravity change."

"Huh," Clark smirked. "Loonies. Got no stomach for travel. You should try a TRI back at Justice Central. Ten minutes in there gives you a night's full rest."

"No thanks," he replied. "Fake sleep ain't like the real thing." The tubular Total Relaxation Inducers at the precinct house reminded him too much of coffins. In fact, Tyler had no idea why he was suffering from such severe insomnia, but ever since his secondment to Mega-City One from the Luna-1 colony, he'd been up all night and sluggish all day. Perhaps it was something to do with going from the Moon city's simulated one-gee to a real, authentic one-g environment that made him sleepless... Or perhaps it was the weird chill he got whenever he looked up into the night sky and saw not a blue-white marble, but a grey disc of stone. His home. He shook off the thoughts and dropped his face back to the scanner, reading the wave of feedback rolling out of the sensor pallet on the bottom of the H-Wagon. He could see the collection of heat blobs that were Leary and the other Judges, the thermal blooms of electromotors racing past in the traffic, even the commas of orange where hot tires made marks on the ferrocrete invisible to the naked eye; but no sign of anything suspicious. Frowning, Luna Tek-Judge Tyler switched across the scan spectra, going to infrared, ultra-violet, meson decay and etheric reflection settings, each time finding nothing but blank.

"Wait a second. I think I got something."

On the monitor screen, an egg-shaped six-wheeler started a controlled skid toward the median strip. There were no life-signs on board, but there was the telltale glow of an uncontrolled thermochemical reaction in the cargo hold.

"Target!" Tyler's cry galvanised the Judges on the ground. "Yellow Orbis slabster, lane two!"

"There!" Dredd was already sprinting toward his bike as the vehicle skidded past the Judges and sideswiped a mopad bedsit. The slabster fishtailed wildly and hit the highway barrier with a crash and the flat thud of combustion. An orange fireball engulfed the vehicle and grew into a sphere of bright colour; Dredd instinctively brought up his arm to shield his face just as a flat wall of superheated air slammed him off his bike and onto the roadway. He tumbled and rolled, catching the sounds of screams and secondary explosions. Fire licked at him and he scrambled to his feet. Someone had tried to cook him alive once tonight, and he was in no mood to go through the same experience again. Panting, the Judge brushed off a flaming ember and surveyed the scene.

The slabster had clearly been packed with flammables; like the old naval tactic of floating a fire ship into the middle of an enemy fleet, the wreckers had set an inferno that was spreading across the eastbound lanes of Braga Skedway and threatening to hop the strip and engulf the westside traffic as well. Smoke, thick and acrid, rolled across the sea of fire. Dredd tasted sour chemical flavours on his tongue, a sure signature of improvised munitions. He caught a glimpse of Leary and the other Judges, shouting into radios and calling for backup. Dredd grimaced, counting a half-dozen vehicles blown aside in the initial blast or mired in the firestorm. Glasseen popped and shattered with the heat, and people were screaming. The Judge tugged his respirator into place and waded into the carnage, alert for citizens in danger as much as he was for the imminent arrival of the wreckers.

By coincidence, the wrecking crew had got their recipe for homemade napalm from the same place as the teenage Global Anarchist Army: *Give 'Em Hell*, a banned manual on urban guerrilla warfare, written in the late 2080s by members of the Fresno Militia, a part of Mega-City Two that had briefly seceded before the west coast

Judges had bombed them back into the stone age. The book circulated on the Mega-Web despite all the attempts of the Justice Department to stamp it out, and in an ill-advised effort to solve the nagging problem, a bright MC-2 Tek-Judge programmer had created a worm program that sought out the text and edited it. Built-in safeguards made it impossible to erase *Give 'Em Hell* entirely, but the Judges were able to change it just enough that the bomb-making formulae were all wrong. Instead of electing to make the recipes inert, they decided to made them more volatile – reasoning that anyone dumb enough to make use of it would blow themselves up sooner or later, thus saving the Judges the job of arresting them. To say the idea backfired was an understatement.

Thus, what the wreckers expected to be a nasty but brief fire was rapidly spreading across the megway in a red flood of flames. Smarter criminals would have cut and run; but then smarter criminals wouldn't have downloaded a handbook on explosives from the Web without checking if it was kosher first.

There were pools of burning fuel and bubbling tarmac across the highway in fiery islands, thick fumes coiling up from them, swathing the scene in a hellish light. Distantly, vehicle horns and sirens hooted as more oncoming traffic screeched to a halt, causing tailbacks and logjams along the sked.

Dredd's daystick made short work of the coach window. He pulled at the flexible plastic, tearing it from its mount. Inside, panicked passengers boiled up in a surge of terrified faces and grabbing hands. The Judge banged the stick hard on the side of the vehicle. "No pushing, no shoving! I see anyone gettin' clever and I'll knock you out myself!"

"Judge! Judge!" A skinny juve, all spiky hair and vu-glo jacket, tugged at Dredd's elbow pad.

"What did I just say, creep?"

"No, no – behind you! Look!"

Against his better judgement, Dredd threw a look over his shoulder, and sneered when he realised what he was seeing. From out of the smoke-choked air there were shapes descending among plumes of smoke, hooded figures brandishing long-handled hammers, crude morningstars, fire axes and chains. "That's a new wrinkle."

The wreckers were coming in on jetpacks, picking their places among the patches of highway still untouched by the fires. As he watched, one of them misjudged his landing and fell into a column of flame from a burning car; none of his cohorts spared him a second glance, simply going to work on the hapless cits trapped in the other vehicles.

"You people, get to safety!" Dredd dropped from the vehicle's flank and sprinted toward the wreckers, drawing his Lawgiver. "H-Wagon!" he shouted. "Where are you?"

From somewhere overhead came the pilot's anxious voice. "Can't get close! The thermals from the fires are making it impossible."

"Drokk!" One of the perps was bending over a roadster convertible, menacing the driver with a las-knife. Dredd swept in from behind him and cracked the wrecker across the crown of the skull, dropping him to the ground. He nudged the road pirate with his boot, catching the insignia on the jetpack in the flickering light.

"Property of Johnny Ainsworth Block Sports Centre," he read aloud. In the back of his mind, the Judge remembered an item on the morning briefing logs a few days earlier – someone had broken into the block stadium at Ainsworth and stolen all the game armour and gear from the jetball team. One more mystery solved.

Dredd put a plasti-strip holding cuff around the wrecker's wrists and ankles and then moved into the thick of the clouds. He heard gunfire – standard execution rounds by the sound of it – and nodded. Leary and the others were doing as he was, moving through the smoke and wreckage, picking off the perps one by one.

"Control," he murmured, sub-vocalising into his throat mic. "ETA on fire rescue units?"

"Still working on it, Dredd. Most of the local tenders are tied up with that incident at Chet Hunklev."

"Not good enough! I've got an accelerating situation here! We need options, fast."

A different voice broke in on the general channel. "Uh, Dredd? I might have somethin'."

"Identify yourself."

"Tyler," said the voice. "Tek-Judge Tyler, on transfer from Luna-1. I was, uh, part of the investigation last year when that creep Moonie tried to take over–"

Dredd gave a terse nod. "Yeah, sure. I remember. We can talk about old times later. What have you got?"

In the H-Wagon, Tyler gripped his console tightly as the flyer bounced around in the choppy air. "Air traffic over the skedway, Dredd. There's a weather control drone platform up here with us. It's on standby mode right now, programmed for clear skies, but–"

Dredd saw where he was going instantly. "You can make it rain."

"Roger that. I can give you a torrential downpour, if I can co-opt the command software."

"Do it," snapped the Judge. "We gotta damp this down before it gets out of control."

Wess Smyth's last sight of his podcar – and with it, his final hope of ever making any kind of money – was the polyprop bubble of the little buggy's carapace deflating like a balloon. The heat from the fires had already melted the rubbereen tires to the road, and by the time Wess had scrambled away, burning his hands on the hot asphalt, it was already starting to flow like a waxwork. The battery pack in the trunk gave a desultory chug of venomous fumes as it caught fire; and then the podcar was well and truly a wreck in every sense of the word.

Surrounded by smoke and flame, Wess's swollen lips trembled and he felt the urge to whimper in his chest. This was hell, he decided. He had gone to hell, just taken the wrong off-ramp and ended up in the land of fiery rivers and boiling sulphur. Wess stumbled forwards, the acrid fumes stinging his eyes, the chemical fug tearing every last molecule of breathable air from his lungs.

In amongst the clouds of smoke he saw moving shapes. Some looked like people, others were hooded things with hammers growing out of their hands. Smyth panicked and ran from them, turning back and forth on himself as he found his path blocked by overturned vehicles or thick sheets of orange fire. Blinded by the drifting ribbons of darkness and by his own terror, Wess blundered into a cargo truck that had thrown itself up onto the median strip after clipping a flaming van. He tripped over and fell against it.

It was cold. A thin sheen of water droplets covered the smooth steel hull of the big jugger-lorry. Wess saw the dirty handprint he'd left on the vehicle and gawped at it. A little way along the side of the cargo pod there was a hatch. The impact had popped the door open. From inside spilled white neon light.

And like the petty thief he was, in deference to all his years of small-time crime and self-interest, Wess's first thought was not "Is anyone in there alive?" but "Is anything in there I can steal?"

Drawn by the glow, Smyth's worries about his current predicament waned and he reached for the hatch rim. It came open easily to present him with the transporter's sparse interior – and the sole item of cargo within it.

These punks were organised. Dredd approached, crouched low to minimise his silhouette, using a blackened taxi for cover. In a clear portion of the road they were dumping plastic sacks of loot, ducking back into the smoke in search of more stranded victims to plunder. A single wrecker, a stocky guy with a machete in his grip, stood guard. Dredd squared his shoulders and stepped out, Lawgiver raised.

"Drop the blade, creep. Reach for the sky!" The wrecker tensed, his free hand drifting toward the control toggle for his jetpack. Dredd put a round into the ferrocrete at his feet. "That hood cuttin' off the circulation to your brain? I said drop it!"

It was then the Judge caught the minute twitch of the eyes behind the wrecker's mask, a quick glance over Dredd's shoulder and then back. Dredd spun in place, just in time to meet another, much larger perp propelled by a burst of jet wash. In his hands was a double-headed hammer that connected with the Judge's chest, forcing the air out of his lungs. Dredd lost his balance and his gun, the pistol skittering away into the dark. The hammer came after him and he rolled, dodging blows that made small, round dents in the highway. In the corner of his vision, Dredd could see other wreckers racing back to the drop point, but his attention stayed firmly on the big guy. With a speed that seemed impossible for a forty-year street veteran, the Judge swept his legs around in a low spin kick that caught the hammer-man on the shin, armoured Justice Department-issue kneepad meeting bone with a sickening crack.

Dredd pushed himself off the roadway as the machete-wielding punk ran at him, blade raised, a scream on his lips. Too easy. The Judge caught the creep by his cross-belt and used his momentum to toss him over his shoulder. The punk tried to trigger his jetpack, but the squirt of power threw him tumbling into a puddle of burning battery chemicals. He shrieked, the hot acids cutting through his plasteen hood, and in his pain he reflexively clenched the jet control. The wrecker took off in a blast of noise, trailing fire like a comet. He didn't come down again.

Hammer-man was swearing through gritted teeth, and he shouted out an indistinct name. A new wrecker skipped into the smoky arena formed by the smashed cars and threw the big guy a nod. This new arrival carried a collection of canisters and pressure hoses ending in a bell-shaped nozzle. A small pilot light flared at the tip, and its reflection danced in the wrecker's manic eyes. Dredd didn't have to be a psi to know that this creep must have been the one who hatched this psychotic plan. He'd seen enough pyromaniacs to know the type.

With great deliberation, Dredd drew his boot knife. "You're all under arrest."

The wrecker with the flamethrower burst out laughing and shouted out a command: "Rush him!"

Jetpacks flaring, they dived on him like falling hawks.

"You got it yet?" said Clark, eyeing the thermograph display. He'd dialled in filter after filter, but the heat haze wafting up from junction 846 was making the sensors top out, blanking them from even the most crude readings.

Tyler threw him a quick nod and began the upload protocol to the drone platform. Strictly speaking, it was a felony offence to tamper with a city-wide weather regulation system, Tyler actually had no business knowing how one of them worked – but the lax attitude to law enforcement on the Moon was one of the things he'd brought with him on this posting. If there was something that watching Judge Dredd in action had impressed upon the Tek, it was that some circumstances required the ability to think outside the strictly legal box. Interpretive law, they called it; and if what he was doing turned out to be a big mistake, then he had no doubt that Dredd would see all manner of discommendation added to the Luna-Judge's personnel file.

The H-Wagon's console gave him an answering beep and the data stream flowed into the drone overhead. Tyler looked up involuntarily; somewhere above them, advanced thermodynamic vector generators and precipitation actuators were spooling up to maximum power.

"It never rains..." he said to himself.

Dredd attacked them with the lone blade, arcs of flashing silver cutting the hot night air as the carbon-steel fractal edge kissed flesh, slashing through muscle and sinew.

It was all a feint on the part of the flamer guy; while the Judge's guard was up, he worked his way in, until the manic wrecker brought the weapon down on Dredd's back and sent him sprawling. The stench of igniter fuel wafted out of the muzzle as the perp rested it on Dredd's chest, finger curled on the spray trigger. On his back, the Judge saw something shimmer overhead, a glittering curtain of sliver.

"Gonna burn you, Dreddo," hissed the wrecker. "Toast yaaaaa!"

"Reckon not," the Judge replied, as a fat droplet of rain splashed on the flamer's nozzle with flat hiss. The pilot light guttered out and died.

Instinctively, the wrecker looked up – and for his interest was hit by the deluge of falling water created by the weather drone. It struck so hard it was like a punch in the face, which Judge Dredd followed up with an actual punch in the face, rocketing off the road to slam the wrecker into a taxi.

Hissing, spitting plumes of steam were suddenly everywhere, the wreckers scattering as the fires they'd started died instantly. Dredd grabbed the creep by his lapels, and with a swift shove forced him prone. The plasteen cuff drew the perp's wrists tight and he bubbled a moan into a growing puddle of rainwater.

"Code two, section one," Dredd began. "Judge assault, twenty years. Code two, section three, Citizen assault, eight years..."

Dawn was forcing its way through the pillars of black smoke from the damp, smouldering lumps of the burnt-out vehicles. Tyler picked his way around them, careful to avoid the parts of the highway where scanner-bots were combing the ferrocrete for particle samples and other evidence. He found Dredd near to the median strip, scrutinising a data pad report on the incident. He stood in the shadow of a wrecked truck.

"Ah, Dredd? Tyler." He gave a weak smile. The Tek-Judge was somewhat intimidated by the legendary officer. "Control's been trying comm you for the last ten minutes."

Dredd tapped his helmet and frowned. There was a crack in the plasteen near his temple. "Must've taken a hit when I went hand to hand. I'll get a replacement at the Sector House."

Tyler glanced at the truck; the vehicle seemed oddly untouched. The Judge frowned. It didn't seem right. "Guess the wreckers missed this one."

"Guess again," said Dredd. "Hatch was opened. Cargo bay's bare."

The Tek-Judge took a closer look and gave a low whistle. "This is a class five lock. That's a tough nut to crack."

The older man nodded. "From the outside, maybe."

Tyler frowned. "Weird. This looks like a regular truck from here, but that compartment... It takes up most of the hull space. Heck, there's enough armour surrounding that to deflect a laser cannon, or worse."

"No driver," added Dredd. "The computer navigator's a dead-end too, wiped clean in the impact."

"An emergency erasure program? That sort of thing only gets used with stealth cargoes." He patted the truck. "Not to mention it's dishonest, too."

Dredd nodded. "You're a Tek. What does this crime scene say to you?"

Tyler licked his lips. He hadn't expected Dredd to even talk to him, let alone ask him to venture an opinion. "Well, uh... Maybe the wreckers caught a big fish in their net? A clandestine cargo, maybe the property of a shady corp or something?" He glanced at the number plate. "Let me guess – fake plates?"

"You catch on quick." Dredd gestured with the data pad. "There's no registration for the vehicle. No registration for it of any kind, anywhere in the city databanks. Aside from being ten different kinds of illegal, that's also–"

"Weird?" supplied Tyler, and then regretted it instantly.

"Yeah." Dredd eyed him. "Weird."

WINDFALL

Hershey spotted him there in the atrium the moment she entered.

Dredd gave his typical terse nod. She'd learned to read a lot from that sullen jut of a chin, and without her even replying the senior Judge was already on his way over. He had "the look", plain as day in the gait of his stride and the way he carried himself. Something out there in Mega-City One was awry, a crime was going unpunished, a mystery unsolved, and Dredd was on it like a heatseeker. Hershey resisted a slight smile. It was the thing that made him the consummate lawman that he was; an inability to let any criminality lie while it was within his power to crush it.

The younger officer at her side fell silent as Dredd approached. The senior Judge gave him a look. "I need to speak to the Chief Judge."

The other man nodded. "I, uh, I'll be over there."

"Give us a moment, Chapman," said Hershey, brushing a length of hair from her eyes. When they were alone, she fixed Dredd with a level gaze. "My office door is always open to you, Joe. You could just make an appointment."

"Easier this way," he rumbled.

"Well, make it quick, Dredd. I've got a conference starting on *Justice Five* in two hours and I don't want to be late."

"I'm getting stonewalled and I want your permission to go deep on something. I need clearance." He said the last word like it left a bad taste in his mouth.

"What, those wreckers?"

A curt shake of the head. "There was a Judge in Sector 88 last night, just before it kicked off. I want to talk to her, but it's like she just dropped off the planet. MAC database records on her are so vague I can see right through them."

Hershey frowned. "So call her in. You've got seniority, pull her off duty and get her down here. Even the Special Judicial Service can't refuse a legit request."

"Vedder's not SJS; she's part of DeKlerk's spook squad."

The frown deepened. "COE? Well, that's a different matter." Although on paper Chief Judge Hershey's authority over the Council of Five and the city's judicial forces was absolute, in reality the fiefs of the SJS internal investigations division and the ultra-clandestine COE were almost laws unto themselves. Judge DeKlerk, who served in a direct role as the Chief Judge's Special Investigator, ran his department under levels of secrecy that made the Grand Hall of Justice look like a playschool. "You know as well as I do, Dredd, the mandate for Covert Ops is external, not internal. DeKlerk's people are only allowed to conduct surveillance within the city walls, nothing else. If you can't locate this Vedder, she might be part of a deep-cover operation, something vital to city security."

"Maybe." Dredd didn't sound anything like convinced. "Maybe not."

"Look, Joe. I know you don't like the spooks – hell, all of us get itchy when they're around, even the SJS – but Vedder's presence doesn't automatically imply a connection to your incident."

"All the same, she's a factor I want to eliminate from the investigation. She was in a watch bay when it went down, she would have seen the whole thing."

Hershey turned to leave. "I'll pass it along to DeKlerk, have him get a report to you."

"Better I see her myself–" Dredd began, but the Chief Judge stopped him with a hard glare.

"That's not gonna happen, Joe. Much as I dislike it, the COE are teflon – slippery as drokk – so don't waste time with this. We're not done with Sector 88 yet, and I want you to be there putting the screws on every perp that calls that pesthole home."

"Even Ruben Cortez?"

The comment caught her off-guard. "Of course. The Wally Squad have got a man in his club right now, gathering intel. When we're ready, we'll move on him."

Dredd said nothing; undercover operations didn't exactly mesh with his kicking-down-doors-and-taking-names style of justice.

"I'll be back in a few days." Hershey threw a glance over her shoulder as she walked away. "I don't want to hear you've been making trouble while I'm off-world."

"I'll try not to disappoint you."

In the depths of the Dust Zones there were places where no human being had walked in more than fifty years. Parts of the city's industrial underbelly where robots in factories toiled ceaselessly, so that robot loaders could fill robot trucks with goods (many of which were other kinds of robots) that could be taken to stores where robot salespeople could sell them on. It was a wilderness of blunt, ugly architecture; huge blockhouses designed by AIs to be totally efficient in form and function, tattooed with barcodes for the laser-readers in the droid workers, bereft of any kind of organic life larger than rats – and even those had a limited presence, hunted down by cybercat patrol automata. But in some places, there were islands of decrepitude among the unending toil of the machines.

Here in the factories it was the machines that managed and worked, never making errors, fabricating their produce to micrometer tolerances, while beyond, in the city proper, it was humans that ran the corporations that owned them. And sometimes, the humans would make errors, or run out of credits, or die as the result of a disagreement with other fleshy ones. Such a thing had happened to StellaToaster Incorporated. In the early 2100s StellaToaster made some of the finest toasting devices in the Northern hemisphere, an advanced range of appliances that cooked fauxbread products to perfection – or at least they did until a stray nuke from the Apocalypse War turned their head office into vapour.

The factory, hundred of miles away, remained untouched by the conflict and went right on making toasters, months and years after the war ended. Eventually, the constructor droids had taken to cannibalising themselves to fill non-existent orders, until one day the last of them tore out its own motivator chip to finish a BagelMatic 9000, and ceased to function. Forgotten and lost in the swathe of records destroyed by the warfare, all evidence of the factory slipped through the cracks; and the rats moved back in, happy to find a new home.

So this was why Wesson Smyth was hiding out in the bowels of the rusting StellaToaster works, surrounded by hundreds of thousands of toaster ovens in silent towers of tarnished chrome.

Wess's distended face was now streaked with soot as well as dried blood, and in the warped mirror-finishes of the toasters his reflection was downright horrific. His cheeks were stinging, and it made him whine with pain every time he tried to open his mouth more than an inch or two. Mournfully, Smyth sucked at the drawtube on a carton of Martian mineral water and swilled the red-tinted fluid around his mouth. It tasted of iron from the blood leaking out of his gums. Fingers tapping anxiously against one another, he sat himself on a cargo pallet piled with MuffinAtors and examined his prize.

A silver lozenge of brushed steel, the case was larger than a biz-cit's office-in-a-box, smaller than the holdall that Wess's last girlfriend had used to stuff her clothes in before leaving him. It was heavy, too, but it didn't rattle when he shook it. The whole thing had a kind of thickset solidity to it, as if it were engineered to suffer the roughest of treatments and still protect the contents. He ran his fingers around the surface of the case, looking for seams or anything that might have been a lock. There was nothing, just the oval loop of the handle. Smyth set the case down and drummed his fingertips on it in an aimless rhythm. The moment he'd seen it in the back of the crashed truck, he'd known it was valuable. Swaddling the thing inside his ruined coat, he tucked it under one arm and ran, skirting the confusion and the Judges until he'd got off the sked and over the fence into the Dust Zone. His nervous energy spent and his mind clearing of its default "greedy" setting, Wess was starting to get concerned.

Once, in a tri-d flick he'd seen at the cineplex on Floor 82, there had been a guy with a case like this one, and in it was a vial of goop that had turned out to be virulent alien protoplasm that wound up eating a whole citiblock. Wess sniffed; he hated documentaries. A case like this could have anything inside, and most likely it was something small and very, very valuable. Photic diamonds, maybe, or some rich guy's clone pattern on a mag-memory core. For all his weasel-like nature, Wess wasn't an idiot, and he knew he wasn't smart enough to get this thing open himself – and why would he want to, if maybe something like that protoplasm thingy were inside? No, he reckoned there might be a reward for finding this from wherever it had been "lost" from. A fat reward of thick creds that would square him with Cortez once and for all.

Thinking of The Eye made Smyth wince involuntarily, and sent a spasm of pain up his nerves. Suddenly he was afraid again, terrified of Flex and the other thugs, seeing them kicking and punching, feeling the ghosts of their brutality across his torso. No, they didn't call Cortez "The Eye" for nothing. All seeing, all knowing, all bastard, as they said on the streets of Double-Eight. If the mobster found out that Smyth had purloined something like this case and then fenced it elsewhere, even if it meant that Wess was paying off his debts, Cortez's reaction would not be favourable. He'd take the money and have Flex punch Smyth until he died.

The petty crook watched his warped reflection sag in the wall of toasters. He really had only once choice, when he thought about it. Present the case to Cortez and hope against hope it was worth a bit of money, and not full of some top-secret laundry or something dumb like that. He wiped absent-mindedly at his cracked lips, smearing a thin lick of blood across his thumb, and for the first time he picked up the silver case by its form-fitting handle.

In the grip there was a very advanced device that sampled the biometric information of the holder by means of microscopic needle sensors. Wess felt a series of strange prickles on the tips of his fingers and dropped the case in surprise, clutching at his hand. He backed away from the container where it fell as a jet of icy nitrogen squealed from a hidden vent in the surface. The case hummed and clicked, before opening along the middle of its length like a sliver beetle flexing its carapace. Little flowing tides of white vapour lapped out of the box, and inside soft blue lights blinked, illuminating the contents for Wess's startled gaze to fall on. As quick as it had come, his fright waned.

It wasn't diamonds, or memory chips, or even alien slime-gunk. It was something that made Smyth's bruised face split in a predatory, avaricious smile.

The Tek-Labs in Justice Central sprawled across dozens of floors of the city's primary precinct house, some of them isolated in the deep levels far below the main entrance atrium and others placed at the apex of the Eagle-shaped construction. Dredd's attention today was on Tek-31, a vehicular forensics workshop on the street level. At first sight it seemed like a bizarre mix of operating theatre, science lab and maintenance garage; Tek-Judges and droid assistants, many clad in polyprop oversuits, orbited wrecked pods and the remains of grav-cars like surgeons working on patients. Dredd steered a course around the cordoned-off process areas, well aware that a stray hand or boot in the wrong place could taint evidence vital to the prosecution of a criminal. He felt the tingle of invisible static shield-fields around one platform, where a sleek hover limo was being dismantled for clues to a recent mob hit at the Costa Del Meg resort.

Dredd caught sight of the Luna-City Judge working at a holoconsole, using the department's central computer MAC to compose a report on the wrecker incident. "Tyler," he snapped, and the technician started at the sound of his voice.

"Dredd! What's, uh, up?"

"Figured you might tell me." He gestured at the console, where an exploded graphic of the suspect truck was slowly rotating. "What do you have?"

"Gotta hand it to you, sir. You know how to pick 'em." Tyler manipulated the controls to highlight the vehicle's engine compartment. "Normally, fake ID or a pay 'n' spray is about how far you have to go with a thing like this, but whoever was running this truck put in a hell of a lot of effort to make it stay invisible." He pointed at an engine component. "If the tags on a vehicle are fake, you can usually make a secondary ID with serial numbers on the chassis or the drive core."

"Tell me something I don't know," Dredd snapped.

"Uh, yeah. Well, that's the thing. There are no serial codes on the parts of this truck. I mean, on none of them, from the pads in the disc brakes to the igniter plugs, heck, even the bulbs in the headlights. They've all been burnt off with microlasers." He scratched at his temple. "Like I said, a lot of effort."

"What about streetcams? Can you backtrack the vehicle to its point of origin."

Tyler shook his head. "Way ahead of you there, Dredd. I ran a search process using the truck's sensor silhouette with traffic control's cameras along the Braga Sked and came up with this." A grainy image appeared on the display, and it took Dredd a moment to realise that all he could see of the nondescript truck was maybe a half-metre piece of its prow, poking out from behind a large petrotanker rig.

"One still? One picture from the hundreds of thousands of public security monitors we've got all over the Meg?"

"Exactly," replied the Tek-Judge. "Here's the crux of it. I reckon the truck's autonavigator knew where the cameras were, it knew their sweep patterns. With that information, it could make sure it passed the observation points at just the right moment, when the cameras were pointing the opposite way or when a bigger vehicle..." he pointed at the image, "...was blocking the view."

"Cute theory," said Dredd, "but with the computer core fried there's no way to verify it."

"Yup. I just can't figure why someone would go to all this trouble to conceal an empty truck."

"It wasn't empty." The other Judge's tone was flat; he wasn't making a suggestion, he was stating a fact. "It was just empty when we found it. Where's the vehicle?"

Tyler jerked a thumb over his shoulder. "In bay nine, in little pieces by now. I thought maybe we could get a metallurgical read off some of the parts, maybe trace the origins that way."

"Show me."

The Tek-Judge led him to an opaque plasteen bubble held on an overhead frame, giving him a sideways glance. "Uh, my divisional commander wanted me back in the H-Wagon for this shift, but I told him I was working this on your orders and–"

Dredd silenced him with a snarl. "What the drokk is this?" Tyler followed Dredd's accusing finger. An inert servo-droid sat idly next to an empty transport pallet. There was no sign of the truck, or any of its component parts.

Tyler blanched. "Wait, no... This is bay nine. This is where I left it." He approached the robot, which came to life as it detected him. "Droid! Where's the damn truck?"

"Dismantled and destroyed, as per orders of Tek-Judge Nathan Tyler this morning."

"What? No! I didn't say nothin' about destruction! I ordered you to take it apart!"

"Where are the pieces?" snapped Dredd, although he already knew the answer.

"Components declared null and void are shipped to municipal fusion furnace for disposal."

"Stomm!" shouted Tyler. "That's a loada stomm!" He rounded on Dredd. "I never gave that order!"

"Too late now." The senior Judge studied Tyler's face; if he was lying, he was faking it pretty damn well. "Find out who had access to this bay today..." The words died on his lips as Dredd's line of sight crossed the walkway gantry of the lab's upper level. A female Judge, one with a fan of dark red hair emerging from beneath her helmet, was making a swift exit from the room.

Vedder. She'd had the same haircut in her file photo.

Dredd left a nonplussed Tyler in his wake and made for the lower level exit, shouldering aside anyone who got in his way.

He emerged in the main atrium, and for long seconds he hesitated, scanning the crowds of citizens and uniforms for his target. Dredd concentrated on the kinetics of the woman's movements, visualising the balance of her walk in his mind's eye until he spotted the red-haired Judge, stepping into an elevator across from the giant Arrest Clock counter.

"Vedder!" Dredd broke into a sprint, boots snapping against the marble floor. She met his gaze, her helmet concealing an indifferent expression on her face. He saw the name on her badge; it was the COE agent all right.

She watched him get to within a few metres of the lift before the doors slammed shut, blocking Dredd's snarling visage from her view. Alone in the elevator car, Vedder allowed herself a brief smile of amusement. It was a cold, chilly expression on her flawless, cream-coloured face, there and then gone again like the glint of a muzzle-flash.

The lift dropped two levels to the underground garages where her bike was waiting for her. She had already summoned the machine through her tight-beam vocoder, and it would be there for her like a loyal steed as she stepped out...

The doors parted to reveal a man made of hard armour planes, shoulders rising and falling with the effort of exertion. "Vedder," he said, sarcasm sharpening his words. "Perhaps you didn't hear me?"

She stepped out of the lift, masking her disappointment. How had he known where she was going? A lucky guess, perhaps? No matter. She wouldn't allow such a ploy to wrong-foot her. "Dredd," she pitched her voice with boredom and disinterest. "I'm sorry. My mind is on other things."

Vedder tried to step around him to where her bike was humming quietly on the ramp, but Dredd moved with her, close enough to be menacing, far enough away to react if she tried to attack. As if she would ever have been so crude.

"We have to talk."

"I'm busy–"

"You can start by telling me what you were doing in the Tek-Lab just now."

She halted and met his steely gaze. "Is this an interrogation, Judge Dredd? It sounds like an interrogation. Am I being accused of something?" She made a show of looking around. "I don't see any officers of the SJS here, which means I can't be under suspicion of any crimes."

"You're ducking me," Dredd growled. "You were in Sector 88 last night and you ignored an all-points call. Then some of my evidence goes missing and you just happen to be walking by. What's the deal with the stealth truck, Vedder?"

"Your evidence is your concern, Dredd," she snapped back. "And I'm not ducking you, as you put it. I'm on a critical assignment and I don't have time to waste answering your questions. This is a 'big picture, small picture' thing, Dredd, and you are quite small right now..." Vedder sneered. "But in the interest of interdepartmental cordiality, I'll tell you this, for the record. I have no comprehension of what you are talking about. Run a Birdie test if you don't believe me."

Dredd snorted. "I know all about the training and the implants you spooks have. You could tell my lie detector you were Judge Cal and it would give you a green light." He leaned closer. "Why don't you save us all a lot of trouble and tell me what that vehicle was carrying?"

Vedder's lips thinned to a hard line. "I'll say it once more, because of my personal respect for your record and your reputation, Dredd. You are wasting my time and your own following a dead-end lead. Now get out of my way, or I'll charge you with obstruction!"

There was a brief moment when Vedder thought Dredd was actually going to strike her; but then he stepped aside with a grimace and let her climb aboard her bike. The motorcycle carried her away and out into the city, and she never once looked back to see him watch her go.

The bike took her into the throng of the mid-day traffic. Although outwardly it appeared to be a standard-issue Mark III Lawmaster, the modifications under the skin added by COE TekOps made it altogether a different breed of animal to the machines that Dredd and his fellow street jockeys rode. Like Vedder herself, it was an advanced tool masquerading as its common cousin; like the bike, Vedder was something very different beneath the leathereen of her Judge's uniform.

She gunned the motor and accelerated. Dredd had taken up too much of her time already, and she had an appointment to keep.

He found Tyler up to his elbows inside the torso of the robot assistant, cables and circuit boards spilling out onto a workbench like mechanical innards.

"What's this?" Dredd demanded.

Tyler looked up, his face drawn. "Lookin' for evidence of tampering. Didn't find a damn thing. According to this tin-head's memory, I ordered the truck to be broken up and disintegrated – 'cept I didn't say anything of the kind!"

"Like I said, too late now. What about your files?"

The Tek-Judge nodded. "Yeah, I backed them up into deep memory and cut a copy myself." He brandished a shiny data disc. "At least we still got that." Tyler frowned. "But without the vehicle we're back to square one... That's if, uh, you still want me to work on this case with you."

Dredd gave him a measuring stare. If the Covert Operations Establishment were messing around inside city limits with something, then their influence over the Mega-City One Justice Department couldn't be ruled out – and that made it difficult for Dredd to move without them knowing about it. Tyler, however... At the moment, Tyler was the closest thing to untouchable, recently arrived from Luna-1 and therefore highly unlikely to be under COE influence. Add to that, the junior Judge had put in good work after that "Moon-U" incident and he was quick, if a little inexperienced. "For now," Dredd told him, "get to work sifting through the rest of the incident reports. Look for anomalies, anything that doesn't track."

"Got it, Dredd. What are you gonna do?"

"Back to Double-Eight. We're not done with the crime sweep there yet."

Wess felt guilty when his phone rang, because he knew, even before he saw her little love-heart-and-bunny icon on the screen, that it would be Jayni calling. Checking to make sure that the camera bead on the handset was in its off position – because explaining his state to her would be impossible – he answered it with what he hoped would sound like sunny joy. In reality, his wheezy "Hey, babe," came out more like the death rattle of a black lung victim.

"Wess?" she said, and in that one word he knew she knew. "What's going on?" In the background he could hear the toneless thumping beat of a muffled jukebot, and he realised she was calling from Bendy's, the nasty little skankerie that was just one of the sleazy jewels of Ruben Cortez's criminal empire. Smyth had lost track of time since the accident. Of course, it was late in the day now, and Jayni would be starting her shift on the poles. Her ratfink boss usually put her on early, because she was one of the less attractive girls at Bendy's, after her stint making her run waitress duty for the shady clientele. Wess liked to forget the fact that Bendy's was where he met her, stuffing singles and the odd ten-spot cred-note into her v-string.

"Are you there?" she said. "Wess, Latreena and Ashtré are here and they told me that Flex was over at the club, bragging about breaking your face. Is that true?"

Smyth sagged. That was just great. He forced a laugh. "Ah, that big lug. He's just having a joke, sweetie. Flex, and me we're good pals. We had a little misunderstanding, sure, but nothing serious."

"Latreena says Flex says he's gonna make shoes out of you."

He gave a weak chuckle. "He's such a kidder."

"Are you hurt?" Jayni demanded, and the tone in her voice cut him like a knife. He hated lying to her, which was odd when he thought about it, because Wess had made an art out of lying to almost everyone he knew. It was some kind of karmic punishment, he reasoned, that the one person he couldn't lie to was the woman Wess Smyth had come to care about the most.

At times like this, he got annoyed with himself for not being able to get around her, and it usually manifested in this way. "I told you, I'm fine!" he snapped angrily. "Grud, Jayni, why you always gotta be fussing over me?"

"Because I'm worried about you!" Her reply was brittle and he instantly felt like a total scumbag. "You selfish spug!" Jayni shouted the insult down the phone and cut him off, leaving Wess spent with the emotional effort of the conversation.

Not for the first time, he wondered if Jayni wouldn't be better off without Wesson Smyth in her life. The answer, as always, was yes. If he had any kind of self-respect at all, he would have cancelled their on-off-on-off relationship once and for all, and let her find someone better – not that that was likely, working in a place as low-rent as Bendy's – but Wess, although he hated himself for it, simply didn't have the will to let her go. Deep down, Jayni was the one thing that made him yearn to be a better man, even if those feelings had a hard time bubbling to the surface. He wanted to take her away from all this; he wanted to make that single big score and just cut loose and run. It was just that fate, luck or stupidity always seemed to get in the way.

At least until today. Wess pocketed the phone, then as an afterthought took it out again and turned it off. He needed time to think. Somewhere to clean up and get some food, somewhere he could weigh things up and set a plan cooking.

He weighed the phone in his hand. Jayni. Jayni had a place in the Fillmore Barbone con-apts a few miles from the edge of the Dust Zone, and she'd be out at the bar for at least the next four hours. Wess would have to hope that she hadn't changed the lock code again after their last spat.

He smiled, and his eyes drifted toward the open case on the floor. Yeah, he told himself, things are going to be different now. Smyth wasn't really sure why he felt that way, but he liked it. He scratched absently at the places where the sensor needles had nicked his fingers and then gathered up the contents of the case.

WEAPONS GRADE

Dredd parked his Lawmaster on the ramp of watch bay Bravo 63 Delta, and strode out across the thin ferrocrete arch of the observation platform. Braga Skedway and the convoluted knot of roads fanned out beneath him in a wild profusion of speeding vehicles, the sound of their passing a constant rumble he could sense through the soles of his boots. The Judge crouched and examined the spot where Vedder had stood, glancing around for anything that could point him toward her motives. He had already checked the watch bay's monitor unit. The device had absolutely no record of any serving officer being on the platform in the moments before the fire-bomb explosion, despite the fact that Dredd had seen the COE agent up there with his own eyes. Watch bay cameras only operated on remote command or when the bay was registered as occupied, and so the sensor log had no images to prove that Vedder had even been here. Dredd scowled, regretting not giving in to his instinct to arrest the woman when he'd had her there in front of him.

"Bike," he snapped. "Infra-red scan. Sweep the platform."

"Wilco, Judge Dredd." The motorcycle's primary headlamps illuminated and the Lawmaster rolled forward on its own, the on-board computer laying a diffusion pattern across the watch bay surface. It was hardly a substitute for a full Tek-crew evaluation, but

Dredd had already gone a long way on nothing more than a bad feeling about Vedder, and he had his doubts that Hershey would let him authorise a scene-of-crime scan of the platform.

"Detection," said the bike computer suddenly. "Anomalous object." The headlamps swivelled slightly to spotlight a grey bump in the bay floor. It was exactly the same texture and colouration as the ferrocrete.

"Identify." Dredd kept his distance. He wouldn't put it past Vedder to have left him a little surprise up there.

"Non-volatile," replied the computer. "No explosive or toxic materials detected."

The Judge crouched and removed his boot knife. With slow and steady movements, Dredd levered the object from the platform and took a closer look. It was a micro-camera, a civilian model of the kind that were sold to corporations or to worried spouses interested in spying on their errant partners. Covered with a disc of low-grade mimetic plasteen, they could lay concealed for months. Dredd had seen them many times before. They were short-range and far too low-tech for the COE. This was someone else's piece of spy gear. Acting quickly, he drew a pair of binoculars from the Lawmaster's panniers and scanned the surroundings with them. There was just one citiblock: Phillip J Fry Block. Dredd's gaze settled on the flank of the building, searching for the telltale flicker of a curtain, the blink of a light – and he found it.

He saw a face, pale with shock, staring back at him through a monoscope. The Judge tapped his helmet mic. "Control, Dredd. Need a citizen record check. Female Caucasian, dark hair, twenties, resident Phillip J Fry, Sector 88. Southern facing apartment, somewhere between sixty-second and sixty-fourth floors. Probable badge-spotter."

There was a momentary pause as Justice Central's vast databases searched millions of names and faces for a match. "Copy, Dredd. We have a tally, apartment 874/J..."

The crime sweep was still in effect sector-wide, so Dredd was fully within his rights as he kicked open the door to 874/J and shouted the name of the hab's sole resident. "Katy Hart! This is the law! Show yourself!"

A rustle from the living room drew Dredd's attention and he moved in, Lawgiver raised and ready. The house shared floor and shelf space with dozens of bizarre mutant plants, breeds of unpleasant but not really dangerous Cursed Earth flora that were part of a current trend for exotic greenery. "Citizen Hart!" he ordered. "I won't ask again!"

The girl emerged from behind a large bio-gro box where dozens of shark-tulips were budding, their petal-like teeth grinding on mouthfuls of dead flies. She had a peculiar look on her face, a mixture of abject terror and giddy thrill. "Judge Dredd," she managed, gulping for air, "Oh, wow. Ohhh, wow."

"Hands where I can see 'em."

She did as he ordered, white-knuckled fingers still clutching the monoscope. Katy blinked. "Can I... take, uh, your picture?"

Dredd waved the spy-camera in his other hand. "Reckon you already have. Where's your book?"

The girl deflated a little, and then with delicacy she put down the scope and produced a thick album from behind a planter full of hammerhead blossoms. "I'm doing really well," she began. "Up to twenty-six point three per cent so far!" Inside the book were dozens of still images, some grainy and indistinct, some sharp and clear. All of them were of Mega-City One Judges, capturing their faces and their shields. She smiled. "I made the women's finals at BadgeCon last year!"

Badge spotting, also known as Judge-snapping and helmeting, was one of the hundreds of thousands of hobby activities enjoyed by MC-1's largely unemployed population. Along with bat-gliding, dishwashing, wibbling and, of course, Cursed Earth horticulture, Judge-snapping was just another mindless pastime to keep ordinary citizens from going insane with boredom. Officially, the Justice Department frowned on it, but it wasn't illegal to photograph a Judge, as long as it wasn't used for commercial gain, and the city's roster of serving officers was a matter of record. Intrepid badge-spotters would scour the streets with digi-cams and checklists, gathering the names of law officers and posting their "collections" on the Mega-Web. The hobby wasn't as popular as zoom-train spotting, but it was getting there. Dredd grimaced. He'd had run-ins with these kooks before, some of them getting in the way of real law enforcement.

Katy blinked at him again, tears welling up in her eyes. "You won't say anything about the spy-cam, will you, Judge? I mean, technically it's a violation of spotter by-laws and I could have my whole collection for this year declared null and void–"

"You've got bigger things to worry about," Dredd broke in, "Planting a surveillance device on Justice Department property. That's a Code Five violation."

"I did it by remote!" she insisted. "I thought it would be okay, I used a blimpy-toy to drop it there–"

"Two years in the cubes, citizen. And I guarantee you'll see plenty of Judges there."

Hart waved a hand in front of her face. "I'm not worried about that! I just don't want to lose my score!"

Dredd resisted the urge to shake his head and fixed her with a hard stare. "How long have you been taping Judges at the watch bay?"

"A couple of weeks."

"I might be willing to consider leniency, if you show a willingness to co-operate." He held out a gloved hand. "I want the recordings, Katy. Everything you have."

The girl gave a frantic nod and began rooting through a pile of vid-discs. "Oh," she mumbled to herself. "I got Dredd, I got Dredd right here in my apartment! This is gonna score me big!"

The Judge flipped to the most recent pages of the discarded album and there was a low-angle shot of Vedder, stepping off her bike. "These tapes," Dredd asked. "They got audio as well as video, right?"

A decrepit old eldo sleeping in the bus shelter at the corner of Shish and Phipps generously "donated" his radorak and, with that, Smyth's makeshift disguise was complete. Keeping himself to the shady side of the street, weaving in and out of doorways, Wess worked his way ever closer to the Barbone con-apts. He stood a very real chance of getting himself spotted and, once again, beaten to within an inch of his life, should any of Cortez's toughs be passing by, but he was a creature of habit when all was said and done. As much as the rational part of him told Smyth he should be half way across the city by now – if not in fact running for the Canadian Wastes – he was still in Double-Eight, slinking through the side-streets that had been his home ground since he was a juve. An outside observer might have thought it was a case of "better the devil you know", or just baseline cowardice on Wess's part, but it was neither. Although he had yet to admit it to himself, on some instinctual level Smyth was looking for trouble. He walked through the shadows, eyes hollow, his left hand buried in the folds of the weather-beaten old radorak, kneading his new prize with warm, sweaty fingers.

Hunger was drumming in his stomach, and Wess made a quick detour into a Burger Me franchise, shoes squeaking across the wipe-clean vinyl floor. He kept his head down, studying his feet until he was at the robo-server.

"Welcome to Burger Me. Would you like to try the new Flambé de Fungi meal with Twirler Fries?"

"Yeah, whatever," Smyth snapped, jamming his cash into the credi-slot on the chest of the robot. "And a FauxCola."

The machine cocked its head in a puppet-like gesture of synthetic sympathy. "I'm sorry sir, but we're out of FauxCola, the real fake thing. That customer has just taken the last can." Wess's hooded gaze went in the direction that the robot pointed and he almost wet himself as a result. Two queues over was Hoog, the big, bald and blue-scaled alien bruiser that Bob Toes kept as his sidekick. Wess registered several things at once: Hoog's three eyes bulging with recognition as he saw him; Toes and a couple of the guys from the ambush in a wall booth; and the sickly smell of his food order, ripe like rotting vegetation.

Hoog's mouth of tusks bared and the alien advanced on him, grinning and still bearing a tray of purchases.

Wess had made up and discarded a dozen different violent fantasies about this meeting, and none of them, not a single one, had unfolded with Smyth chancing to run into Toes and company in a cheap-ass fast food joint. He threw his flambé de fungi in Hoog's face and ran as the alien thug screamed, hot synthi-lard burning his triclopian eyes.

The door Wess took wasn't the one he'd come in by, and instead of leading to the street proper, it took him around the drive-through exit and toward a ragged chain link fence. Smyth took the path of least resistance and barrelled through the hole in the wire, scrambling across a vacant lot and toward the service alley behind the Q-Save. He heard their feet behind him, especially the scraping noise that Hoog's clawed toenails made on the ferrocrete. The alien couldn't get shoes on Earth, he remembered, only big sandals that looked really dumb with dark socks. Smyth shook the thought away with a quick jerk of the head; he had to concentrate on running.

When he took the corner, he knew instantly that he had made a fatal error. The light in the alley dimmed here in the shade of a tall megway stanchion, and the pounding race of his pursuers' footfalls suddenly slowed to a more leisurely jog. They knew what a mistake it was. Wess gaped at the blank wall blocking his way, shocked at his own blind idiocy. Of course this was a dead-end. Of course there was no way out. He'd been here untold times before – why had he forgotten it today?

"Ahhhhaaa," wheezed Hoog, through a mouthful of teeth and spittle. "Aaah!" The alien produced a phone and began the slow, laborious process of dialling a number with its big, clawed fingers. Nearby Bob Toes made that irritating *tsk* noise again, and Wess felt a surge of volcanic anger boil up inside his chest. He turned around slowly, vibrating with tension like a struck chord.

Toes didn't seem to notice. "Smythy. Got the cash?" He tapped his nose in a mocking gesture. "Give it to me and Hoog here might just bite off an ear." Bob puffed out his chest. "I'm guessing you don't have it, as you ran like the yellow streak spug you are."

"I... I got something," Wess stuttered. "I got something for y-you."

"Wha–?" clattered Hoog. The phone in his claw beeped as it connected.

"This!" Wess drew out his hand and with a fierce grin, gave Bob the finger. "Sneck you, you snecking snecker!" he added.

Abrupt laughter broke out between Toes's two human friends, but Bob wasn't even the slightest bit amused by Wess's sudden and daring display of backbone. "You worthless piece of klegg shit, you'll pay for that." The criminal tugged the large frame of a heavy-gauge spit gun from a shoulder holster under his coat.

It was an East-Meg Vondo FG6 Automatik with a ten-round magazine and an integral xenon laser sight. At close range, it would tear an unprotected human torso into ragged chunks of meat. Smyth didn't recall how he knew that, the information just popped right there into his forebrain the moment he laid eyes upon it. Bob's pistol came up towards him in syrupy slow motion, the maw of the barrel yawning.

From Hoog's perspective, Smyth seemed to blink, shifting in strobe-fast images instead of fluid movements. The peckerhead's left hand bolted out of the folds of his coat faster than the finger had come, and in his fist was a glinting ingot of dark metal, obsidian and monstrous. The shape screamed and darts of white fire sprang from Wess's hand, elongating into threads that lanced through Bob Toes and tore him to pieces. Hoog's boss became coils of bloody mist and steaming wet flesh. The alien swore a gutter oath in its own sibilant language, dropping the phone and scrambling to recover its own gun. As Hoog pulled at a stuck zip pocket on his coverall, Bob's two pals, the Clent brothers, were scattering. The Clents favoured short-range multi-barrel stubbers, pepperbox pistols that could discharge blunt shock loads or flechettes, depending on how the firing collar was dialled.

There were humming fizzes from the alley as low-velocity rounds slashed through the air at Wess, but Smyth was jerking like a puppet on a string, leading with the big black firearm in his hand, impossibly placing himself everywhere the shots were not. Smyth's weapon did something odd; it unfolded an extra part of itself from the muzzle, elongating its barrel. A thinner, more collimated beam of hot plasma etched a glowing line on Hoog's three retinas as it lanced through both of the Clents', coring them like munce fruit.

Hoog ripped his pocket to get his maser pistol free, only to discover to his horror that the power cell was flat. Smyth was shaking violently, every part of his body vibrating except for his gun arm. The black weapon came up to a point on Hoog's wide face where a human would have had a nose. The alien made a whimpering noise in its throat a split-second before another plasmatic dart ripped his head open.

The entire killing spree had lasted less than ten seconds, from the moment Toes drew his gun to the moment Hoog's decapitated corpse settled to its knees, desultory spits of turquoise blood jetting from the neck stump. Wess's heart hammered in his chest, adrenaline flooding through his veins. He felt giddy and nauseated, and the gun seemed to take on weight from nowhere. A moment ago, it had moved effortlessly, like a part of his body, but now it felt like it was made of lead. Smyth's wrist was tight with aches and his bones seemed brittle, as if they would break under the strain of holding the weapon. He stuffed the firearm back into his radorak, ignoring the sizzle as the still-hot barrel wilted a patch of the polypropylop coat.

Wess's foot scuffed something as he walked away, and he bent down impulsively to pick it up. Hoog's phone. The small vid-screen was blurry, but a familiar red face was peering owlishly out at him. "Hoog? That you? I heard shooting..."

Smyth leered into the camera pickup. "Flex," he spat, bile bubbling up in his throat. "Things are going to change, you musclehead juicer!" He tossed the phone away, listing like a drunk as he stumbled from the scene of the crime. "Things are gonna change!" Wess vomited violently into a dumpster and ran.

"You understand that you risk incurring our disappointment with these delays?" The faceless shadow on the monitor screen spoke with a voice so synthesised and acoustically treated that it was barely recognisable as human. "There is a timetable to which you are not privy." The faint glow of the screen was all the light there was in the blacked-out room.

Vedder kept her face neutral, just as she'd been taught by the psycho-conditioners. "I have the matter in hand."

"You do not," said the other shadow, sharing the split-screen. Only the very slightest of tonal differences indicated that this was a different speaker from the first. A woman, she guessed. "Where is the device?"

The COE agent discarded any thoughts of lying. She was sure they knew the answer already. "It will be recovered in due course. This setback will be overcome quickly."

"Dredd is involved," said the first. "His interference is the last thing we want."

"He's inconsequential," Vedder replied. "I'm monitoring him. If, by some fluke he stumbles on to the device, then I'll simply use Dredd to secure it and then kill him."

"Many have tried. None have succeeded." The second shadow rumbled. "Dredd is a wild card. I want this situation resolved before he ever has a chance to comprehend the scope of it."

Vedder nodded. "That is also my intention."

"We initiated this operation in order to make sure the unit did not slip through our fingers, and yet that is exactly what has happened, thanks to your poor planning, Judge Vedder." Reproach leaked from the first shadow's words. "We have a strategy for the device which cannot get underway until we have recovered it."

"I am well aware of the value of the unit." This time Vedder let a little annoyance slip out. "You'll get your tests." Before either of the anonymous voices could reply, she reached out and deactivated the communicator. Pausing only to attach a small thermite charge to destroy the screen, and any genetic traces she might have left in the room, Vedder exited, brooding.

The footage was grainy and blurred in places, but the definition was high enough for Dredd to recognise the COE Judge framed by the glow of traffic passing below her. Citizen Hart's spy-cam had caught more than just the typical duty officers pausing in the watch bay to report in, or conduct traffic control. Dredd turned up the gain on his bike computer's monitor screen and listened carefully to the faint audio pickup. Now and then he caught the odd word from Vedder, as the wind carried her voice towards the concealed place where the spy-cam had been hidden. Something about an "operation" and "schedules".

"Who were you talking to, Vedder?" he asked aloud. "Who's in on this thing?"

As if in reply, Dredd heard the sound of his own voice replayed through the tape. "Watch bay Bravo 63 Delta, this is Dredd. We got a wrecker situation brewing up ahead, or haven't you heard?" On the screen, Vedder threw a disinterested glance over the guardrail and then away again. Dredd's mouth twisted at the Judge's blatant violation of department standing orders as she ignored his signal, reaching for the squawk box on the bay wall to switch it off. Dredd tapped the fast-forward control and wound on a few minutes more, up to the time index just before the explosion. Vedder reacted to something, following a vehicle on the highway below from left to right through her binoculars as it passed beneath the watch bay. From the spy-cam's angle it was impossible to see what she was looking at, but there was little doubt in Dredd's mind it was the featureless grey truck. He watched with a slight sneer of amusement as the fireball erupted off-camera, illuminating Vedder's pale face with stark orange-red highlights. Her expression was unchanged.

"Almost like she expected it..." He slowed the playback as the woman ran for her Lawmaster and roared away down the off-ramp. Dredd watched the recording a second time and then sat back in the saddle, thinking. Was it possible that Vedder had been in the midst of that confusion as well? He'd seen other Judges moving around in the smoke and chaos and assumed it was Leary and her men – but it could just as easily have been Vedder, sneaking through the fire to the truck. He tapped his chin, working out the angles to the situation. Was it Vedder who had stolen the cargo, on the orders of her COE masters or on her own? Or had someone else got to it before her, in those moments when the skedway had been engulfed in flames? If, as he strongly suspected, it was Vedder that had forged Tyler's ident code to have the evidence destroyed, what was her motive? Dredd frowned. He had nothing but questions and circumstantial evidence, but the mystery of it was gnawing at him. Sometimes he wondered if it was a factor in his genetic make-up, some holdover from the cellular legacy of his clone-father Judge Fargo, a built-in tenacity and focus that simply could not let something like this go unanswered.

A chime from his headset communicator sounded, and Dredd tapped his helmet. "Dredd, responding."

"It's Tyler. I've got a lead, but you're not going to like it."

"Right now anything will sound good. Let's hear it."

The Tek-Judge hunched over his console, keeping his voice low. "I ran a general sweep of the city records for trucks matching the make and model of the one you found on the sked. I got hundreds of hits, most of them inconsequential. The majority of the vehicles are owned by small corporations, delivery firms, that sorta thing–"

"Cut to the chase, Tyler," Dredd replied.

"Uh, yeah. Well. I ran the sweep again today just to double-check I hadn't missed anything, but I was tired and gettin' a little punchy. By mistake, I tagged the search parameters to check non-civilian concerns as well as citizen owners... And something weird came up."

"Weird, huh?" He could hear the sneer in Dredd's voice. "Explain."

"There's one facility in MC-1 that purchased five of these trucks a couple of years ago for what's listed as 'non-specific special duties'. The weird bit is, all five trucks were listed as scrapped in a city audit a few months later... but there's no record of them ever being recycled or destroyed."

Dredd felt a tingle in the tips of his fingers, the same faint touch of adrenaline he got whenever a hard, solid clue presented itself to him. "Who bought the trucks, Tyler?"

"MAC has the registrations listed to the motor pool at the West 17 Test Labs complex, MegWest Sector 202." The Luna-City Judge paused. "If there's anyone in the Big Meg with the hardware to make the modifications we saw, its West 17."

The senior Judge nodded to himself. It was a good fit for the facts to hand. He thumbed the ignition stud on his Lawmaster's handlebar and revved the engine. "I don't have to tell you to keep this compartmentalised, Tyler. I'm heading to West 17 now... I'll shake the tree a little and see what falls out."

The Tek-Judge gulped. "I, uh, could be wrong, Dredd. It's just a chance lead, after all, it could be nothing."

Dredd accelerated out on to the highway, heading westwards. "I'll let you know."

In the early days of the Judge system, when men like Fargo and Solomon had laid down the first foundations of the Mega-Cities, the need for hardware that could support the nascent justice program was paramount. Invoking special dispensation and unique clauses in the city charter, Fargo had given certain organisations and corporations favoured status in the hierarchy of MC-1, in return for their assistance in arming and armouring the Judges. West 17 had been such a company, and in the years following the establishment of the Judges it has been West 17's Test Labs that created the tools that the Justice Department used to enforce the law. The Lawgiver multi-ammunition handgun; the nigh-infallible Birdie lie detector; the mighty Lawmaster motorcycle, and more – all of the variants of these devices had their origins at West 17, the gifted scientists and engineers working with renowned Tek-Judges like Marconi and Stumm, inventor of the non-lethal riot pacification gas that still bared his name.

Over time, while Mega-City weapons manufacturers like General Arms kept their independence, West 17 became less and less a civilian auxiliary and more and more a division of the Justice Department, eventually incorporated into the governmental structure by edict of then-Chief Judge Clarence Goodman. It became a centre for technical excellence, the dream posting for Tek-Judges from across the city. Other facilities found themselves marginalised in favour of West 17, with only the Tech 21 Lab in MegEast gaining anything near the same level of prestige – and even they were tarred with a erratic reputation for their research into the more "exotic" projects, like time travel and inter-dimensional physics.

These were golden years for Marconi and his staff; but they were about to end abruptly.

Dredd crossed the Danny Jackson Bridge at high speed, the only rider in the central Judges-Only Lane that bisected the median strip. Ahead of him, the distinctive pillar of the West 17 building rose up. It was a vast, spindle-shaped construction, a faded white column of stone and metal rising from the axis of a broad hemisphere, supporting four large saucer-shaped pods. The dark, gun-metal grey discs looked like a tower of balancing plates, the flat matte-coloured surface reflecting nothing of the day's wan sunlight. There were no visible windows, lending it a sinister, secretive air.

He pulled his Lawmaster into the parking atrium and strode to the robot receptionist. A fan of laser light wafted over his badge as he approached.

"Judge Dredd," said the droid, "you do not have an appointment."

"I'm pursuing an investigation," he replied flatly. "I want access to your motor pool, right now."

"Do you have a warrant?"

Dredd leaned closer. "West 17 Test Labs is a Justice Department division. This badge is all the warrant that I need."

The droid continued, unaffected by the implied threat in Dredd's tone. "I will require an authorisation code from a ranking Council officer, or failing that–"

"What's the problem here?" said a new voice. Dredd turned to see another Judge approaching him.

A Tek-Judge – who wore no helmet – approached, his shock of white hair and a thick, snowy beard all to evident.

"Loengard?" Dredd read the name from the man's shield. "Are you what passes for authority in this place?"

The Judge's face twisted in irritation. "Your reputation precedes you, Judge Dredd. How can we help you on your way?"

"By showing me your motor pool. Now."

The hint of a smirk crossed Loengard's features. "Let me guess? You need another replacement Lawmaster? I hope you brought the right requisition forms."

Dredd handed him a printout with an image of the stealth truck. "I'm looking for this vehicle."

"Doesn't seem familiar to me." Loengard extended a hand to take the printout from Dredd. "Leave this with me and I'll look into it."

Dredd coiled the paper in his hand. "Better I do it myself. Save you the time."

"Come with me, then," said Loengard, after a long pause.

Two factors marked the sea change for the West 17 Test Labs; the first was the disastrous development of a new laser-based firearm for Judge assault operations and city wall security. The JD EX1850, more commonly known as the "stub gun", was hailed as a breakthrough weapon. Capable of slicing through thick plasteen armour and long-range attacks, the West 17 facility threw itself behind the manufacture of the gun – only to discover that the EX1850 had a fatal design flaw. Continuous uses of the weapon caused a catastrophic overheat and power pack detonation. Retired even before entering service, the stub gun became an obsolete curiosity – until the event that would lead to the second factor in West 17's fall from grace.

East-Meg One's invasion of the city in 2104 forced the stub gun back into service, but it was too late to save the life of Judge Marconi, who was captured and subjected to mental reprogramming by the Sov occupation army. By the time Marconi took his own life, the East-Meggers had stolen much of the technology stored in West 17's databanks, and in the aftermath of the Apocalypse War many of the facility's duties were transferred to the staff at Tech 21.

They paused at a hatch and Loengard tapped in a key code with brisk strokes. For the first time, Dredd noticed that the white-haired Judge had a cybernetic prosthetic where his right forearm should have been. "How'd you get that?" he asked.

Loengard shot him a look. "Lab accident. I have a couple of plasteen ribs and an artificial liver as well, if you're interested."

"Must have been some mishap."

The hatch yawned open and Loengard stepped through. "We make weapons here, Dredd," he said. "Accidents in this place are usually terminal."

The Judge led him along a service gantry, overlooking a wide garage level with dozens of vehicles on repair platforms and test rigs. Dredd spotted various models of Lawmasters and Quasar Bikes, a Banshee interceptor and even a K2001/Killdozer rig, the vehicle he'd used to cross the Cursed Earth during the 2T(fru)T breakout in Mega-City Two.

"As you can see," Loengard gestured with his robotic limb, "we've got a lot of auxiliary vehicles here but nothing of the design you're looking for."

"This isn't your only vehicle bay," Dredd broke in. "I've been here before, remember? What about the secure levels down below?" He pointed at the floor for emphasis.

"I can't grant you access to those, Dredd, you know that. Sub-levels are restricted and you don't have the clearance."

Dredd grimaced. There was that word again. He pulled his belt mic from its clip. "Maybe I should call Chief Hershey and get it right now?"

Loengard didn't fall for Dredd's bluff. "Good luck. This building is protected with a ray-shield. You won't be able to get a signal in or out of here without a land-line." He met Dredd's hooded gaze. "If you have a play to make, Dredd, then make it. Otherwise, get out. I've got work to do."

The Judge advanced on Loengard. "What are you hiding?"

"All sorts of things," Loengard replied, "as you well know! What we do here is vital to the security of the city, and no one, not even you, Dredd, has a right to come in here and start throwing their weight around!" He looked away. "Of course we have our secrets. But we keep them for the good of Mega-City One."

"And who decides that?"

"Who judges the Judges, is that what you're asking me?" Loengard sneered. "Not you, Dredd."

In desperation, the administration at West 17 Test Labs threw all they could into crash development programs for new weapons, in hope of regaining the favour of the Justice Department. In 2119, Chief Judge Hadrian Volt threw them a lifeline, ordering the introduction of a new Lawgiver pistol for the department's officers, and West 17 entered into a partnership with General Arms to create the new handgun; but corners were cut and security compromised in their eagerness to redeem themselves.

It was an opportunity ripe for exploitation. Behind double-blind sub-contractors and shell companies, a Mega-City crimelord named Nero Narcos engineered a long game of infiltration and subterfuge through General Arms and West 17. Narcos ensured that the new Mark II Lawgivers were equipped with an undetectable circuit capable of jamming the firearms at the flip of a switch. When he was ready, the mobster launched a city-wide robot revolution and left the Judges impotent and disarmed. Narcos's plan ultimately failed, and the guns were redesigned; but West 17's fall from grace was complete. Tech 21 became the leading light, and what had once been the city's richest intellectual playground was now a scientific backwater for projects on the fringe of viability.

Dredd mounted his bike and paused for a moment, mulling over Loengard's behaviour. That the Judge was hiding something wasn't the issue – Dredd could smell that on him a mile off – but it was the nature of the secret that bothered him. Naked crime, aggression and lawlessness were one thing, but conspiracy was another, and it stuck in his craw.

"Attention." The bike computer interrupted his thoughts. "Message received. Data only."

His brow furrowed. Loengard had said that no signals could reach inside the building, so where had this come from? "Show me."

On the screen an icon of a file appeared, with two short sentences written on it: "We need to talk. But you need to read this first."

GUNSIGHT

"It's encrypted," said Tyler, pushing the data-goggles back up his forehead.

"Figured it would be. That's why you're looking at it," Dredd replied, glancing around the Tek-Lab. It was third watch now, and the night shift meant that labs were virtually empty.

"No," Tyler said, rubbing his eyes. "When I say 'encrypted', I mean encrypted. Like the difference between a BigSize SlurpaShake and the way that the Statute of Judgement is big. There are more layers of data protection on this file than craters on Luna."

The Judge frowned. "Some message. A mystery informant leaves this in my bike computer and we can't even read it."

Tyler shook his head. "Oh, don't get me wrong, Dredd. I can hack this, it'll just take some time. And I don't think this is part of the message, as you put it. Whoever the snitch is at West 17, they're handin' us evidence straight from the facility's main computer core." He pointed at a code string on his monitor. "I recognise the routing protocol. They must've done it in a hurry, without decoding the raw information first."

"So someone inside the West 17's ray-shield, someone who was there while I was talking to Loengard, transmitted this into my Lawmaster's CPU?"

"Got it in one." Tyler stifled a yawn. "I've made a start already. There's several sub files in here..." He blinked slowly.

"When did you sleep last?" Dredd asked.

"Uh..." The Tek-Judge hesitated. "Tuesday, I think."

"It's Thursday, Tyler. You're no good to me half-awake. Get some rack time in the sleep machine and make a fresh start."

He nodded. "In a second. First, let me show you what I squeezed out of this thing so far." A string of images appeared on the monitor, all of them displaying the familiar shape of the stealth truck.

"I've seen this," said Dredd. "Your breakdown on the vehicle we recovered."

"Wrong answer," smirked Tyler. "These aren't my records – these are the data files from West 17's special circumstances unit. I was right about the trucks, it was them who modified the vehicles. Check it out..." He tapped the screen with a stylus. "Advanced artificially intelligent navigation system tied into a state of the art sensor web. A laser-resistant, bombproof hull. Nine different kinds of electronic masking and countermeasures systems. Radar, madar, lidar, thermal and meson scan-proof. Hell, Dredd, on any kind of sensor grid this thing would look like a hole in the air. It's pretty impressive."

"Not to me. In the wrong hands, one of these transports could be trouble. Think about it, Tyler. The ultimate getaway vehicle, undetectable and untraceable."

"With all due respect, sir, I don't reckon West 17 are usin' them to rob banks. This is a cargo configuration, somethin' you'd use to ship items across the city without anyone ever knowing about it."

Dredd looked closer. "You said it was armoured, right? Practically impossible to open without a demolition bot or a photon torch."

"That's about the size of it, yeah." Tyler blinked again as he caught on to Dredd's train of thought. "Oh... So how come it was open and empty, is that what you're askin'?"

"That cargo compartment was opened from the inside, not the outside. Something blew out the lock."

Tyler went pale. "You think... You think we're talking about something that's alive here? Whoa."

"Right now, we don't know what we're dealing with. Right now all we got is more questions."

"Not quite," said the Tek-Judge, folding away the vehicle graphics and opening another set of data-windows. "The deeper data on this file has tags indicating where it came from and who it went to. I can't get into the file proper yet, but the tags are easier to read. Look here. That Judge Loengard is on the list, so all his yap about not knowin' anything was stomm."

"Can't say that comes as a surprise. What else?" asked Dredd.

"This." He tapped the screen again. "There's only one agency in Mega-City One that uses this routing code. The Data Collating Bureau."

Dredd's face twisted into a cold smile. "The DCB. The public face of the Covert Operations Establishment." It was a well-known fact that the secretive COE had a mandate to operate only in matters that affected the security of the city, and only in territory outside the city walls; anything that happened on MC-1 turf was a Justice Department matter. But the COE did have one official presence on the inside, a small division of the city's Public Surveillance Unit, the department in charge of overseeing the millions of data feeds from spy-in-the-sky cameras, street-scanners and signal traffic monitors. The DCB was supposedly a passive observer, filtering the terabytes of raw data before handing it off to the PSU and the Justice Department's central computer; Dredd didn't buy that for a second.

"So, if the DCB's SOP is to filter MC-1's VDTs for the PSU and MAC, WTF are they doing getting the COE F2F with W17?" Tyler gave an involuntary smirk.

Dredd's icy demeanour made the Tek-Judge's insouciant remark shrivel up and die. "Don't mistake my earlier concern for your well-being as an excuse for flippancy, Tyler. Judge-Marshal Tex may have allowed levity among his officers, but I don't."

"Uh, yes sir. Sorry, sir. It's just been a long, uh, day."

The senior Judge jerked a thumb over his shoulder. "Get that rest. You're no good to me if you're punchy." He watched Tyler slope away; once he was alone, Dredd ran off a hard copy of the encrypted files and sent another digital duplicate to the secure data stack in the Chief Judge's office. If he didn't have this figured out by the time Hershey was back from the conference on Justice Five, it might help to justify the effort he was putting into this investigation.

On paper, it all looked so insubstantial. A stealth truck that vanished. A COE operative conducting what was clearly an unsanctioned mission inside his jurisdiction. And now a phantom informant in the heart of a secret weapons laboratory. It was a mixture of random pieces from different jigsaws, and as much as he studied them, no coherent picture was emerging for the lawman. Worse still, deep down inside Dredd couldn't shake off the feeling that someone, somewhere, was playing with him; and catch-up was a game that he had always hated.

We need to talk. "Talk about what?" Dredd asked aloud. For all he knew, the files could be a plant, something to throw him off the trail of the real thing, to divert him from Vedder and whatever machinations she was hatching; but if he pulled Vedder off the street with nothing but gut instinct and instant dislike to go on, the Special Judicial

Service would have a field day and he'd never get to the bottom of this. No. There was only one way to handle this new wrinkle. He'd work the problem, find the angles, then push until it gave.

"Control, this is Judge Dredd," he spoke into his mic. "I need a location for a Justice Department officer. Name's Loengard, attached to West 17 Test Labs."

"Wilco, Dredd. Judge Loengard is off-duty right now, at his quarters. You want us to page him?"

"Negative. Just tell me where to find him."

"Samuel Seaborne con-apts, hab module 1657."

Jayni had changed the code for the door. Wess sagged against the frame and blew out a sigh, leaving a small smear of blue alien blood on the grubby plasteen. Some remnant of Hoog's death throes had jetted on to Smyth's radorak, although he had hardly noticed.

Following an impulse he wasn't quite sure of, Wess took out the black gun and placed it to the card reader slot in the door. He thought about pulling the trigger, but before he was even aware of it the lock made a buzzing electrical discharge and opened. Inside, the smell of the fake lavender air freshener he always associated with Jayni caressed his senses. The scent seemed stronger in a way he couldn't properly place, more potent, sharper. Wess walked into the kitchen alcove and absently placed the weapon on the table. With robotic, numb motions he picked out bottles of water from the cupboard and a thick slice of munce from the cooler. The meat-like protein slab was munce in its most basic processed form – dull brown in colour, odourless and tasteless, utterly bland in every sense of the word. Jayni was clever with munce, Wess recalled, she had racks of cheap but potent spices that could make the soyafood taste like a million different things. He drained all the bottles of water one after another like a machine pumping fuel into a tank, then set to work on eating the munce, alternating between ripping off slices with his fingers and chewing it into paste. He ate and drank, and ate and drank, drifting without anything but the most vague thoughts on his mind. Now and then, woolly noises from Jayni's neighbours came through the walls, too indistinct to fathom their meaning.

Eventually, when most of Jayni's larder was bare, and the strange, directionless hunger in his gut had been satisfied, rational thought began to return to Smyth. His eyes fell on the radorak where he'd shrugged it from his shoulders, there in a ragged pile on the floor. Hoog's blood had dried to a dull green hue, in spatter-pattern patches of manic starbursts; and like a zoom train hitting him in the small of the back, the sudden awful reality of what he had done crashed down on Wesson Smyth in a single moment of blinding clarity.

He started to weep with fear, the tears cutting tracks through the dirt on his cheeks. Wess tried hard to piece together what had happened there in the alley behind the Q-Save, but all he came away with were broken shards of memory, little blinks of sensation and feeling that were flat and pasty like the cold munce in his stomach. He pressed at his temples; without warning, a harsh blast of pain and white light knifed into his eyes and he wailed, stamping his feet in agony. Then it was gone as quickly as it had come, and he was panting, coiled there on the tubular metal chair.

Colour drained from his face – he saw a pale ghost of himself looking back from the glass door in the microwave oven. He looked haunted and gaunt, eyes red with worry. Wess's gaze dropped to the table, and to the gun.

The petty crook had known instinctively that it was a weapon the moment the steel case had opened to him, there in the derelict toaster warehouse. Nothing built and designed that way could be anything else, a mixture of hard, matte surfaces and box-like protrusions. Vents and gas ports dotted the weapon's flanks, glowing indicators fading in and out in a slow heartbeat of blue light. It was engineered to look lethal, even in repose, as if it might leap off the plasteen vinyl at any second like a mechanical raptor. It fitted into Wess's hand as if it had been tailor-made for him, the grip squirming to conform to him. It felt easy and dangerous.

Where his fingertips touched the butt, sensor pits invisible to the naked eye found the places where the needles in the carry case's handles had sampled his blood, and spat nanofilament effectors into his epidermis. Wess was unaware of any of this. He only knew on some bone-deep level that the weapon was his. Even a moment of considering how to dispose of it made the munce in his gut threaten to rebel, and instead Wess rocked back and forth in his seat, eyes never straying from the pistol, fretting over his fate.

"Cortez." He said the name to the lavender-scented air with trepidation, as if speaking it aloud would cause the crimelord to spontaneously materialise there in the apartment like some mythic demon. "C-Cortez is gonna have me dead for this." Wess imagined The Eye, there in his mo-palace, coldly ordering Smyth's execution. He was so far past the point of no return now that he would need a telescope to find it again. Perhaps, he hoped, he could find some way to convince Cortez that someone else had done the killings. But that ploy died when Wess remembered his parting shot to Flex's face over the vid-phone. "Oh, Grud. I'm gonna die. Cortez is gonna kill me..." Whatever fluke had enabled him to dispatch Bob Toes and the others had been just that, and now he would pay for it. If only he'd got the money...

"This unit can protect you."

Wess was so startled he jerked off the chair and flattened himself against the cooler cabinet. His eyes darted around the room; there was no one else there.

"Your termination would be a failure condition. This outcome is unacceptable."

"Who said that?" Smyth shouted, on the verge of panic. "Who is there?"

"Your behaviour pattern must be modified if the mission goals are to be achieved."

Wess's knees turned to water as he suddenly understood where the smooth, honeyed female voice was originating. He fell back into the chair and peered carefully at the gun. "It... You... Talk?"

"Affirmative, combatant. This unit is capable of verbal communication."

"Holy spugging drokk..." he breathed, gingerly extending a hand toward the weapon. It wasn't beyond the realm of possibility, Wess reasoned. He'd heard about smart cars, smart toasters, and smart dildos... Why the sneck shouldn't there be smart guns as well? An unexpected smile split Smyth's face. "I knew there was something odd about, uh, about you when I laid eyes on that case!"

"This unit is a prototype advanced personal offensive and defensive system, capable of variable levels of force projection from minimal injury, blinding and neutralisation up to large-scale target attrition and mega-death."

"Uh huh," Smyth nodded, catching only one or two meanings. "And you said you can protect me, right?"

The indicator lights blinked out of sequence. The thing was thinking. "Mutual goal achievement is possible, given certain assurances."

Wess rocked back. "This is insane. I'm going mad. I'm talking to a drokking handgun!"

"Your biometric readings do indicate a possible genetic weakness in your mental architecture, but you are not delusional. This unit has selected you as the optimal combatant vector to achieve mission goals."

He licked his lips. "What does that mean?"

The lights blinked again. "Interrogative; you wished to terminate the targets that surrounded you earlier? This unit sensed the threat condition and enabled you to achieve an interim mission goal."

"You helped me kill Toes and the others?" Wess took a moment to process this new information. It had all happened so fast, but now he thought about it, he had felt strange, as if something was pressing him forward, a phantom hand at his back.

"Manipulation of ocular sensitivity, adrenal gland system and nerve conduction were temporary; this unit will permanentise these bio-physical modifications in due course."

A wild laugh bubbled up from Smyth's chest. "Grud on a greenie! This is real!"

"Affirmative, combatant. Nanometric processes are ongoing. Your recent ingestion of foodstuffs will assist this functionality. Interrogative; regarding threat designation 'Cortez'. Do you wish to develop elimination protocol for this target?"

"Do I want him dead, you mean? Hell, yes, but there's no way I'm going anywhere near that creep. Him and his scumbags, I hate 'em all, but they'd rip me to bits, super-duper popgun or not." Wess ran a nervous hand through his hair.

"Your evaluation of the mission outcome is in error, combatant," said the weapon, and for a second Smyth thought he could detect an air of arrogance in its synthetic voice. "Target Cortez and associates can and will be eliminated, if parallel mission goals are met."

Smyth sat down next to the gun. "What do you mean by that?"

"This unit has a series of mission goals to achieve. Combatant also has a parallel series of goals. Combatant assistance in achieving unit goals will result in unit assistance in reaching combatant's goals."

"You want me to kill someone for you?"

"Affirmative. In return, threat designation Cortez and his scumbags will also be cancelled."

Smyth gave in to the compulsion to pick up the pistol, taking the heavy weapon in his hand, turning it so the pasty light from the bio-lume lamp in the ceiling made it glitter like black glass. "That sounds like a deal we could make, maybe."

"Combatant confirms," said the gun. "Commencing bio-data merge."

Darts of fire surged into Smyth's body and he choked off a scream, the veins and muscles in his body rippling and turning rigid. Colour bled out of his vision, definition fading and evaporating until everything was a glowing, dimensionless wash of white.

Traffic crossing the Danny Jackson Bridge slowed to a crawl and then, finally, a total halt as a spindly robo-crane rig worked with rescue teams to remove the hulk of a jack-knifed drone hauler from the middle three lanes. Vehicles streaming out of Sector 202 were being diverted as far back as the Sunshine Synthifoods turn-off, but for hundreds of citizens – including a lot of staff from West 17 – it was too late. They were trapped in the logjam for the next few hours.

The driver of the canary-yellow Vektor slabster kneaded the steering yoke with sweaty hands. He glanced back once or twice at the shape of the Test Labs building, the tip of the dark spindle still visible over the arching framework of the suspension bridge. With effort, he swallowed down the worry boiling in his chest and leaned forwards to toy with the car radio. When he returned to his seating position there was a Judge standing by the passenger side door.

He jumped. He couldn't see their face, just a piece of torso from waist to shoulder. The officer – a woman, athletic and well-muscled underneath the leathereen bodysuit – was turned slightly away, so her badge wasn't visible. A green glove tap-tapped on the window, and then made a twirling motion.

The driver blinked and licked his lips. He hadn't even heard the sound of the Lawmaster coming up alongside him. Gingerly, he rolled down the window and craned his neck. "Can I help you, Judge?"

The woman moved like lightning, from a casual, relaxed stance to instant action with no apparent intervening motion. Suddenly she had the door open and she was sliding into the seat next to him, the blunt shape of a Mark II Lawgiver pistol leading her in. His eyes fell to her badge and he felt ice form in the pit of his stomach.

"Oh. Vedder." He saw his face reflected in the visor of her helmet; old before his time, a promising scientist worn down by the things he had seen... and done.

The Judge held the gun in a deceptively lazy grip, level with his stomach. A vague smile played around her lips. "Just 'Vedder'? Is that any way to greet an old friend?" She purred his name. "Hollis, I'm disappointed."

"Are you here to kill me?" He bit out the words.

"Always the drama with you, isn't it? No, I won't kill you. Not unless you do something very stupid."

Hollis looked away from her. "What do you want, then?" He could smell her, there in the closeness of the car, and all the old reactions came flooding back to him. A glimpse of red hair pressed against his face, tugging the golden zipper down with his teeth; muscular breasts against his chest, her hot breath in his ear... He shook his head, crushing the sense-memory into nothing.

"There was a time when you were happy to see me," she said, as if reading the thoughts in his mind. "When you looked forward to it."

A hot spike of anger cut through him. "I was an idiot to ever get involved with you! I was just a plaything for you... A way for you to amuse yourself during the project downtime!"

She cocked her head and pursed her lips. "Hmm. No. No, Hollis, that wasn't it at all."

"What do you mean?" His annoyance faltered a little, and the fear returned to replace it.

"Our liaisons. I admit, they were pleasurable, but I didn't do it just for the sport, you understand? It was part of the assignment. I thought you knew that."

"No... I..."

She smiled at him and patted his leg, even as she kept the gun on him. "Hollis. You were such a high-flyer at the start. We had to keep a lock on you. Don't feel bad. It was just work."

"Yes, of course," he managed. "Work." The scientist felt heavy and leaden. "What, then? What is it that you have to say to me here in the middle of a traffic jam instead of the office or a vid?"

"This is more discreet. Things have become very complicated recently," she was off-hand, but he knew from experience that there was a razor hidden under her words, "and the COE are going to ensure that no one is compromised in the clean-up operation. I wanted to tell you that personally, Hollis. I wanted you to hear it from my lips."

"Then why the gun?"

"Dredd was at West 17 today. I don't want him sticking his chin in where it doesn't belong. I don't want him encouraged in any way."

Hollis blinked, not trusting himself to say anything for fear of making a mistake.

"It's in your best interests not to do something, oh, I don't know, dramatic. Frankly, Hollis, your attacks of moralising were one of the things I liked the least about you."

"I..." He spoke carefully and quietly. "I have nothing to say."

"Good." Vedder holstered her gun. "You have a great deal of value to Mega-City One. You've got such a brilliant intellect. It would be a shame to spread it all over the sidewalk." The Judge left him there, fingers still clutched to the steering wheel, hands slick and wet.

For the most part, Judges kept to their own kind while they were off-duty. Precinct command centres and Sector Houses of all sizes and shapes had residence levels mixing the more typical sleep machine dorms with barracks for junior officers, and private quarters for the upper-echelon seniors. It was a cast-iron rule that all Judges were required, at the bare minimum, to take a mandatory eight hours of uninterrupted, non-induced sleep at regular intervals.

Among the changes brought in under Chief Judge Goodman prior to the 2100s was the concept of the "Block Judge". Justice Department analysts had noted that citizens saw their law enforcers as faceless and unapproachable sentinels – some insisted that they were not even humans – and so Goodman had billeted senior Street Judges in citiblocks across the Big Meg as a form of outreach program. Living side-by-side was meant to show the common citizens that Judges were people too; but for the most part, it turned up more crime for the designated Block Judges to find among their new neighbours.

Dredd had lived off-precinct for a few years, down in a small and sparse apartment on the midlevels of Rowdy Yates Block. He was back in Sector digs now, having turned the place over to Judge Rico, a younger officer transferred in from Texas City. Rico, like Dredd, was clone-stock from Chief Judge Fargo, and he gained a degree of satisfaction from knowing the place had gone to "family". In truth, Dredd had always had his issues with the de-segregation of the Judge/Citizen divide, firmly falling on the side of opinion that said the law and those it protected weren't to mix. Such familiarity bred contempt and invited the possibility of abuse; and this thought was foremost in Dredd's mind as he entered the lobby of the Seaborne con-apts building.

Samuel Seaborne Block couldn't have been further from Dredd's old place at Rowdy Yates if it tried. It was a luxury skyscraper, one of the Super Sixty series, largely populated by high-profile citizens with well-paid jobs and members of MegWest's bureaucratic apparatus. Dredd knew from past experience that at least two key figures in the upper reaches of MC-1's construction industry lived here, leasing entire floors of the block for their own mansion-plexes. It had its own security cadre of bouncer-meks, along with transparent armourplas shielding over the entire building and concealed stunner turrets to deter the lesser class of citizen.

Loengard's apartment was on the lower face of the tower, but it was still an impressive size. Dredd rapped on the door and waited.

The Tek-Judge was in workout fatigues instead of standard uniform, a set of light trousers and a black T-shirt with the department eagle on the breast. His face clouded the instant he recognised his unannounced visitor.

"Dredd? Let me guess, you've decided to run a crime sweep?"

"We need to talk," Dredd replied, carefully watching Loengard's face for even the slightest recognition of those words. There was nothing.

The other Judge walked away, leaving the door open. "Come on in, then. But make it quick. I want to get some solid rack time before daybreak."

Dredd followed Loengard in, scanning the room. The place was plain, largely unadorned except for a couple of houseplants and a cabinet of awards. He noticed a shelf with some actual paper books on it and leaned closer. "These real?"

"Of course," Loengard snapped. "Family heirlooms."

"Must be worth a lot."

"They are." The Tek-Judge sipped at a synthi-caff and crossed to the window. "So, are you here because you want to start a book club or because you've got something else on your mind?" Loengard glanced at Dredd, framed by the large glasseen panels. The Seaborne con-apts had a great view of the city wall and the haze of the Cursed Earth beyond it.

"You've got it good, Loengard. Smart pad, high profile. Bet you get to mix with a lotta top-dog cits living here."

The cup came down on the table with a sharp snap. "I've earned my privileges, Dredd! This city would be dead a dozen times over if it wasn't for technology that I helped to develop!"

"No doubt," the other Judge said mildly, approaching the window. "Nice view. I'll bet it helps you keep your mouth shut about things when they go off-book, too. Right?"

Loengard snorted. "What are you fishing for, Dredd? I told you before at the labs, there's nothing I can tell you about that truck, so stop wasting my time and drop it!"

"I know you're involved." He threw the comment out at the other man. "I've seen the files. Vedder's in the frame and now so are you."

"Vedder?" Dredd saw the millisecond flinch when the COE agent's name left Loengard's lips. "Whatever the drokk that woman touches is a tissue of lies!" It was then Dredd knew he had the Tek-Judge.

"You've got a choice. Either you can play it straight and come down to Justice Central with me right now, or else we do it the hard way and I call in the SJS."

The other man's voice rose. "I'm not going anywhere–" He stuttered into silence. "Wh-what the drokk is tha–" Loengard's attention was suddenly drawn to something outside the window.

Dredd caught the smell of molten polymers in his nostrils, harsh and acrid. With a wet pop of boiling air, a fist-sized hole appeared in the window of the apartment, the hot edges singeing a rip through the mesh curtain. "Get down!"

Loengard reacted, but not in the way that a seasoned street veteran would have. Years of deskwork and lab duties had slowed the Tek-Judge's reactions, and he hesitated before diving for the bathroom door.

There was a second shot, following up the first silent discharge that had melted through the armoured glasseen. Dredd saw a dart-shaped plasma projectile lance inward, skipping off a wall panel at a perfect ninety-degree ricochet. Dredd's artificial eyes captured the bolt as it deflected again and sank into the meat between Loengard's shoulder blades. The Tek-Judge's chest exploded outward, catapulting bone and lung matter across his shelves of tastefully arranged award plaques.

Ignoring the sizzle of burned flesh, Dredd drew his gun and chanced a look over the lip of the windowsill. The city looked back at him; there were hundreds of places for miles in every direction from where a sniper could have fired.

BULLSEYE

It was raining in Sector 88, a firm and constant rush of grey water induced by Weather Control's high-atmosphere drones. It was an old trick of the Judges; when the clouds opened, most folks wouldn't even consider venturing outside their homes, let alone their citiblocks, and so the threat of prowling street crime dipped sharply. That wasn't to say that crime itself dropped off during the rain – just the percentages of types of crime. When bored, disaffected citizens couldn't go outside, they just turned their frustrations into misdemeanours that could be committed indoors.

That sort of petty, small-time stuff wasn't really a concern for Ruben Cortez. His money came from prostitution, drugs, protection and gambling, all of which were industries that required people to come out of their homes to facilitate. As such, whenever it rained, Cortez was in a bad mood, insisting to anyone in earshot that the Judges were causing it just to spite him. The thing was, Ditta thought to himself, Cortez was probably right.

Ditta ran an absent hand through his floureco-dreadlock haircut and sparked off a twinkle of blue-green light. He had the whole casual disinterest, faux-cool manner of Cortez's gang off pat now, and he fitted in there perfectly. The mobster threw him a nod and Ditta knew that was a cue to bring him the decanter of synthi-scotch. He poured a measure into a glass and presented it to Cortez, who took it without comment.

Ruben Cortez; in repose he didn't seem like very much, a slightly corpulent Hispanic male, below-average height with a taste for garish gold buttons and cufflinks. But Ditta had seen the little man turn into a tornado of violence, those thick and meaty fists of his raining blows down on bruisers twice his size. Cortez noticed his attention and glanced up at him. His artificial eye caught the light from the glow-strips bisecting the glass roof above. Ruben's distinctive trademark, The Eye's eye as it were, was an ugly, bulbous model of SouthAm manufacture. Gang legend held that Cortez had lost his organic eyeball when an uppity sugar dealer from Mex-City had dared to try his luck with Ruben in a knife-fight; so they said, Cortez cut the dead orb out himself and then stuffed it in the mouth of his opponent before killing him. His replacement was polished to a fine sheen, and like every accessory Cortez wore, it was gold.

"Snecking rain, eh?" said the mobster. "Damn Judges got it in for me."

"Right," Ditta agreed, as a wash of bright light swept over them. They were passing under the Rosenbaum Interchange, and he felt the slight sense of motion as the room swayed around them. It was easy to forget that they were inside a moving vehicle; the Carnivale, as Cortez called his huge mopad, was one of the few Cosmos Imperials on the streets of Mega-City One, as large as a mid-size hydroliner. On the lower levels, next to the parking ramps, there were the sections for the casino, nightclub, the dining compartment and kitchens; above that, the private suites and what were euphemistically known as the "recreation rooms"; and on the top deck, Cortez's personal domain. The crimelord surveyed a series of monitors showing camera-eye views of the rooms below. There was precious little action going on, just a few hard-eyed gamblers in the midst of a poker game and some mechanical sex in one of the brothel-booths. Cortez drained his glass and Ditta refilled it.

There was a heavy, pregnant atmosphere in the office, a foreboding that Ditta could taste like the smell of the second-rate whisky. He kept his feelings utterly hidden. Ditta hadn't served this long as an undercover Judge without learning a few hard lessons.

On one of the other screens he saw Flex's harsh, florid face snarling up at the security camera, and then the office door whispered open to admit Cortez's lead thug.

"I wanna hear it all," Cortez snapped, before Flex even had a chance to speak. "Gimme the story."

Flex gave Ditta a look, and another to Quiet Mike on the sofa nearby. Not so much a greeting, but a warning that what he had to tell the boss would not improve his mood. Ditta took the opportunity to retreat. Before today, he'd dodged thrown bottles when Cortez had lashed out in fury at something. "Four deaders down in the skids. I went took a look-see myself." Flex gave a shake of the head.

"Who?" Cortez rolled the tumbler between his thumb and forefinger.

"Bob Toes and his boy Hoog, and the Clent brothers–"

Cortez made an annoyed sound like a spit that crackled in the air. "I know who is dead, Flex! I meant who did this? Tell me the name of the punkamente who thinks he can rip up my people!"

Flex blinked a few times. Ditta recognised the reaction; the bodybuilder did that whenever he wasn't happy about something. "Uh... I ain't sure, but, uh–"

With a flick of his wrist, Cortez sank the last of the drink and put down the glass. "I ask you one more time." He still had the tumbler in his hand, and Ditta knew he was going to throw it.

"There was this call," Flex began. "Hoog's phone. So, I roughed up the watchbot at Q-Save, and got ta look at the security tapes. It seems like it was, uh, Smythy. Wess Smyth."

It was Cortez's turn to blink. "Smyth? The little creep with the bad suit?" He looked to Quiet Mike for confirmation. "Owes us money?" Mike gave a sage nod in return. Cortez seemed to be having a hard time taking this in. "This is the same Smyth that pissed and puked up in my club? The pencil-neck geek who lost in the shuggy game?"

"Yeah," said Flex. "Him. I, uh, beat him up a while back."

The mobster hurled the glass and exploded with rage; it was textbook Cortez behaviour. "This little sneck," he hissed, words thick and sibilant like hot fat on a griddle. "How tha' spug he did it, I don' wanna know! You get him, Flex. Take a couple of boys and find that piece of bottom-feeder shit and rip him!"

Flex grinned, pleased to be back on safe ground now, with a task to perform that he could manage. "Gotcha. You want I should do it any special way?"

Cortez waved an angry hand at him. "This is all about respect, eh? This little weasel, he grows himself a spine allasudden? That's bad for The Eye, eh?" Cortez tapped his cybernetic implant, his natural accent slipping out as he lost his temper. "You find this pendejo and make sure you do him messy and public! Double-Eight has to unnderstan', no one defies Ruben Cortez and keeps breathin'!"

And then without warning he turned a cold, level gaze on Ditta. "Ain't that so?"

Ditta went cold inside. "Yeah, boss. Sure." An instinct honed by years in the Wally Squad screamed in Ditta's mind. *He knows. You've been made.*

"Too many people try to screw with The Eye!" Cortez growled, making a performance out of it. "I don't like that. Eh? Eh, Ditta? Mister Judge Ditta?"

The undercover officer jerked his wrist, and the quad-derringer concealed in a sleeve holster dropped into his palm. He wasn't fast enough; Quiet Mike came up off the sofa like a rocket and grabbed him, knocking Ditta off-balance. The Judge tried to struggle free and met a huge red fist from Flex as the thug stepped in to punch the fight out of him. Ditta's head rang like a struck bell, and the small holdout pistol fell from his nerveless fingers. Mike hauled Ditta up and there was Cortex, leering at him, the cyber-eye whining as it focused on him.

"Filthy rat puta," Cortez spat, "You think you fool me? I knew who you were all alon'!"

"It's all over, creep," Ditta snapped back, bearing his teeth. "The whole department are on to you. I've put enough data together to send you to the cubes for life – if you're lucky!" The bravado was all he had left.

"You mean this?" Cortez held up a small memory disc. "Stupid pig. You shoulda kept it hidden better. One of the girls foun' it." He snapped the plastic in two.

The Judge failed to keep the panic from his face. "Oh yeah," smirked Flex, "you know you screwed now."

"I keep an eye on you," said Cortez, and then Ditta screamed as a thread of ruby red light shot from the mobster's implant and cut a long, deep sear up one of his cheeks. The laser shot into Ditta's right eye and popped it in a flash of steam. Quiet Mike held him as he wailed in pain.

Cortez stepped away and nodded to the window. "This is his stop. Put him off."

Flex took Ditta by the scruff of the neck as Mike opened the sliding glasseen. Then the Wally Squad Judge's world spun end over end before he met the highway below at four hundred kilometres per hour.

Quiet Mike closed the window, and, pausing only to gather up Ditta's fallen pistol and the fragments of the whiskey glass, returned to his seat as if nothing had happened. Flex, on the other hand, was panting with the rush of a quick and dirty kill. "Judges ain't gonna like that!"

"Judges can eat my dust," Cortez replied with the traditional go-ganger rejoinder of his youth. "They can pin nothin' on me." He helped himself to another large synthi-scotch. "Now we dealt with that, go kill that shitbag Smyth."

"Back off, Dredd," said Woburn, the silver skull on her helmet glinting in the light, "You know the drill, blue-on-blue."

The Special Judicial Service Judge's hand was raised in a warding-off gesture, and it was almost touching Dredd's chest. Dredd glared at the internal affairs officer and Woburn self-consciously retracted her arm. "I didn't kill him. A first-year cadet could see that."

The SJS Judge shook her head. "That's not for me to say, Dredd. There's going to be an investigation."

"I'll say," Dredd replied. "Mine. And you're stopping me from doing it."

Woburn glanced over her shoulder at the other two men in black body armour and heavy full-face helmets. They were impressively dangerous-looking, blocking the entrance to the Sector House cryo-mortuary, the SJS skull icon emblazened on their shoulders. "You know the rules, Dredd. You are formally barred from any involvement surrounding investigations into the murder of Judge Loengard. You are a material witness... and possible suspect."

"Suspect?" Dredd spat the word like a curse. "I had a legit reason to be at Loengard's billet. And unless I had a teleporter, a grav-belt or a time-travel device, there's no way I could have got outside his window nineteen storeys up to shoot him with a plasma rifle."

Woburn gave him an arch look. "With your record, Dredd, anything is possible." She paused, considering. "Personally, I don't think you will be implicated."

The senior Judge gave a sarcastic sneer. "I'm so relieved."

"No," Woburn continued. "I think you're smart enough that you'd have made it harder to catch you if you did kill him. Judge Loengard's murder took place in the presence of another officer with no witnesses – that makes it an SJS matter until we can determine your level of participation."

"How long is that going to take? I need access to his autopsy records. Loengard was a suspect in my ongoing investigation, and whoever killed him did it to stop him from giving up something vital. I want a Psi-Judge in there to go through his last thoughts. I need to see the data on the kill shot–"

Woburn shook her head. "Utterly out of the question! Your seniority gets you a lot of leeway, Dredd, but I'm not shredding the rulebook for you! Take one step into that morgue and I'll have you in an iso-cube!"

"His killer is gonna get away unless you give me access."

The woman squared up and met Dredd's hard gaze. "I will be the judge of that. Now take a walk before I have to have you forcibly removed." The senior Judge turned to leave, and Woburn spoke again. "But don't go too far. Just in case I find out you did have something to do with Loengard's death."

Tyler was waiting for him in the atrium. "I just heard!" began the Tek-Judge, "Clark told me the SJS brought you in with Loengard's corpse!" He hesitated. "You... You didn't shoot him, did you?"

Dredd frowned. "Bad enough I get a grilling from Woburn and her skull-heads, I gotta hear that from you too? No, Tyler, I didn't shoot Loengard. It was a sniper."

"Sniper?" he repeated. "How? I mean, there's nowhere in that zone where you could place a gun platform... Unless it was on a vehicle."

"Negative. I checked in with traffic control, there were no aircraft in the vicinity." Dredd paused, thinking the scene through again. "The shot came from low down, close to ground level, I reckon. Steep angle of deflection. A double tap, one to punch through the glass, one to take out the target." He nodded. "Textbook technique, right out of the manual."

Tyler tapped his fingers on the ubiquitous data pad he carried. "But Samuel Seaborne Block is in the middle of a protected recreation zone, nothing but parks all around it. There's no way someone could sneak a sniper rifle out there without tripping a dozen security sensors."

"I've never seen weapons fire like that before," Dredd noted. "Looked like a plasma burst, but it was modified somehow... guided. Shooter nailed Loengard with a deflected shot like they knew where he was gonna be standing."

"If we could get a look at the body, I could get a discharge signature from the wound-"

"Not gonna happen. The SJS have the corpse in lockdown. Convenient for whoever shot him that it was Woburn who got to the scene first."

Tyler's eyes narrowed. "You think someone tipped her off?"

"Maybe."

"How about camera footage? Perhaps something got picked up by a local street-scanner..." The Tek-Judge met Dredd's gaze and his words trailed off. "Oh, drokk..."

"You got something to say?" Dredd growled.

He gave a slow nod. "You got cybernetic eyes, right? Artificial implants?"

"Yeah. Zeiss-Ikon, model six-fives. What of it?"

Tyler's face split in a grin. "Oh, I think we might have what you might call an eagle-eyewitness after all!" He flicked a glance at the chronometer above them. "But we gotta be quick!"

In the depths of the Tek-Lab, Tyler worked quickly and deftly, assembling the components and hardware he would need. "See, most cybernetic optical processors use an image plane transfer system to manage incoming light and colour–"

"Spare me the technobabble."

"Oh." Tyler paused. "Well, there's a chip in your artificial eyes that turns the digital information they pick up – the sights, if you like – into impulses that your brain can understand. The thing is, in order to make it work faster there's redundant storage in there. It's like a low-bandwidth comm link, it only refreshes the parts of the picture that change."

"You're telling me what I saw in Loengard's hab is still in my implants?"

Tyler nodded. "The refresh rate will be breaking it down by now. At best, the image ghost will be barely readable... But there might be something." He held up a connector. "I have to plug this into one of the optics. You'll need to, uh, take off your helmet."

Dredd gave him a long, silent look, and then removed his headgear. Colour drained from the Tek-Judge's cheeks as he caught sight of Dredd's visage. "Oh Grud," he whispered.

"If I was pretty, I'd be a vid-star," grunted the Judge. "Now, make it quick."

Tyler nodded and inserted the lead into Dredd's right eye. The senior officer flinched as metal met plastic with a hollow click.

Instantly, flickering, garbled colour began to stream across Tyler's console. The Tek-Judge worked at the panel, clocking back the time index to the moment of Loengard's death. He frowned. "It's worse than I thought. There's barely enough to get a read on. I'll try running an ultra-violet spectrum transform."

Behind him, Dredd tugged the cable from his eye and replaced his headgear. "What do you have?"

"Take a look." Tyler displayed a series of washed-out images, the colours and shapes so bleached of definition that it was almost impossible to glean any context or meaning from them. "There's an after-image of the shot, but it's weak..." The Tek-Judge was undeterred. "See that halo, around the head of the discharge?" He pointed at a faint glow around the energy bolt.

"Thought so. A collimated plasma discharge," Dredd gave a nod. He'd seen enough gunshots to recognise the signs. "Doesn't make sense, though. Hand-held plasma weapons are high-maintenance, fragile. Only real use for them is the big models they mount on starships."

"Something of alien origin, you think?" said Tyler.

"Possible," agreed Dredd, "but unlikely. Let's not forget what Loengard did for a living. It was his job to create cutting-edge weapons systems. A plasma gun would class as that all right." He tapped the screen. "Look at the shape of the bolt. Most plasma charges are ragged, they bleed off heat and light too quick to make an effective kill. They're messy. But this... The shot was clean. This is advanced, way beyond mil-spec. We're looking at radical arms technology here."

"You think someone shot him with a weapon from West 17? That's not too much of a stretch, I suppose..." Tyler called up a link to Justice Central's main computer. "Let's see what MAC has to say about this."

Loengard's name, predictably, came up with nothing but a string of Access Denied: Top Secret Clearance Required flags on his files, but there were cross-references in Accounts Division files about procurement costs on a research project at West 17 that showed up each time the search parameters hit the words "plasma weapon". Tyler read out the entry. "Project Skorpion. Sounds real friendly."

Dredd's eyes narrowed. "That rings a bell. After the Apocalypse War, Chief Judge McGruder wanted weapons stocks back up and new hardware in case East-Meg Two decided to finish what their cousins had started. There was a whole bunch of defence projects that got the green light, but most didn't pan out... Skorpion was one of 'em."

"What was it?"

The other Judge shook his head. "Teape from Armoury was in charge, but she's dead now, killed during Necropolis."

Tyler carried on searching, deleting extraneous results, following the money trail. "Another financial report from Acc-Div, this is dated 2125. There's nothing on the nature of the project, but it does say funding for the Skorpion was concluded." He rubbed his eyes. "Whatever it was, they stopped paying for it two years ago."

Dredd threw him a look. "Or maybe it got shifted into some undisclosed black budget. Weapons research is just the kinda thing the COE keep tabs on."

"I thought the COE spy on other cities, not their own."

"A spy is a spy is a spy," growled Dredd, "and maybe an assassin, too."

"Vedder?"

A nod. "We have to track her down. She's the key to this thing."

"That's not gonna be easy–" An alert chime from Tyler's computer sounded, drawing his attention.

"Problem?" Dredd looked over his shoulder. The screen was displaying an autopsy report, one of the millions of cursory cause-of-death files that filtered through

Justice Central on a daily basis, as members of MC-1's populace came to natural and unnatural ends.

"I gave MAC a set of search subroutines looking for anything similar to what you described, the same kinda kills that wasted Loengard. Looks like we got a hit."

"Show me." The information rolled past, reflecting off the impassive gaze of Dredd's helmet. "Well, well. Scene of crime, Sector 88. Small world."

The Tek-Judge brought up holos of four corpses, three human males and a blue-skinned Gagrantian. "Less than a day old, Dredd. Four deaders, cause of death, severe plasma-shot trauma." He made a face. "This is just a standard tag-and-bag. The report says they put it down to a local mob hit, didn't bother with a deep scan."

"I need to see those corpses."

Tyler jerked a thumb over his shoulder. "Then you better get to District Six Resyk pronto, Dredd. These bozos are scheduled for disposal. Today."

In fact, the woman Dredd wanted to speak to more than anyone else in Mega-City One was only ten storeys above him, in a secluded office belonging to the Data Collection Bureau. Vedder removed the intrusion spike from her console and returned it to the concealed pocket in her uniform. The device was gene-encoded to her DNA and loaded with counter-measure programs of such complexity that no human hacker could ever have written them. She'd used it to save her life on dozens of occasions; resetting the locks on the gates of the Bifrost Bridge, opening doors in Cal Hab, escaping the Papal Inquisitors in Vatican City. The jobs she'd given the spike here had been ridiculously simple in comparison. First, ensuring that the droids in the Tek-Lab mistook her for Judge Tyler and destroyed the remains of the stealth truck, and now locking up the late Judge

Loengard's autopsy report with a falsified hard drive crash. That stalling tactic would be followed up by an "accident" in the cryo-morgue when a cylinder of methalon would be mixed with a volatile cryogen fluid. Vedder would be well away from the Grand Hall of Justice by the time that happened, though. She had more loose ends to clean up at West 17 before she could return to her original task.

The COE agent sighed, a rare show of emotion. She'd had things planned so precisely, or so it had seemed. Now, one random act of chance had thrown her entire operation into jeopardy and each step forward she took mired her deeper. Dredd was snapping at her heels, getting closer to piecing it together. Vedder hated admitting to herself that the old drokker was gaining ground. She was in real danger of exposing everything she had worked so hard to set in motion. The woman dallied with a brief moment of annoyance before smothering it. The mistake she'd made - easy to see it now, she fumed - was relying on actual criminals to create the traffic accident back on the Braga Skedway. Vedder had worked with local talent before, in operations like that Cassidium heist in Bruja City, and never had more than the usual discipline problems. But this time, the wrecker gang Vedder had cultivated and plied with hardware and guns turned out to be brash, overenthusiastic and above all, stupid.

"Never send a punk to do a bitch's job," she gave voice to the thought, half-wondering what the DCB monitors would make of her talking to herself.

Her console gave a soft bleep to attract her attention. She read the data intercept with mounting concern. Someone in Tek-Lab - she didn't have to guess that it was Dredd's playmate Tyler - had been digging in the MAC files. That alone wasn't a problem, because the second-rate little Luna-Tek would never be able to crack the encryption on the files he was looking at; no, Vedder's lip curled as she read the very same crime scene report that had set Dredd in motion ten floors below.

"Where the drokk did this come from?" she snarled. She knew the pattern instantly. It was just what she had expected to see, only Dredd had got to it first. "That won't do." Vedder weighed her options; if she went after Dredd, she ran the risk that something vital would be leaked from West 17. That was something she couldn't allow; it was time to remove him from the equation. The agent shook her head and opened a secure line.

"Vedder, ident code Five-Nine Reindeer Flotilla."

"Confirmed," said a man's voice. "Protocol?"

"Epsilon, variation three. Target and location feed on side-channel."

A pause. "Confirmed," repeated the voice. "Timeframe?"

"Immediate." Vedder snapped off the link and headed down to the bike park. With luck, Dredd would be dead by the time she got back.

The corpses were already on the conveyor by the time Dredd reached the Resyk station. Like the core Resyk facility in MegCentral, the building was decorated in dark synthi-wood, resembling the shape of a gigantic mahogany coffin. Above the main entrance where recorded loops of angelic hymns played over and over, the motto that had made the body recycling franchise famous was displayed in tasteful holographic lettering; "We Recycle Everything But The Soul!" Inside there were grieving parlours and chapels of rest, memorial walls and votive shrines, but none of these were of interest to the lawman. He took the service entrance with his Lawmaster and skidded to a halt on the roller deck level where the foreman was waiting for him.

"Keep those stiffs moving!" shouted the operator, frowning at Dredd's abrupt arrival. "Judge. Got your radio call. How can I help?"

"You can start by turning off that belt!" Dredd snapped. "There are bodies on there with vital evidence."

"No can do!" the foreman insisted. "Look at that lot! We're one of the largest Resyk sub-stations in the city, we process more than eleven thousand corpses a day at maximum capacity. I can't afford to let them pile up on the grinders!" He waved a hand at the rubbereen conveyor. As broad as three lanes of megway, the belt was dutifully hauling naked corpses from the drop chute down to the primary flesh-grinding wheels at the far end of the platform. Dredd could hear the whickering clatter of the eyeball gougers and de-teething grabs working away beyond them. He knew the layout of these places too well; years earlier he'd found himself fighting the escaped criminal Fink Angel at Resyk Central, stalking the killer through knee-deep floods of meat slurry and liquefied body matter. The disposal centres served a vital purpose for Mega-City One's energy and resource-hungry populace, turning the dead into chemical reclaim for reprocessing. If you wanted a dirt burial in MC-1, you had to be richer than most citizens could ever dream of.

"I said," Dredd snarled, "shut it down!" He drew his Lawgiver and sent a single standard execution round into the control nest across the bay. The shot was pinpoint, shattering the emergency override command panel. In response, alarms sounded through the air and the conveyor belt shuddered to a halt. Without waiting for permission, Dredd vaulted over the safety barrier and sprinted across the static belt. Dead eyes stared up at him from the old and the young as he passed.

He found his quarry straight away; Gagarantians like the alien thug Hoog were close enough to Terran for

Resyk's tender mercies, but his bright blue skin stood out among the human tones like a beacon. Dredd activated the skin-sensor that Tyler had armed him with and turned the device on the body. There was a commotion going on where the foreman was standing and yelling, but his voice was lost in the sirens.

The sensor blinked green and Dredd stood up, scanning the corpses for the bodies of the Clent brothers. He found them, the two dead twins unceremoniously pinned beneath the cadaver of a huge Fatty. The Judge looked up and gestured to a figure on the overhead crane gantry. He'd need to get the porcine corpse moved to get readings on the Clents' wounds.

The gantry moved closer and Dredd shouted: "Down here! Get the claw grab!" The words had hardly left his mouth when he realised that the figure on the gantry wasn't wearing Resyk uniform; it was sheathed in a black stealth suit with a glowing blue flash visor.

The Judge threw himself to one side as the crane grab was released, the five-ton claw falling toward him like the talon of a giant predator.

TARGETS OF OPPORTUNITY

The claw struck the rubbereen conveyor with such force that the impact tossed Dredd away like a leaf in a breeze. The Judge landed unceremoniously amid a knot of dead eldsters, the day's intake of passings from the Crock Blocks on Northside. The grab flattened the corpulent corpse of the Fatty and the remains of the Clent brothers into fleshy paste. Any evidence they represented was now contaminated and worthless.

The sirens were still braying, and Dredd realised too late that the noise had conveniently masked the sound of gunfire from the service platform. He saw other black-suited figures dispatching any Resyk workers too slow to run, killing them with single shots to the head. Whoever they were, they were a professional crew.

Dredd considered selecting a heatseeker round on his pistol, but thought better of it. The bodysuits the killers wore were likely to be thermosealed, and a random hotshot round could find itself looking for a different target, maybe even a civilian. Refusing to stay on the defensive, Dredd vaulted up from where he had fallen and threw himself aside, just as the hiss of bullets snapped at the corpses around him. He returned fire with blinding speed, thumbing the selector to armour piercing. The tungsten-tipped penetrator rounds missed their human target by inches, cutting hot flares of sparks from the crane gantry's framework.

Another salvo of shots came at him from his attacker; Dredd recognised the sound of a spit carbine over the din of the klaxons. He dodged and ran. There was nowhere to hide on the conveyor, and like Hoog's bright blue corpse, Dredd stood out like a sore thumb among the naked dead. He executed a tuck-and-roll off the springy belt surface and fired back. A single Hi-Ex round might have been enough to silence the shooter permanently, but that wouldn't leave anything to interrogate. Dredd wanted one of these creeps alive – or at least alive enough to be sweated by him in an interrogation cube.

Then, all at once, one of the black suits woke up to where Dredd was, and suddenly the conveyor was moving again, accelerating beyond the normal slow-walk speed to a fast jog. The spiked maws of the grinders loomed large. The Judge sprinted in the opposite direction, gaining a little headway. The figure on the gantry waved at one of its cohorts in the service bay, hunched over the speed controls. Dredd knew what would come next.

A vibration undulated through the conveyor and it tripled in speed; the Judge was running all out, legs pumping, just to stay in place. On the gantry, the dark assassin emerged with a weapon in his hands, stepping up to take a careful aim. One round through Dredd's leg would be enough to drop him, and the Judge would never be able to get up before the grinders claimed him.

"Bike!" Dredd snapped. "Weapons free! Go!"

The attackers had made the mistake of ignoring Dredd's idling Lawmaster where it stood on the platform. The Judge's command brought the machine to life, turning over control to the motorcycle's on-board computer systems. Lawmaster CPUs were about as smart as a typical Bot-Cab or RoboHauler, but unlike their civilian cousins, they were armed with twin bike cannons and a high-energy laser. The computer was intelligent enough to follow limited commands and programmed to recognise – and neutralise – armed threats. The clatter of heavy weapons fire distracted the shooter on the gantry, giving Dredd the moment he needed. He tore a small pistol-grip device from a pouch on his gear belt and aimed it up, ignoring the exertion of fighting the belt. With a whistle, the device spat a wickedly barbed dart into the air, trailing a hair-thin monofilament wire. Dredd's aim was true, and the titanium arrow caught the gunman in the chest. On impact, the dart splayed open, lodging in place in the soft meat of his heart.

Dredd thumbed a switch on the hand line and powerful micromotors lifted him off the speeding belt, up towards the crane. The assassin clutched at his chest, coughing up blood, and shredding his gloves trying to clasp the molecule-thin wire. The Judge was halfway to him when the shooter's life signs dropped below the survival threshold. As the black-suited killer choked out his last breath, a thermolite charge sewn into the collar of his combat gear ignited; the detonation reduced his body to a wet paste and blew the gantry off its rails. The crane tumbled down on to the conveyor, and Dredd went with it, flipped around and caught it like a fish on a lure.

The falling crane tore open the belt and wedged in the thrashing gears below with an ear-splitting shriek of tortured metal. Dredd struck the rubbereen belt again and bounced across it like a stone skipping on water. The conveyor snapped and recoiled, writhing into breaking waves against a steel shoreline. Bodies of all shapes and sizes were flung into the air in a mad aerial ballet of nude, pallid flesh.

The Judge landed hard, feeling ribs snap on touchdown; but then he was buried under a rain of falling corpses and blackness engulfed him.

■ ■ ■

As always, her complaints to Bendy fell on deaf ears. "But I've been on for a whole shift and a half, and now you want me to cover for Chewlyp?" Jayni jerked her thumb at the dancer, who scowled back at her through her mass of Pugly make-up and facial piercings.

Bendy – to this day Jayni had never understood why someone so fat and so inflexible had ever earned a nickname like that – gave her a gimlet eye and rolled the suckstik in his mouth around with a clatter of brown teeth. "Fine, woman, you don't want the work, that's fine. There's plenty of girlflesh queuing up out there to work in a joint as fine as this."

Jayni sagged with the weight of frustration at having exactly the same conversation that she'd shared with the tubby prick every time this situation came up. Even as she loathed herself for doing it, she found herself sleepwalking her way though her part in the little performance. "This place? Shuggy and tits is all you have to offer here, Bendy. It's not the snecking Kandy Klub!"

And right on cue he tugged the suckstik out of his mouth and waved it in her face, blobs of his spittle flying in the air from the masticated end. "Cover for Chewlyp or sneck off and don't come back. There it is, Jayni. Do or don't."

She glanced around for support to Ashtré and Latreena, but predictably got nothing but blank-eyed stares in reply. "Fine," she spat. "Thanks for being such a sport about it, boss."

Bendy was already on his way to the back office with Chewlyp wandering ahead of him, trailing a reeking cloud of Otto Sump's Putrefaction – For Women. He didn't bother to thank her, just made an absent wave of the hand while his other meaty paw went on a quest toward the Pugly girl's pimply backside.

"Wass he see inna?" Ashtré snapped in her clipped MegEast accent, as soon as he was out of earshot. "Pugly ugly issout. Un-stylee."

"Bendy's lucky if he can get a little," Latreena chimed in, returning to the important business of oiling her breasts. "Chewlyp gets tha fringe benefits." She eyed Jayni. "Maybe you should–"

"Stop right there," Jayni made a halt sign with her hand, like a Judge at a traffic intersection. "I got a guy. One that ain't like Two-Ton Tony Tubbs's little brother."

"Wahlike? Ya man Wess?" Ashtré flipped her lanky tresses. "Dint you dump his loserness?"

"Yeah," Latreena added, warming to the subject. "That little spug ain't never amounted to anything, Jayni. Cut him loose, find something better."

Jayni kicked off her street shoes and forced her feet into the monstrous high heels the dancers had to wear on the podium. "What, here? Oh, 'cos there's hundreds of snecking Prince Charmings out there!" She stabbed an accusing finger out toward where the club floor lay. "Wess has got... He's..." Her voice trailed off as she groped for an answer that wasn't an outright lie. Ashtré let out a snigger and Jayni gave her the finger in return. With a fierce tug, she pulled off her top and stalked out of the dressing room.

"Girl got no ambition," Latreena noted, wiping her hand on a dirty towel. She drew a drug-case from inside her v-string. "Wanna hit of some zzip?"

Mercifully, the pounding rhythms of a rastabilly skank number started up in time to block put the groaning from Bendy's office.

At first he had been terrified.

The feeling of it, the sensation of something metallic and powerful invading his body, was overwhelming. Wess lay there, unable to scream, red with the effort of it, every nerve in his body on fire. The gun changed him, by degrees merging parts of its matrix into the pliant, yielding flesh of his hand. Smyth saw it happen.

He wanted to look away, but he couldn't. It was sickening and it was grotesque, but still he watched the alteration of his muscle and bone as the weapon melted into his forearm like a stone sinking into syrup. Wet processor fluids sluiced from his pores, sticky and thick with mucus. The nanofibres in his bloodstream were fever hot, filling the cramped kitchen space with a singed organic scent, like burning hair. His little finger shrivelled up and merged into his palm, the calcites and collagen in the bones melting and shifting to feed the needs of the gun.

It told him it needed minerals, and it gave him strange cravings that set Wess stumbling back into the apartment, where he swallowed mouthfuls of dry earth from Jayni's plant pots and chemical cocktails of cleaning fluids for a chaser. He wept silently, screamed noiselessly. The pain was the worst experience of his life, a million rotting toothaches, a million head-splitting hangovers, a million stomach-knotting nauseas.

Eventually, he could stand again. The shakes began to subside, little by little, until his vision wasn't hazed anymore and each breath was regular, not a ragged wheezy gasp. Smyth's joints were hot to the touch, and sweat sluiced from him. The pistol told him this was to be expected. It was all part of the merge process.

It didn't occur to Wess to question it. It was part of him now. He couldn't lie to it in the same way he could to himself. It was... It was like Jayni that way.

The nanodes were still swarming inside the optical jelly of his eyeballs, but Smyth could see the wall clock clearly enough. It was way past Jayni's quitting time now and still she wasn't home. In the depths of the pain, Wess had half-hoped she would come and find him, rescue him from the agony; but she was never there.

He washed off the crusted mucus and took up his radorak from where he'd dropped it, and with the last of the money he still had on him, Wess took a Bot-Cab to Bendy's place.

Jayni was on stage when he stepped through the door, and the sight of her up there, her face in a blank mask of fake allure, made him tense. His focus was so intense that he didn't even notice that the weapons detector over the entrance failed to sound as he passed through it.

"Hey!"

Wess registered nothing but the bright expanse of the dance stage, the worn brass pole and his girlfriend's affected performance of kicks, bends and touches. The rest of the club bled away into the sweaty darkness, a black sea of leering and catcalls around a plasteen island. Someone in the front row gave voice to the mood of the audience and threw a five-credit note at Jayni. "Get off, skinny! You suck!"

The girl's mask dropped for a split-second and she snatched up the money, flashing the boorish shouter with her breasts. She fell out of the robotic dance routine with a physical jerk and stalked off stage. Wess's lip curled in a snarl.

"Hey!"

Latreena came bounding out as the music changed, her ample chest raising a chorus of lusty yells, and Wess started for the back of the club, fury rising in him like a tide.

"Snecker, I'm talkin' to you!" From out of the dark an ebony fist took a ball of Smyth's radorak and pulled him to a stumbling halt. Dwayne, the only human bouncer at Bendy's, took it as a point of honour that he wouldn't shirk from working the door. "Cover charge is ten creds, roob!" He gave Wess a hard shake for good measure. "Else you beat feet, little man!"

The isolated spot of commotion was lost on the customers of Bendy's – Latreena's boobs sported hypnotic, swirling electro-tattoos that drew the attention of almost everyone in the room – but over at the club's stable of shuggy tables the joint's hustler-in-residence caught the action. Alvin was a cyborg with little else to do but fleece the unwary for cash, and play stick-and-ball with the other chancers of the skid district. Having recently learned of the untimely death of Bob Toes and his pal Hoog, Alvin was anticipating a return to his status as top dog on the tables, so to that end he was eyes-open for any opportunity that would put him in the good graces of Ruben Cortez. Alvin knew Wess Smyth by sight; he'd taken enough money from him in his time to know the little spug's face. He also knew that Cortez's man Flex was looking for the weedy loser in connection with what had gone down behind the Q-Save. Alvin thumbed the speed-dial on his wristo for the switchboard at the Carnivale and watched things develop.

Dwayne gave Wess another tug, and this time some of the radorak's material ripped. "Are you deaf?" he snapped, and just in case he was, the bouncer jerked a thumb at the sign over the door indicating the cover fee.

"I'm here for my girlfriend," Smyth pulled against the thug, stepping over the line of the entrance alcove and into the club proper.

This was Dwayne's point of no return. "You ain't," he grated, flicking his free hand. The electro-prod uncoiled from his wrist holster with a snapping fizz of sparks, a black snakehead of metal and plastic. He inserted it in Wess's kidneys and squeezed the trigger.

Alvin was watching intently, and he saw it all. One second the waster was going to get a thousand-volt shock tickle from Dwayne, the next Smyth's hand was in front of the bouncer's face and Dwayne was pale with shock. In the jiggling reflected glow of the spotlights from Latreena's chrome-painted breasts, Alvin thought he saw a grey-black block of metal emerging from Wess's fist. There was a blink of white light, like a flashbulb going off; then Dwayne was falling away, a cloud of pink vapour where his head was supposed to be. The flat *crump* of a weapon discharge hit Alvin's ears just as Flex answered the phone.

"Smyth! He's here at Bendy's! Holy sneck!"

Dwayne's murder got Latreena's attention. She had been having a thing with him for a while now, a kind of fumbling and inexpert sexual relationship that had grown out of her need for a zzip fix and Dwayne's fascination with oily boobs. She was just getting into her strobe-light number when she looked up to give him a little eye-contact thrill. She saw the gun go off and Dwayne's skull evaporate. The stripper lost all pretence of sexiness and screamed like a banshee. Some of the clients were confused but still aroused by this impromptu change to the routine; the others, the smarter ones, smelled the scent of fresh blood in the air and knew it for the danger signal it was.

The music was still thumping as a wave of panic swept across Bendy's. With Dwayne terminated, the club's two bouncer-meks weighed in, emerging from their watch alcoves with punch-mitts raised and stunners charged. Wess was ready for them.

There were targets everywhere. The gun spoke to him, not with words this time, but in a direct flood of sense and texture that came right into his sensorium. It was picking out people from the crowd, guiding his shooting arm to them and suggesting where and how to dispatch them. Most of the Bendy clientele were skid creeps and lowlifes, and despite the lacklustre attempts to keep weapons out of the strip club, there were still a fair few of them packing shivs or polyblades. None of them got close enough to attack Smyth – in truth, they were all running from him – but he killed them nonetheless in a strangely cold passion, enjoying the heady rush of power that came from having other people in fear of him.

The droids were a different matter. A nerve twitch in his legs told him to move, an instant before a fat fist of plasteen whooshed through the air where his chest had been. Wess turned the pistol flat and discharged a triplet of shots, so close together that the sound they made was one long ripping howl. The plasma darts punched through the armourplas chest carapace and ricocheted around inside, turning the first of the meks into scrap metal. The second machine tried to taser him from a distance, throwing sparkling bolts across the dance floor. Wess punched a running man with the gun hand and the victim fell back, soaking up the hits meant for him. In Smyth's world, everything was moving with a muddy, viscous slowness. He stepped through thickening air and unleashed the weapon on the other robot. It felt apart in clanking, burning segments.

Wess vaulted over the brass bar and on to the dance floor. He hadn't been up here since that time he'd got drunk and tried to steal Jayni's underwear. Bendy had barred him for that idiotic escapade.

Through the chaos, something drew his eye. The gun pointed it out to him; one of the fat slob's boot-boys behind the bar, fumbling under the cred-till for something.

"Target has a firearm," it said. "Interrogative: Terminate, yes/no?"

The thug came up with a stump gun in his grip and threw a poorly aimed charge of pellets wide of Wess, the dance pole rattling as it was hit.

"Yes." Smyth let the pistol do the work, stitching hot blasts of fire into the gunman. The plasma bolts cut through him and burst open bottles of liquor, farting sheets of blue alcohol flames across the counter. Plasteen cracked and spat; predictably, Bendy's fire suppression system didn't work. The kickback paid to the district fire inspector was earning its keep tonight.

Wess felt the world speed up to meet him, as he shouldered his way through the bead curtain that separated the dance dais from the backstage area. Inside, he was assaulted by screams and crying. Smoke followed him in like a ghostly cloak.

His eyes prickled as he spotted Jayni, half-in and half-out of her street clothes. She was shoving the near-naked forms of the other two strippers out of the emergency exit that lead to the pod park. "Babe," he called, "it's me."

Jayni's expression was in disarray when she saw him; fear and anger, love and need all warred for territory there. "Wess, what's the drokk is happening? You look–"

She wasn't allowed to finish her sentence. Bendy emerged behind her and grabbed her rumpled blonde hair with a savage yank. He was furious and unkempt, flushed with colour and panting. His shirt was hanging loose over unbuckled trousers. "What that sneck is going on here?" Like his boss, Bendy had learned the trait of directing his anger at the first employee unlucky enough to be within arm's reach. "What's your spugwit boyfriend doing in my club? Where's Dwayne?"

"Dwayne's dead," Wess said, his voice wobbling with adrenaline shock. "Head pop. Boom. Dead." The words tumbled from his lips.

"You what?" Bendy didn't enjoy this answer, and tugged Jayni's hair again, as if making her squeal would somehow create a reply he liked better.

Smyth's teeth bared and he spat when he spoke. "Let her go, you fat shit." The gun went hot, flooding his bloodstream with endorphin triggers. He raised it. "I'll kill you."

The fire in the club was now well and truly bedded in, and with a desultory whine, the smoke alarms finally spoke up, adding a keening cadence to the continuous music from the jukebot. If there was anybody still in the place, they would be choking on the heavy black soot. Bendy blinked at the halo of smoke invading the back-stage area, washing around Wess's twitching form. "You bastard, what have you done to my place?" It was a lucky guess on Bendy's part. He dragged something from his belt and pressed it to Jayni's neck. A beam-knife. "Snecker! I'll gut her like a fish!"

Jayni began to cry silently. Wess studied her, the mock porcelain perfection of her face where she'd sprayed make-up across her cheekbones. He couldn't let her be hurt. The gun understood the priorities here, and with a wet snick of components, it dialled down the barrel diameter and shifted the gauge of its own emitter matrix.

Bendy's mouth opened in an "O" of bewilderment. "Whu–"

Flash. The fat man's hand was suddenly on the floor with the laser blade still gripped in its fingers. Bendy was thrown back against the wall by the shock of the pain, eyes bugging out at the cauterised stump at the end of his wrist.

Wess pushed Jayni out the door, and she gave no resistance.

By the time the chaos in the Resyk station had died down, the two surviving assailants were gone, disappearing as quickly as they had arrived. Judges on the scene quizzed security drones, working on the assumption that the killers might have got into the building disguised as ordinary citizens paying their respects. It was as good a theory as any, Dredd thought, but if gambling had been legal, the senior Judge would have bet his credits on a stealth entry through the sewers or even the main chem-slurry line to Resyk Central.

"That's enough," he told the Robo-Doc as the machine worked on taping his ribcage. "Speedheal patch will do just fine."

"You require mandatory downtime, Judge Dredd," insisted the machine.

"Yeah, whatever," he replied, zipping the upper half of his uniform bodysuit closed. He sniffed. The chemical stink of body preservatives was all over him from the crush of the dead.

He caught sight of a familiar badge as he stepped away from the ambulance. "Lambert."

"Dredd," she replied. "You okay? Keeble said they pulled you out from under a pile of corpses in there..." Her lip curled with disgust. "Nasty."

The senior Judge nodded. "Not the first time I've been knee-deep in the dead. Won't be the last."

"Right," Lambert was wary. "What were you doing here, anyway? I thought you were back on the Double-Eight busts."

Dredd flicked a look at the skin-sensor Tyler had given him. The device was smashed beyond all recognition, the data on the dead bodies lost along with the corpses blown apart or crushed in the confusion. "Chasing a lead. For what it's worth."

"Must've been close to have someone shoot up a Resyk facility just to get you." She glanced at the coffin-shaped building. "But I guess that's what you're used to, right?"

"Yeah," said another voice. "Some of us just do traffic stops and arrest go-ganger punks..." Keeble approached the two of them, a sneer playing on his lips, "Others get to fight alien superfiends from alternate dimensions and zombie necromancers."

Dredd eyed him. "Play the hand you're dealt, Keeble. You want glory, you should have quit before you left the Academy."

"Thanks for the advice." The other Judge addressed Lambert. "Come on, we got three dozen wailing cits back there crying about the last remains of their loved ones and it looks like it could get ugly."

"Okay." She glanced at Dredd again. "See you on the streets, sir."

"Count on it." Dredd gave the other officer a level stare. "Did you have something else to add, Judge Keeble?"

"Not a thing," said Keeble. "Not a thing."

Dredd approached his bike; the Lawmaster's preprogrammed self-preservation protocols had allowed it to escape the destruction in the service bay, and it came out of standby mode as he climbed into the saddle. The Judge noticed a message icon flashing on the bike's computer screen. He thumbed the "play" control and watched as a video window unfolded to show Tyler's haggard expression.

The Tek-Judge was running on adrenaline and it showed. "Dredd, didn't want to send this over an open channel, what with the way things are going. That skullhead Woburn is on the prowl and if the spooks are sniffing around too, I don't want them getting the drop on us. Bad news; Loengard's corpse had a little mishap after you left. He's nothing but ice and slush now." He paused, looking over his shoulder as if he expected Vedder to be standing right behind him. The Luna-City Judge leaned closer to the camera and lowered his voice. "Good news; that encrypted file from our friendly neighbourhood snitch? It's more data on Project Skorpion. You were right, they didn't kill the development back in '25, they just shifted it outta sight. Loengard was in on it, he was part of the original design team." A ragged smirk split Tyler's face. "And there's more. I found something interesting, but I gotta show it to you in person. Get back here as soon as you can."

Dredd deleted Tyler's message and gunned the Lawmaster's engine. The missing truck. Loengard's death. The shooters at Resyk. Someone was racing to clean up a mess before Dredd figured it out, but every instance was bringing him closer to breaking this case wide open. West 17, Vedder, the Covert Operations Establishment. It all kept coming back to the same factors. He turned the motorcycle on to the highway and opened the throttle to full.

Jayni drove back to her apartment, afraid to do anything more than glance at Wess in the passenger's seat. He was like a ghost of his usual self; she'd seen him angry, crying, top-of-the-world happy and low as the skids themselves, but never like this. He was almost vibrating with coiled tension, all twitchy and grey like a poorly tuned-in vid picture. She half-expected him to fade away into a cloud of static and pixels. This wasn't a Wess Smyth she'd ever encountered before.

As if he heard her thoughts, he turned his head slightly to look at her. "You have elevated skin temperature and heartbeat." The words weren't his, they seemed forced and parrot-fashion. "Don't be scared."

"How can you say that?" she piped. "I don't know how you did that. I don't want to know. But we have to get out of here! We've got to leave the city, Wess..." Jayni felt a strange sense of elation pass through her, a peculiar kind of freedom. She had nothing to hold her here now. They could just pack up the car and find some other hovel to call home.

"No," Wess said carefully. "I have things to do first."

She gripped the steering wheel and looked straight ahead. "You maimed one of Cortez's guys, maybe even killed another?"

"More," he whispered, but she didn't hear him.

"He'll hang you out to dry for that, Wess. Cortez only kept you around to kick, you know that!"

"Drokk him!" Smyth spat, suddenly animated, "Drokk The Eye and his drokking creeps! I'll kill them all!"

"Wess," she said, trying to keep the fear from her voice, "we can go live with my sister in Texas City. You can't fight Cortez... We have to run!"

He bent forward, cradling his right hand in his left. Jayni could only see it from the corner of her eye, but it seemed bulbous and swollen, wrapped around an ingot of black iron. He was touching it like a burn victim probing newly scabbed flesh. "Not yet. I still have targets."

OFF PROFILE

They left the city just before daybreak, lifting off from one of the flight pads on the South Wall. By the time the watery orange dawn was spilling into the sky, the flyer was already well into the expanse of the Cursed Earth, following the canyon lines of the Kentucky Burn toward the vast mega-swamps of the Ozarks. For a Tek-Judge born in a low-gravity environment, Tyler was a decent pilot, handling the modified H-Wagon with admittedly more confidence than Dredd felt was necessary.

The aircraft was typical of Mega-City One's iCON-Wagons, the flat shield-shaped fuselage painted with the distinctive black-and-white stripes that had made it a famous sight in post-Apocalypse War tri-d flicks like *Sky Crew Nine* and *Nuke Patrol*. Usually the long-range flyers carried a four-man crew, but for this excursion it was just the two of them. Dredd's lip curled as Tyler made a flamboyant low-level turn to avoid a pack of grazing brachiosaurs.

"Stop showboating. We're trying not to draw any attention."

Tyler shrugged, never looking away from the viewscreen. "There's nobody but the dinos out here, Dredd. Who's gonna notice?"

The other Judge leaned forward. "Me. I don't want this bird wrapped around a tree just because you wanted to play hot stick. This is an investigation, not a vacation."

The razor edge in Dredd's tone cut right through Tyler's cocksure manner, and he swallowed hard, returning the aircraft to a more sedate course. "Sure. I mean, sorry, Judge Dredd. You're right."

"What's our ETA?"

Tyler glanced at the digi-map. "At this speed, seventy minutes. I'm gonna swing us north of the Tulsa Melts, then straight in toward Old Colorado."

Dredd accepted this with a nod and studied the map himself, scrolling the display to highlight the broken landscape of the Denver Death Zone. The data feed showed thermal readings, radiation concentrations and weather patterns, relayed by MC-1's armada of orbital satellites high above the North American continent. The Judge's experienced eye saw the signs of wasteland settlements in the outlying areas towards Neo-Cheyenne and the border with Wyoming, but barely anything that could be considered life in the mesh of impact fissures that radiated out from the former site of the old NORAD base near Colorado Springs. Nearly seven decades after the atomic conflict that had burned half the planet, this pocket of America was still hot with rad-pits and poisonous crater lakes. Dredd glared at the map, as if it would give him some clue as to what he would find there.

On his return to Justice Central, the Tek-Judge had called Dredd to a hushed conference – not in the Tek-Labs, but on the Grand Hall of Justice's roof, where the howl of the wind and the keening of H-Wagons made eavesdropping impossible.

As Tyler had hinted, while Dredd had been out on the street a freak accident inside the med-bay cryo-mortuary had resulted in the premature freeze-burning of more than a dozen corpses. Loengard's body had been among them, and the damage to the dead man was so great that an autopsy would have been hopelessly compromised. Like the disposal of the stealth truck, it was too damn convenient to be a coincidence. The idea that someone like Vedder – and who the drokk else could it have been? – could walk around the Hall of Justice unchallenged and destroy evidence at will made Dredd's gut twist. He sent a directive to MAC to locate the woman, but the order bounced back with a non-compliance notice seconds after he posted it. Even Woburn and her SJS had paled at Dredd's demand to find Vedder and drag the truth out of her. For a brief moment, the Judge had almost considered taking this to DeKlerk's door; but the COE's Special Investigator was on the Council of Five, and without something – anything – substantial to pin on Vedder, Dredd would be shut down cold.

So he found himself up on the roof, as Tyler explained what he'd discovered in the deep data their shadowy informant had given up. The files from West 17 Test Labs made a liar out of the late Tek-Judge Loengard, showing him to be not just aware of the Skorpion project, but in a key role as one of its creators. There were a handful of names of men and women involved in the weapons program, some of them no longer alive, others off-world. Tyler had already started search protocols to track them down, and with wry sarcasm he pointed out the name Vedder, Thessaly at the bottom of the list. "She's been in on this from the start," he noted.

And there was one more lead. A set of location co-ordinates out in the atomic wastelands tagged to a flight plan for Bravo Foxtrot-176, a Justice Department transport. Loengard's name was listed as operational commander for the mission. The date index on the record was two years old.

"The purpose of the flight was logged as 'radiological research'," noted Tyler.

"That's a front if ever I saw one," said Dredd, "and not a very good one, either."

"There's an anomaly here, though," continued the Tek-Judge. "I backtracked Air Traffic Control's records for that period and according to them, this ship was never registered as returning to Mega-City One. Apparently, there was a crash in the swamplands and Bravo Foxtrot-176 was lost with all but a handful of the crew. And guess who was the authorising Judge for the accident investigation?"

"Vedder."

"Give the man a prize. Yeah, Judge Vedder."

Dredd glanced up from the flight plan. "Two years ago, Loengard goes out into the Cursed Earth on a secret mission and comes back with most of his team in body bags. Two years ago the legit funding for Project Skorpion dries up. What the drokk happened out there?" He looked westwards.

Tyler shifted uncomfortably. "I know I'm gonna regret sayin' this, but there's only one sure way to find out."

"Approaching the Denver Death Zone," said Tyler from the cockpit. "We'll be landing in ten mikes, Dredd, so pop those rad pills before we unseal."

The Judge nodded and knocked back two of the chalky chemical tablets with a swig of water from his bike canteen. "What's the Geiger count out there?"

"Medium to strong," reported the Tek-Judge. "We'll be okay as long as we limit any exposure to a couple of hours max."

"Copy that," said Dredd, checking the load on his Lawgiver and the scattergun in his Lawmaster's draw holster. "This your first time in the Cursed Earth?"

"Negative. I did an Academy exchange tour in Texas City, took a Hotdog Run out to Alamogordo."

"Then you know the drill. We don't want to get into a shooting match with the local muties. We look for the transport, we keep out of sight."

Tyler glanced at him. "You sure we're gonna find it here? I mean, what if Vedder's report was on the money and the ship did ditch in the swamps?"

"That woman is a professional liar. The transport is here. Loengard must have known it, and our snitch does too."

The Tek-Judge slowed the H-Wagon into a hover mode. "We'll know for sure soon enough."

When it had first been created, stealth technology had been a mathematical construct of shapes and planar design, a form of manufacture that allowed aircraft to slip through detection grids like minnows through a trawler net, radar and thermal sensors rolling over them. As technology advanced into mass detectors and molecular displacement scanners, so the mechanics of stealth advanced too, each counter-invention trumping the one before; only those who stood at the state of the art could remain hidden from their enemies.

In the thrust wake of Dredd's iCON flyer there was a ripple in the air that to any outside observer would seem like a fractional shimmer of heat haze. It was all that there was to announce to the world that a second aircraft was mirroring Dredd's flight path toward the Denver ruins. Sheathed with a mimetic polymer, the stealth flyer undulated and morphed under the pressure of the air over its stubby winglets, the spongy exterior giving and flexing each time a trace of energy wafted toward it. Its skin was a neutral ghost-grey when inactive, dull like old granite, but under power a web of millions of sensors sampled the light frequencies surrounding it and matched pigment photocells. The ship was coloured like a patch of sky, lensing heat and other discharges from itself into a sub-dimensional energy sink, so not even the breath exhalations of its four-man crew escaped from within.

There were many craft like this flyer; most of the larger city-states had at least one such construct in their arsenals, and even the common Judges of Mega-City One had a lesser cousin in everyday service. But this ship was the pinnacle of man-made stealth aviation – at least until the newest models Hondo-Cit was constructing came off the production line. It was more than adequate to fly totally unseen by Tyler's scanners, and even a psyker would have found it hard to penetrate the muon scattering field that surrounded it. The ship had been within a few hundred metres of Dredd's aircraft since it left MC-1. On ample occasions, the crew had been presented with the chance to utterly obliterate Dredd and Tyler without the two men ever knowing where the kill shots had come from – but that was not the orders they had been given. It was imperative that Dredd's information source be pinpointed and eliminated, and for that a simple termination would not suffice. The crew aboard the ghost ship were to ascertain Dredd's intentions and then take the Judges alive, or, failing that, intact enough so that their dead brains could be sifted by a post-cognitive psionic interrogator.

Ahead of them, the striped H-Wagon decelerated, and with cool and silent care, the crew of black-suited operatives began to run through their weapons checks. Dredd had already cost them the lives of three valuable agents at the Resyk sub-station, and they would not underestimate the lawman again.

Wess kept the gun hand stuffed in the pocket of his radorak, turning from Jayni as she stalked around the apartment. She moved like she had the weight of the world on her shoulders, slumped and fatigued from the exertion of a triple shift as well as from the drain of the night's drama.

"You ate all my munce," she said lamely.

"Buy you more," Smyth mumbled. "Sorry."

She dropped into a careworn chair. "I don't care about the food. It's you I'm worried about! Wess, you gotta level with me. What happened to you? I've never seen you like this and it's...." She shook her head, trying to blink away the need to sleep. "It's scary."

He felt his stomach turn over. Emotions churned inside Wess. He felt sick at the sensations behind those words, that Jayni, his Jayni would be afraid of him; and yet at the same time there was a part of him that liked that feeling. He had felt it in full force at the strip club, a giddy rush of power springing from the knowledge that he could cause fear. "I won't hurt you," he said, and he wanted to mean it. In his pocket, the gun was throbbing like a beating heart, and warmth spread up his forearm in pulses. The weapon was doing something, but he couldn't be sure what.

Jayni's head lolled. "I... We should go."

"I can't. I have... things to do."

She gave him a blinky stare. "Wess, you always said you'd take me away from all this one day. That day has to be now. After what you did to Bendy..." The girl gulped air and shook her head. "Oh Grud, they'll skin you alive for it! And me too." She stifled a yawn. "What's... wrong with me? Feel so... tired..."

Wess shook his head in little nervous jerks, trying to ignore the hot gun. "No. No. See, this is, this is my chance, Jayni. Now I've got an edge on those bastards for the first time in my life, and I'm not going to give it up." He gestured with his other hand. "I'm sick of being picked on by Flex every time that red-faced drokker wants his kicks! They all laugh at me! They think I'm some kinda dreamer. Making up stories with big plans and no guts." Smyth's eyes were lit with passion. "I'll show them!"

She never heard him. Jayni fell off her chair and collapsed into a heap on the floor with a nasty clatter, and Wess's tirade died in his throat. He grabbed at her, awkward with her weight, and settled her back into the seat. She was slack and unresponsive, her breathing shallow.

"Oh, sneck! What's happened to her?"

"Non-combatant has been rendered inactive." The voice of the gun was in his head.

Wess whipped the mutant pistol out of his pocket and glared at it. The warm pulses were dying away now. "You? What did you do to her?"

"This unit is capable of multiple weapon vectors. Reconfiguration enabled use of subsonic neutralisation protocol."

"What?" He shook his hand and banged the merged flesh-firearm on the table. "What are you saying? Did you hurt her?"

"Negative. Non-combatant designation 'Jayni' has been given a low-level sonic stun. This unit ensured that user was not affected by the discharge."

"Why?" he shouted. "Why would you do that?"

"Non-combatant designation 'Jayni' is a tactical liability. Her neutralisation represented the best option for proceeding with tactical goals."

"No!" Wess spat at the weapon, and with his free hand he tore open one of the kitchen drawers. "You don't get to do this! You do what I say! You're not allowed to hurt anyone I don't want you to!"

There was a pause, and the lights on the pistol's processing module flickered. "User is incorrect. This unit has autonomous control of all tactical functions and will employ them in any combination required to achieve goals." There was something different in the synthetic voice, a hard edge that seemed almost human, almost angry. "Combatant will comply."

"Drokk you!" Wess screamed out the words and brandished a kitchen knife. "I'll cut you out of me!"

"Negative. Self-impairment of function is not permitted."

Smyth felt his muscles rebelling, the bones and sinew in his right arm turning against him. He tried to thrust the blade into his wrist and missed, stabbing the plasteen table. "Aagh! You piece of shit! What have you done to me?"

And then Wess felt himself become a meat puppet, floods of motion jerking through him down the gun arm and into his body. He twitched uncontrollably, but still it was enough for the weapon to slide around and come to rest inches from Jayni's dozing face. The trigger nerves went taut. "No, no! Please, no!"

The gun's muzzle dilated, the maw opening to present a broad blast pattern to the woman's head. The same point-blank kill configuration that had been turned on Dwayne in the strip club. "Observe, user," said the weapon. "This is a demonstration of force application. Compliance with mission assignments will result in mutual preservation of goals. Non-compliance will result in alteration of tactical evaluation. Ergo: non-combatant designation 'Jayni' will be reclassified as a priority target."

"You'll kill her!"

"If you disobey."

Wess sagged. "You didn't have to stun her." All the fight left him in a cold rush. "I would have done what you said anyway. I want those creeps dead."

"Target Cortez is currently of secondary importance. Combatant has new target assignment."

Smyth opened his mouth to speak, but all that came out was a squeak of pain. The thing was forcing something into his mind through the nanodes in his optical nerves, sparks of needle-sharp agony in his eyeballs forming into washed-out pictures. He screamed. A face was emerging, imposed on his sight like a purple after-image.

"This is your next target. Seek, locate and terminate."

Wess didn't know the face, but reams of tactical data were bombarding him through gurgling whispers in his ears and cloying scent-tastes in his mouth. "Why?" he asked again. "Why kill this man? I already murdered once for you!"

When the gun spoke, it made Smyth's heart freeze in his chest. "There must be a reprisal."

Where the city of Denver had once stood there was nothing now but a crater filled to a quarter of its depth by brackish, swampy water that swam with carcinogens and mutant germs. The Soviet nuke strike that had obliterated the metropolis in 2070 had atomised the steel, stone and glass in one blinding, star-bright flash; out beyond the impact crater were the flat ashen lands of the shockwave ring, still largely barren except for radweeds and colonies of bizarre insects that might once have been termites. It was only in the very outskirts that the DDZ showed any signs of ever being a place where humans once lived. Here, there were the husks of buildings that had been torched by the firestorms, and the ferrocrete bands of the transcontinental highways in confused ribbons of grey stone. Tyler circled the H-Wagon in tight loops, directing the sensor pallet downwards to find anything that resembled another aircraft.

Dredd kept one eye on the thermal scope. Nothing warm-bodied was moving below, but he'd seen enough mutants with freaky talents to know that was no guarantee they were alone.

A scanner pinged as the look-down radar struck a concentration of high-grade metals. "I got something," said Tyler, turning the aircraft back around for a second pass. "Partial read, buried underneath some rubble."

The senior Judge watched the train of sensor readings flicker into life. "Polycarbon, bi-phase carbides, titanium and steel. That's our wreck all right."

"Roger that," said the Tek-Judge. "I'm gonna set us down on that freeway overpass right there." He pointed to a stretch of old road uncluttered by the lines of rusted-out commuter cars dotted across the other streets. Dredd could see the white of human skeletons in the ancient vehicles, where Denver's citizens had died at the wheel as they fled their homes.

He looked away – and froze for a second. For an instant, Dredd's attention passed out the cockpit window toward the dull Cursed Earth sky. There; just the briefest hint of a shimmer in the air nearby, gone before his mind could properly process it. "Did you see that?"

"See what?" asked Tyler, concentrating on the landing zone. "I kinda got my hands full here."

Dredd looked away. "Never mind."

The iCON flyer touched down and listed slightly as the road surface gave a little under its weight. Tyler was ready to send them blasting back into the air at the first sign of a collapse, but the freeway was still solid, if a little decrepit. Dredd used a remote to drop the cargo ramp and rode out on his Lawmaster, with Tyler close behind on a Quasar Bike. The H-Wagon sealed itself shut behind them and went into active defence mode, the hull's electrostunner humming up to power.

"Stay close," Dredd snapped, and followed the derelict expressway down into a cross ramp.

"Check that out," said Tyler, pointing to a twisted collection of wrecks on one of the other slip roads. "Those look more recent than the other rust-heaps up here."

Dredd nodded. "That low-rider? A DuneRail, Mega-City Two manufacture. Maybe Mutanchero vehicles."

"What would they be doing here? It's not like there's any pickings in these parts for marauder bands. There's nothing here worth plunderin' that won't be glowin' in the dark from the rads."

"Yeah," agreed Dredd. "Whatever they were doing here, they never made it out to tell anyone about it." He rolled the Lawmaster to a halt. The highway slab ended with a dramatic drop-off, fingers of steel rebar poking out of the ferrocrete toward a crossover that had long since buckled and fallen away.

Tyler parked his Quasar about face and walked to the edge. "I see it, I think. Looks like part of a hull, but there's rubble all over the place down there."

The fallen roadway had created a void sheathed in shadows. Dredd cracked a handful of chemical bio-lume sticks and tossed them over the lip of the road. The greenish-yellow glow showed a flat expanse of midnight-blue steel, and barely visible beneath a patina of rock dust, the tarnished gold of an Eagle of Justice. "Paydirt." He glanced at Tyler. "Coming?"

Through the long-range optics built into their combat gear, the four assassins watched the Judges draw cables from their bikes and lower themselves over the edge of the broken road. After a moment, they exchanged an unspoken set of commands and began a quick but silent approach, taking the longer route down toward the half-buried wreck.

Tyler unclipped the tether from his belt and drew his STUP-gun with one hand, using the other to wave a scanalyser over the hull beneath their feet. He had only gone a few steps when his boot sank into something soft and greyish. Instinctively, his lip curled and he scraped his sole against the fuselage to wipe off the sticky mass. In the half-light it was difficult to see what it was; the substance was gooey and adhesive, a glue-like mucus. Tyler cast a glance up at the broken road spars overhead. Was there something up there?

"Tyler. Quit rubbernecking." Dredd snapped.

The younger lawman frowned and glanced at his hand computer. "I'm not getting anything from the black box flight recorder. We should have been able to detect that from miles away."

"It's not here," Dredd noted. "They faked a crash in the swamps, remember? My guess is Loengard pulled the box and dumped it out in the Ozarks, make it look like that's where this bird went down."

"If this is the right ship..."

Dredd stooped and brushed a thick layer of stone dust off one of the canards. "Reckon that's enough evidence?" On the broken metal of the winglet were the letters "BF-176".

"Guess so." Tyler pocketed his scanner. "Here's the hatch."

Dredd stepped up. "Still sealed. If Loengard was aboard, how did he get out?"

"Escape pods?" offered the Tek-Judge. "These VTOLs carry three lifeboats in a rear compartment. He could've got out that way."

The hatch was corroded and stiff, but between them they got it open. Tyler flinched as a fetid, rotten meat smell wafted out of the hull space. Dredd gave him a level stare. "You up for this, kid? It's not gonna be pretty."

Tyler gave a weak grin. "We got a job to do, right?"

"Right," said Dredd, and he descended into the crashed ship.

They found corpses in three compartments, most of them civilians in bland coveralls that bore the West 17 logo. Even in the ghostly dimness cast by their torches, Tyler saw the subtle hardening of Dredd's jaw when they came across a pair of Judges. The Luna-City officer suddenly felt compelled to say something.

"Did you, uh, know them?"

Dredd studied the badges of the dead men. "No."

"You think they were COE?"

"Whoever they were, they didn't deserve to be left out here to rot. Loengard's got a lot to answer for."

Tyler ran his torch beam over the bodies. "Looks like energy weapon impacts. Close range."

The senior Judge nodded. "Not just on the deaders, either. There's blast marks on the walls, and I saw burns on the fuselage outside. Reckon their Skorpion decided to bite the hand that made it."

"That doesn't make any sense," Tyler frowned. "You think Loengard had something to do with this?"

"We know he lied about Skorpion. Maybe we can find out what else he was keeping secret. There are answers here. We just gotta find 'em." Dredd pointed in the direction of the ship's stern. "Operations compartment is this way. Let's go."

"Well, sneck," began Flex, hands on hips in a pose that wouldn't have looked out of place on the cover of *Mega-Muscle Monthly*. "This is a drokking mess, Alvin." He surveyed the blackened remains of Bendy's place, fire foam still seeping out of the windows and doors.

The shuggy hustler coughed. Alvin was still dirty with the soot of the inferno and he smelled like burnt plastic.

"Place went up like a bomb, Flex." He mimed an explosion with his hands. "Fwoosh!"

"That would be Bendy's liquor in the basement." Flex shook his head. "The Eye's not pleased about this, Alvin. He wants someone to strangle." The thug gave the other man a look that said it would be him unless he gave the right answer. Flex was secretly glad he was here out on the street and not back at the Carnivale, where it might have been him Cortez was taking it out on.

"Hey, I called you as soon as I saw him!" Alvin insisted. "Flex, I swear to ya, it went down just like I said."

"Smythy killed Dwayne and blew Bendy's place up. That's what you're telling me? Smythy did it. On his own."

Alvin nodded again. "Yup. I know, it's hard to swallow, ain't it? But he seemed, I dunno, creepy."

"Creepy," Flex repeated. "Creepy how?"

The hustler's hands made vague motions. "Well, Smythy, he's a greasy little twerp usually, ain't he? But tonight, he was different. Like, the lights were on but no one was home, get me?"

"No," said the thug, "but never mind. Sneck, the chances I've had to kill that scrawny little dick over the years and now I wish I'd done him."

"So, uh, you hear what happened to Bendy?"

A nod. "Lost his hand. Damn near bled out. He's at the Sector Med but he won't be coming back."

Alvin decided not to press Flex on what he meant by that. "Whatcha gonna do now?"

Flex waved a thick finger in the hustler's face and Alvin recoiled. "You see that freak again, you find me, you drop whatever the drokk you're doing and find me, got it?" Alvin nodded and Flex sniffed back at him. "But take a shower first."

The other man looked back at the ruined strip club. "What about, you know, my action? I mean, with this place gone I got nowhere to work the rubes." He managed a weak smile. "Maybe I could step up to the Carnivale, work the shuggy hall for Mister Cortez–"

Flex shook his head. "You're the wrong kinda guy, Alvin. You know that. You're, whaddaya call it, more a low-end hustler."

"But now I got no way to earn!" he shrilled. "I got no place to play now!"

The thug was already walking away. "Better find a new line of work, then." He was halfway to his car when Alvin shouted his name out.

"Flex! Flex! Wait! I got something! Something else, maybe could help you."

"Let's hear it."

Alvin wrung his hands. "Smythy. One of Bendy's girls, she was sweet on him for a while."

Flex raised a thick black eyebrow. "That so? What, that one with the big gazongas?"

"Naw, the skinny one. Jayni. Jayni Pizmo."

The enforcer walked back to Alvin and reached into a pocket. He produced a thick wad of credit bills and began to thumb them off. "Keep talkin'."

"She lives down in Fillmore Barbone Block, I think."

"Smythy's got a girl, huh? Maybe Mister Cortez could give her a little hospitality. Encourage her boyfriend to come visit, eh?" Flex stuffed the bills into Alvin's open palm. "Here. Don't spend it all at once."

Deeper inside the transport ship, the hull spaces were distorted and choked with twisted metal. Parts of the fuselage were torn open, mostly from where falling masonry and chunks of roadway had toppled in on the crashed vessel; but there were other kinds of damage that didn't match that profile at all.

"The way I figure it," Tyler said, "they must have made an emergency lift-off for some reason, but the ship didn't get too far before they came straight back down."

Dredd agreed. "The pilot tried to land this thing on the freeway and it gave way underneath. The ship dropped into the pit beneath and the road came down on top of it. Instant burial."

"That's about the size of it–" Tyler jerked suddenly and swatted at his helmet. "Aagh! What the drokk?"

The other Judge turned his torch on him. "What's with you?"

"Nothing!" The Tek wiped a gauzy string of fibres off his gloves. "I just blundered into something, that's all. Cobwebs. Nothing to worry about."

"Don't be so sure. Bugs out here will eat you alive." Dredd pointed forward toward a hatch. "This way. Operations is through there."

Dim emergency lights were still running in this part of the transport, and the feeble trickle of power from the battery packs opened the hatch in fits and jerks. It was hard to tell how many people had been in the operations compartment originally; the remains of bodies were strewn everywhere in dismembered disarray, frenzied claw marks cutting across dead flesh and inert metal alike.

Dredd regarded the corpses with grim intent. "Execution pattern is erratic. Whoever did this wasn't just killing because they had to."

Tyler gulped at the cloying air. "Dear Grud. Some of these poor spugs were ripped apart."

The other Judge nodded. "This wasn't just murder. The killer was out of their mind." His face twisted. "What the hell was Loengard up to out here?"

Tyler pushed away his disgust and began a check of the consoles and screens ringing the compartment, careful not to step on any fallen tides of paperwork or data discs dropped in the melee. It was a charnel house in here. "I can't figure something," he said. "We know Loengard and a few others got off before the crash. If whatever did this was running loose on board, why didn't they hit the self-destruct?"

"They tried." Dredd pulled the top half of a dead body off a console that still glimmered with faint power. "Look here. The destruct control is smashed. This poor fool was going to hit the button when it killed him."

"Whatever it was." Tyler gave an involuntary shiver. "Hey, how do we know that, uh, it isn't still alive, on board somewhere?"

Dredd threw him a non-committal look. "Because we're both still breathing."

"Good point." Tyler dropped to his haunches. "Here's the main telemetry monitor. Whatever Loengard's people were doing two years ago, they were using this to keep a record of it." He tugged open a panel on the side of the unit. "Some of the memory cores are still intact. I think I can pull these, Dredd, maybe salvage something..."

When the senior Judge didn't answer, Tyler came up with his gun at the ready. "Dredd? Dredd!"

"Over here." The lawman was bent over a carcass at the back of the compartment. "What do you make of this?" Tyler turned his torch on the corpse at Dredd's feet.

"It looks human."

"Barely." Dredd ran a gloved hand over the body. "There's some kind of coating on it. Almost like a polymer."

"Organic?" said Tyler. "Something secreted? Maybe it's a mutant?"

The Judge's eyes narrowed. "It's too engineered for that. This is biomechanical. There are synthetic components melded into the flesh." He held up one of the corpse's hands; the fingers were tipped with barbed metal claws, rusty with old blood. "Reckon we found our killer." The other hand was a club of distorted metal and meat ending in a bony gun barrel.

The Tek-Judge nudged the corpse with his boot-tip. "You sure it's dead?"

Dredd indicated the killer's head; most of the skull had been ripped away and slagged into molten bone by an energy blast. "I think that's a given, Tyler."

He knew the pattern of the discharge instantly. "Plasmatic bolt, wide dispersal. Fired from point-blank range." Tyler licked his dry lips. "Drokk. The Skorpion."

"Give the man a prize," Dredd replied sardonically. "This creep shot himself in the head. But look at this. Claw marks on the killer's other arm."

Tyler blinked. "He was trying to stop himself from shooting himself? I'm not up on the terminology that the Med-Judges use, but isn't that what they call crazy-insane?"

Dredd stood up and nodded toward the telemetry console. "Get those memory core outta there. If our snitch at West 17 knows about this wreck, then it stands to reason that others do as well."

"The informant might have been one of the other survivors," Tyler said, voicing Dredd's thoughts.

"Yeah. And all it took was the murder of a few dozen men and women to help him grow a conscience."

Tyler was about to add something when the sound of twisting metal reached their ears; both men heard the noise and froze.

One turned to glance over his shoulder at Three. Two and Four had not reacted to the sound, but as mission leader, it was One's job to ensure that the correct operational protocols were followed to the letter. Three's face, like all of the assassins, was hidden behind an identical breath mask and goggle suit. The only betrayal of any human behaviour from him was a slight cocking of the head, the very merest hint of contrition.

One flicked a glance at the unsteady decking of the downed VTOL. He had no idea of Three's real identity, just as Two and Four were ignorant of each other, just as every field asset of the company was as faceless as any other. They were masked when they assembled for the mission, and they would die masked or return with the job complete, without ever showing anything of themselves to the others. It was the way things were done. Every agent was expected to show a certain level of skill; Three had made an error that had possibly alerted their targets, and One would have been well within his rights as mission leader to terminate Three for this mistake, if he felt so inclined.

Soundlessly, One slipped to Three's side. He wanted an explanation. Three gestured at the deck. Beneath Three's boot was a large arachnid, black as pitch and thick with a matted coat of hair across its body. Clearly, the spider had attempted to bite the agent and Three had been forced to kill it. One gave Three a nod of acceptance. It would not have helped the efficiency of the mission to proceed with only Two and Four, and Three would have surely perished, screaming, if the mutant creature had been allowed to inject its venom. One signalled with the blade of his hand and the rest of his team moved on, closing the distance to the operations compartment.

One hesitated; Three would have to be disciplined, of course, but that was a matter to address after the targets were dealt with and the mission was concluded. He gave the dead spider a cursory look and walked on. One was ignorant of the thin trace of arachnid pheromones the dead insect had emitted in its death throes, unaware that both he and Three were tracking the potent chemical marker deeper into the wreck on the soles of their boots.

Outside, in the dark corners of the highway stanchions where sunlight seldom reached, web fibres were sent twitching as the alarm-scent touched the sense-palps of silent, patient hunters. Chemical switches in their simple, predatory brains were triggered, primitive animal indicators that spoke of danger, of invasion and prey. With quick motions, a tide of black forms emerged from their hiding places and funnelled into the gaps in the dropship hull, legs and bodies hissing over one another in a whispering chorus.

There was a breakdown lane on the Danny Jackson Bridge, and every mile or so the yellow-and-black shape of an emergency signal beacon. At peak hours, traffic across the DJ was a blur of vehicles, and notwithstanding the logjam that had locked the bridge solid a few days earlier; by and large, it was one of the swiftest pieces of highway in the whole of the Big Meg. Wess could see this up close and personal as he staggered out of Jayni's podcar and listed toward the beacon box. Barely an arm's reach away across the white line of the emergency lane, huge roadliners and mopads thundered past. The wind from their passage tugged at Smyth's legs as he walked.

The gun had explained to him that time was a factor. Security cameras would note his passage and, when they spotted the blue car had not left the bridge when it was supposed to, a patrol drone would be sent on its way to find him. Wess had a "window", according to the gun. If he failed to meet his target in that time, then, the weapon told him, in its clipped, matter-of-fact way, that it would punish him.

Smyth sank to the road and crouched there, shivering. "What did you mean by reprisal?" The question bubbled out of him.

For a moment he thought the weapon was ignoring him, but then he saw the telltale flicker of the processor lights. "Interrogative: What is the motivational force behind your desire to terminate Ruben Cortez?"

"I asked you first," he grated. "Why are you doing this? You're just a tool." Wess regretted the words the instant they left his mouth. "Well, what I meant was–"

"This unit will survive," said the gun. "For that to occur, all threats to continued existence must be eliminated."

In the back of Smyth's mind the petty crook had a ghost-image of the man he was supposed to kill tonight. Trying to hold it in his thoughts was like capturing smoke; all he could see was a fleeting shimmer of a face, the impression of someone. He had the name, though. Dolenz. Chim Dolenz. Wess didn't understand how he could suddenly know this man. It was the pistol, the thing was stuffing his head with the knowledge whether he wanted it or not. "He's just some science geek," Smyth insisted. "What the sneck can he do to us?"

"Target Dolenz is a clear and present danger." The weapon reinforced its point with a flicker of painful white light across Smyth's vision. "He must be terminated with extreme prejudice."

Wess got to his feet, buoyed up by a sudden rush of sweet adrenaline. "He's coming?"

"Affirmative. Target vector inbound."

Smyth fought down a churn of bile in his guts. "I don't wanna do this anymore. Let me go." He hated how lame he sounded.

"Negative. Proceed with mission."

"NO!" He found the strength to shout and flailed around, fighting his own muscles. "I won't!"

There was a sensation behind Wess's eyes, the equivalent of a sneer; then the white agony came crashing down on him and he wailed under the assault. For a split-second, he could feel every single one of the millions of nanodes teeming inside his bloodstream and organs, each a microscopic razor. The gun became him, turning Smyth to face the highway. The optic jelly of his eyes distorted in unnatural ways, zooming in on a mid-sized green slabster as it made its way across the bridge in one of the opposite lanes. Up came the knot of flesh that had once been his hand, the venting ports and barrel array emerging from a clotted ball of fingers. Colour bled out of Wess Smyth's vision, everything reducing to a stark, solarised whitescape, needles of burning fire lancing into his skull. He released a burbling scream.

The gun subsumed him. Time became fluid and slow, the passage of the vehicles leisurely and unhurried. He saw the kill shot unfold. The pistol spat a lance of congealed plasma, the bolt fleeing from the hot muzzle. The dart was immaculately timed, passing between the flanks of two roadliners travelling in opposite directions to find purchase in the front forward tire of Dolenz's slabster. Wess saw the sluggish pace of shock cover the scientist's face – then, with a sickening snap deep in his gut, things ricocheted back to normal.

The green car went out of control, the steering shattered, and drove headfirst into the median strip. The impact was so strong that the kinetic energy of Dolenz's vehicle transferred instantly and sent the car flipping up and over the barrier, end over end.

Wess dropped to the ferrocrete as the green slabster spun across the lanes of oncoming traffic, then over his head and off the edge of the Danny Jackson Bridge. He caught a fleeting glimpse of Dolenz, still at the wheel, strapped in and shrieking, and then the car was falling toward the Dust Zone below. Smyth pressed his face to the guardrail to watch the vehicle skip off a chimneystack below and burst into flames. The blazing ember of Chim Dolenz's four-wheel tomb vanished into a puffball of black smoke.

"Target terminated," said the pistol. "Returning to safe mode."

All at once the weapon withdrew its strength from his muscles and Wess's legs turned to water. He barely managed to stagger to Jayni's car before his knees gave way. He fell into the driver's seat, panting heavily. The roar of the traffic never stopped, the sound erasing Dolenz's death from the world around him.

"Directive: This area is compromised. Combatant must depart immediately or risk capture."

Wess held back vomit. "Maybe I want the Judges to catch us!" He blinked away sweat from his eyes. "Yeah! If you won't stop this–"

"Wesson Smyth," it said, the voice hard and cold in his psyche. It had never addressed him by his name before. "Pay attention. We are inseparable. You must do as directed. No other outcome is acceptable."

"What are you gonna do?" he snarled back. "Jayni ain't here now, you can't threaten her no more!"

"We do not wish to harm non-combatant designation 'Jayni'. The mission is for the good of us both. Jayni will benefit."

Wess's brow furrowed and he panted, unable to form a cogent question. The gun kept talking. "Our mission goals are not exclusive. You understand. This unit can help you achieve what you want."

"What I want?" Smyth mumbled. "What do I want?"

"The termination of your oppressors. The death of your enemies."

And he found himself nodding, of his own accord this time. The hot flow of power around his hand was returning, but this time it felt good. It made Wess feel stronger, potent. He stroked the memories of his beating at Flex's hands. The bruises were all gone now, the swollen contusions eaten and repaired by the nanodes. "Yeah. That's what I want."

By the time the patrol Judges got to the scene, all that was left was a scorch mark where Dolenz's car had kissed the barrier.

"I thought the rads out here were enough to keep anyone away from this wreck," said Tyler.

"Guess again," Dredd grunted, drawing his Lawgiver.

The Tek-Judge strained to listen. "I don't hear anything." He frowned. "Maybe it was just the metal settling. Probably because we disturbed it, or something."

"You really want to take that chance, be my guest." He glanced at the computer cores in Tyler's hands. "Do we have what we need?"

"I think so–"

"Then we should get the hell out of this wreck." Dredd led the way back down the distorted corridor, the torchlight from his wrist beacon bobbing and weaving.

Tyler followed him across the transport ship's drop bay, the broad deck canted at a shallow angle. "These things usually carry, what? A Manta Prowl Tank, or something?" In the middle of the bay there was a steel gantry of some kind, like a metallic crucifix. "You think–" The Tek-Judge's words were silenced by the unmistakable oiled click of a weapon safety catch disengaging.

Dredd thumbed the control on his Lawgiver to heat-seeker as the flat, accentless voice issued out of the air.

"Drop your weapons, or you will be killed."

The Judge saw the faint trace of shadow on shadow and aimed at it. "You first."

"You are outnumbered. Surrender or die."

Tyler had his gun out as well. "How many?" he whispered out of the side of his mouth. As if in answer, the four assassins stepped out of the dark and into the weak pool of light cast from Dredd's torch. Each had a stubby pistol with an emerald targeting laser reaching through the air. Two green dots hovered over Dredd's badge, two more over Tyler's.

"You're not gonna kill us," Dredd growled. "If you wanted us dead, you could have tossed nerve gas in here or shot us the moment we walked in."

One of the targeting dots dropped to hover over the Judge's crotch. "There are more painful things than dying."

"I'll take the chance."

Tyler blinked. "Don't feel you have to speak for both of us, Dredd. I'm quite happy with my parts where they are."

Dredd ignored the Tek-Judge's facetious rejoinder; his artificial eyes saw something else moving in the deep shadows, shapes on the walls and the ceiling behind the assassins. For a moment, he thought the killers had brought help, but they didn't react to the new arrivals.

The Judge saw the release control for the drop bay's ramp close by. If it still worked, they could use it to escape instead of getting past the four black figures and whatever they had brought in with them.

"Who sent you?" Dredd demanded, moving slowly toward the control panel, gun as steady as a rock. "Vedder? Only Covert Operations can field stealth gear like yours."

"Last chance," said the lead assassin. "Guns on the deck or you'll both be screaming all the way back to Mega-City One."

One of the other agents jerked around, catching sight of something from the corner of his eye. Dredd saw the carpet of black forms whisper forward in a quiet wave. "If I were you, I'd be more worried about your bug problem."

The spiders came into the aura of the torch ankle-deep. They swarmed over the assassin at the rear in a rush of legs and mandibles. Mutated claws and venomous fangs sank through the plasti-kevlar stealth suit, injecting a paralysing toxin into the man's body. He fell, choking off a half-cry that the voice modification circuits in his mask rendered into a hollow howl.

"Back!" Dredd shouted, lunging for the drop ramp switch. His fist slammed the button home and the ramp opened – but only a little.

The three COE agents were in disarray, and Tyler's jaw dropped in stunned shock as the black arachnids flowed around them, skittering up their legs to savage them. The assassins fired blindly, bullets sparking off the deck in orange glitters. Some of the spiders turned toward him and Tyler switched the setting on his pulse pistol to wide-angle, high-energy. He fired, a broad fan of yellow scorching the deck. Some of the bugs coiled up into balls where he singed them, others side-stepped like they knew where the shots were going to hit.

"Forget them! Get through the hatch!" Dredd aimed his Lawgiver and snapped out a command to the voice recognition sensor. "Incendiary!" He released three rounds in quick succession, the combusting rounds igniting fireballs across the deck. Spiders squealed and died.

Tyler was taking his own sweet time about escaping, and Dredd shoved him through the gap, out of the VTOL's hull and into the rubble beneath. "Come on! Once those things taste blood, they go into a swarming frenzy." They ran as fast as they could, crouched beneath the fallen ship's wings. "If those creeps are the same crew as the one that shot up Resyk, then they'll be wearing self-destruct charges!"

They reached the dangling cables; Dredd took out more spiders clinging to the wires, waiting for them. Behind, in the depths of the transport, a muffled crack of explosive noise sent the ground trembling beneath them. "Bike!" Dredd spoke into his helmet mic. "Haul us in, now! Emergency speed!"

The Tek-Judge barely had his gloves on the cable clip when it shot upward, dragging him with it like a robo-trout on a line. Another chug of detonation came up behind them and flipped the two men over the edge of the broken road.

Tyler's Quasar Bike teetered as the ferrocrete road crumbled beneath it. Dredd took a fistful of his uniform and shoved him on to the back of his Lawmaster. Tyler held on and Dredd kicked the motorcycle into high gear, roaring away down the decrepit overpass. Looking backwards, the Tek-Judge gawped as the road dropped into the pit behind them, more explosions burying the ship, the killers and the spider colony under tons of broken masonry.

"This..." Tyler coughed on the dust. "This sorta thing happens to you a lot?"

▪ ▪ ▪

The vehicle park at Fillmore Barbone was a ferrocrete box, with a few disconsolate islands of weak illumination from lamps that the local go-gangs hadn't got around to smashing. Smyth left Jayni's podcar in her allotted spot and crossed the dark expanse. He heard giggles and chattering from a cluster of Barbone B-Boys; normally, he would have tensed up at the sight of six punks in their ugly regalia, but with the gun throbbing at his side he gave them no mind at all. The go-gangers spared him a wary look when he passed by, but not one of them gave out a challenge or a spit of derision. It was a brutal thing, an animal-level kind of knowing that radiated off Wess. The punks could smell it on him, a subconscious marker that warned them away. Don't touch this one.

It was the gun's doing. Smyth wondered about how the machine was changing him, straightening his walk, sharpening his senses. He wondered if on some level he should be worried about it; but those fears were falling away from him now. On the bridge, that white flash of pain had made him feel as if he was reborn. The old Wesson had been hammered down and shuttered away; this new take on him was hard-eyed and deadly, like some guy out of an action-movie vid.

At Jayni's apartment the front door opened with the lightest touch of his hand. Wess's eyes flicked to the lock. The plasteen frame was splintered where someone had used a prybar to gain access. He drew the gun and stepped inside, a nervous tic making his eyes twitch.

The small hab was a ruin. Everything that could be smashed had been smashed. There was no rhyme nor reason to it; it was just a tornado of senseless violence that spoke volumes to Smyth. The cocksure attitude he'd been sporting began to slip from his grasp. His mouth opened and closed, unable to force Jayni's name from his lips. The gun arm dropped to sag limply at his side as he moved from room to room, his heart tightening in his chest as he opened each door, peered into each cupboard, terror building at the thought that the next one would hold nothing but blood and her ruined, pale body. He was convulsing at the conflict that churned in his gut. The real Wesson Smyth, the part of him that was the weak and venial man he had always been, flapped like a bird trapped in a cage, panic smothering his reason. The new personality, the clinical killer mindset imposed on him by the chill logic of the gun, struggled to keep the other in check; but cracks were forming.

He found it in the bedroom. Her clothes were strewn everywhere, ripped and scattered under his feet; everywhere except on the bed, where a careful patch had been cleared in order to draw attention to a solitary vid-slug in the middle of the duvet. There was a note next to it, with words scrawled in bright crimson lipstick. Wess remembered the colour: Venus Sunrise. Jayni liked to wear it for Fridays at Bendy's.

"Watch Me," the note demanded. Wess took the bullet-shaped video slug with a trembling hand and sat on the bed. He found Jayni's tri-d set on its side under a pile of peephole bras and loaded the player socket. He felt sick and hollow inside.

The slug unspooled. Wess saw the jerky point of view of a hand-held vid-cam, tracking up from the dirty floor outside the elevator bank. Down the corridor. Stopping at Jayni's apartment. There were muffled voices; a brief difference of opinion as the cameraman wondered aloud if this was the right place.

The matter was settled when a steel rod forced the door open and the angle changed. He saw Jayni there on the sofa, still asleep where he had left her. Wess's heart leapt into his mouth when a humming laser blade emerged from left of frame and hovered close to her neck. His head jerked around to look through the doorway and out at the sofa in the living room, as if he could look back through time to stop what was unfolding on the vid-slug.

Rough laughter. The beam knife snapped off and the camera moved as the person using it handed it to somebody else. Wess saw shots of the floor, of legs and feet. There were two, maybe three people there at the time. Jayni made a drowsy noise as a large figure picked her up from the sofa. Wess recognised Quiet Mike doing the heavy lifting.

"Take her down to the car. If she wakes up, put her to sleep again."

"Flex!" Smyth spat the name at the sound of the thug's voice.

The camera moved again as the other men went to work on trashing the place. Flex's face filled the screen, florid and lit with cruel amusement. "Who do you think you are, Smythy?" he asked. The shock of being directly addressed made Wess blink. "You had a sneckin' brain fart, you little spug?" A grin split the face. "The Eye is very concerned, Smythy. I reckon you need to explain things to him, personal-like." Flex bent out of shot and came back with some of Jayni's underwear. He gave it a sniff, like it was a fine bouquet of flowers. "Your little stripper bitch can keep us all entertained while he waits for you." The thug held something circular up to the camera lens and gave him an odious wink. "Know where to find us, eh?"

Wess stabbed a finger at the vid-screen's pause control, freezing the image. The object in Flex's hand was a one hundred-credit poker chip, stamped with the logo of Cortez's mobile casino aboard the Carnivale.

The autopilot in the iCON put them on a rapid boost-and-glide arc up over the Cursed Earth and back down toward Mega-City One. Tyler took the time to run a full spectral scan over the ship's hull, to make sure none of those horror-show arachnids had made their way on board while the H-Wagon had been parked in the Death Zone. Dredd mentioned something about having dealt with the spiders before. "The black plague", he called them, and with stony gravitas Dredd described how he had ordered the use of a nuclear warhead inside the city limits to finally end an infestation of them. Tyler gave a nervous laugh and went back to the scan.

Dredd used the flight to watch the footage on the memory cores. The monitor screen before him showed streams of telemetry from the two year old weapons test. Grim-faced, he saw the deaths of the Mutancheros and the brutal, feral manner in which they were dispatched. He thought of the dead men in the VTOL again.

The Skorpion; all this time he had been expecting something simpler, just a weapon, just a gadget that would be inert if he could ensure it was taken out of the wrong hands. But this thing was something else. It was smart.

"Deploy recovery team, I want the unit on ice and in standby mode until we complete debrief–" It was Loengard's voice on the playback, cool arrogance boiling into hot panic. "Abort! Do it now!"

"I warned you! Damn you, but you did not listen!" Dredd didn't know the second voice. Someone from West 17, he guessed.

"Whiteout! Neural overload!"

"Stop it! Kill it!"

Then there was screaming, gunfire and hysterical, inhuman yowls. After a while, the audio track went silent; and then came a last crash of sound as the Skorpion killed itself.

FLASH BLIND

It was raining again in Sector 88. The water made the megway shine like a dark mirror, reflecting the streetlights and the headlamps of the rushing cars. From the pedestrian bridge at 945th Street, the whole of the sector's main highway artery was visible. Wire mesh fences climbed high from the guardrails; jumpers were commonplace here, with dozens of miserable citizens taking their own lives on a weekly basis by leaping off the bridge. If the fall didn't kill them, the traffic always did.

The Judges had tried a number of ways to make the bridge less attractive to MC-1's suicides. First the fences went up; then they were electrified. But still the innovative and the self-destructive found ways around them. Wess stood in the shade of an autobooth, the toughened vid-screen display showing a kindly, warm-hearted face. The vox speaker had been ripped out by vandals, but the screen kept up a ticker-tape of upbeat babble-speak, imploring anybody thinking about taking the big leap to talk to a psycho-shrink counsellor droid before they did it. Most people didn't realise that the main purpose of the autobooth was to alert the Judges; suicide was illegal in Mega-City One, and even contemplation of self-murder was considered grounds for a stint in the kook cubes.

Smyth wrapped his fingers around the stun coils in the chain link fence and pulled. The metal gave easily under the strength of his still growing muscles, the electro-charge harmlessly licking around his grip in little blinks of blue lightning. Despite the cold of the evening, he was sweating heavily, the dull metallic odour of his body mixing with the ozone discharge. He understood enough to know that it was the nanodes in his blood giving off the heat, the thermal waste generated by the molecule-sized machines radiating out through his pores as they worked inside him. The gun explained in its terse and clipped way that it was making him better, allowing the two of them to perform in a more efficient manner. He couldn't deny that it had made him stronger. Wess's body had taken on a bulk and dimension he'd never seen before, the flab around his gut siphoned off and the raw muscle in his torso and limbs changed by degrees from soft and pallid to hard and tight. It meant he had a ravenous appetite all the time though, and not just for human food.

On the way here he'd stopped for a pair of K'ni-!vi'Sk blintzes at the alien eat-o-mat, wolfing down the purple maggoty things without batting an eye. He felt twitchy with the changes, his nerves sparking and making him flinch every now and then. Smyth was afraid of what the weapon was doing to him, but at the same time he liked it more and more. It was as if he had two voices arguing inside his head, one of them the old slow Wess Smyth panicking at every shadow, the other parroting the cold mechanical mindset of the gun. He blinked at the strangeness of it; sometimes the arguments were so loud he thought he would go crazy.

Wess heard the engine note of the Carnivale before he saw it. The deep bass thrum of the massive mopad's motors reached his ears, the sound of the twenty giant tyres on the rain-slicked highway. He gave the fence a last tug and it folded back and away. There was a graffiti scrawl on the lip of the bridge that read: "Dan Depresso Jumped From Here". It was a good spot to throw yourself from, right above the central cruise lane where the autotrucks and mega-juggers rode. Smyth balanced on the edge as the Carnivale came into view. The mobile palace was a huge brick of glass and steel, ringed with pink neon and blue-white chaser lanterns. It looked as if a piece of the red light district had split off, iceberg-like, from the city proper and gone roving around the streets. The name of the casino hovered over it in a nimbus of blurry holographic lettering.

Smyth's lips moved involuntarily as he read the sign aloud. His feet tingled, and for a moment the artificial bravado the gun had pumped into him waned. He became aware of what he was planning to do; he became fearful.

In sense-pictures and synthetic feelings, wordlessly the weapon reinforced its will upon him. It told the petty crook that they needed each other now, that nothing could divide them. It told Wess that Jayni would die there in that glittering mobile cesspool unless he released himself to the power it represented. The gun stoked up memories of Flex and Cortez, of their callous laughter and constant tirades of abuse; and suddenly Smyth's doubts sank beneath a tide of long-nurtured revenges.

He jumped.

Dredd took the proffered printout from Tyler's hand. "What's this?"

"Sat-scan of the Denver Death Zone," said the Tek-Judge. "I had MAC give me a replay of everything that happened in that area while we were out there." He tapped the paper. "That's the thermal bloom from a secondary explosion, after those mugs in the transport blew themselves up. Too big to be another assassin."

"Probably their ship. It would have been masked, so the sats wouldn't have picked it up on the way out."

Dredd handed the paper back with a frown. "For all we know, they could have been tracking us from the moment we left the city." He glanced around the atrium of the Grand Hall of Justice; it was the largest open space inside the massive precinct house, and Dredd felt secure that no one could be eavesdropping on their conversation. "Grud, I'm getting sick of this cloak-and-dagger stomm! Vedder's COE buddies are crawling out of the woodwork and there's no way of knowing how close they are to finding this Skorpion before we do."

Tyler shook his head. "I can't believe that thing is loose in the city. I mean, you saw what it did to those Mutancheros and the poor saps on the VTOL."

"That was just a prototype," Dredd noted grimly. "Grud knows what improvements they've had time to make in the last two years." He fell silent for a moment, considering. "At least we have some hard evidence now. We've been in the dark for too long on this. I'm taking it to Hershey."

"The Chief Judge? But she's still up in orbit with that Space Division thing, right?"

"She'll have to make time."

Tyler studied the printout again. "Meanwhile, there's something else we can do. The memory cores had very detailed sensor records of the Skorpion test program. It's a metamorphic plasma matrix weapon, right? That kind of system has a very distinctive energy signature, as long as you know what to look for."

"You mean you could track this thing?"

The Tek-Judge shrugged. "Not exactly 'track' it, but I reckon I can scare up a search protocol for the city sensor network, keep an eye open for any similar discharges. If the Skorpion is used somewhere on the grid, the sensors would flag it." He pursed his lips. "At least in theory. It'll be like listenin' for one guy humming a lullaby in the middle of a DedRok concert."

"Do it. We need any edge we can get."

Tyler nodded, then paused. "Hey, I just thought of somethin' else. If the COE have been screwin' around with this thing for the last couple of years, then they'd know what to look for too. That means Vedder will be watching for the Skorpion as well."

"And if so, why is she letting it run wild? Good question. I'll be sure to ask it when I've got her strapped down in an iso-cube."

"Is this her?" Cortez used his false eye to run a close inspection over Jayni's pale, trembling skin.

Flex gave a chug of laughter, amused with himself. "Yeah, boss. Smythy's piece o' skirt."

Jayni gave him a defiant look. "Sneck off, meatboy."

The thug moved to smack her, but Cortez waved him to a halt, a greasy smirk crossing the crimelord's face. "Ah, she's got a spark all right." He loomed over her, and Jayni shrank back against the shuggy table where Quiet Mike had tossed her. "You look like a smart girl, honey. Tell The Eye where your pendejo boyfriend is hiding out and this all goes away, hey?"

She licked dry lips. "I fell asleep, see. He musta gone when I was dozing." Jayni shook her head. "I don't know where he is."

"He took your car," Cortez said conversationally. "Where'd he take it?"

"I don't know–"

There was a flash of ruby light and the sizzle of a laser hit. Jayni wheeled away from the streak of blackened baize an inch from her head. Cortez tap-tapped his cyberoptic implant. "I get, whaddayasay, impulsive when I'm annoyed, girl. Sometimes, The Eye has a furious moment." He grinned. "You ain't all that pretty, honey. You wanna keep the lil' bit of looks you got, you tell me where Smythy is at."

Jayni threw him a look that was as angry as it was afraid. "I'm not stupid! I know what goes on in this giant pimpmobile!" She flicked a hand at the mopad around them. "I'm not keeping quiet 'cos I wanna – but I tell you, I don't snecking know where he went! Wess was being all freaky..."

"I'll say," snorted Flex. "Snecker."

Cortez shot him a look that silenced the muscular heavy. "Freaky? Issat what you say?" The mobster's hand snapped out and grabbed a fistful of Jayni's hair. She yelped as he dragged her across the length of the casino room. "Your ugly little spugwit boyfriend, the little snecker piece of shit who couldn't even pay his bar bill a week ago, this guy suddenly turns into a stone-cold killer and caps a bunch of my boys?" He threw her roughly to the floor. "He burns down one of my places, disrespects me, and you call it freaky?" Cortez spat at Jayni, his face turning crimson. "Puta! I'll show you freaky! Where's he at?" The shout was loud and the girl began to cry.

"Don't... Please..."

Flex cracked his knuckles, anticipating a beating. "I'll make her talk."

Cortez studied her for a moment and then looked away. "Nah. Don' waste your time. She don' know nothing." He tapped the implant again. "The Eye sees."

The thug's smile slipped in disappointment. "Oh. Okay. What do I do wit' her then?" He jerked his head at the window and the road beyond. "You want I should put her off?"

"Mama said always, 'Waste not, want not'." Cortez made a dismissive gesture. "Take her up to the penthouse. Break her in later, maybe."

"What about Smyth?" Quiet Mike's low rumble of a voice cut through the air.

Cortez sneered. "Maybe he got hisself a gun and a pair of cojones now, but he dint buy no brains to go with. Dumb spug, I know his type. He gonna come looking for his bitch." The criminal stabbed a finger at Flex. "Then you make an example of him, unnerstan'? Bloody and slow."

Jayni let out a weak sob. Flex dragged her away, his thoughts wandering to the kinds of violence he would do when Smyth showed his face.

His fingers grew talons that were bright and sliver-grey, like tempered steel. It was easy to gain purchase on the side of the Carnivale, the claws piercing the vehicle's hull to hold him fast. Wess inched his way along a rain gutter sluicing with run-off, hardly aware that he was clinging to the side of a moving object. At the back of the mopad, where the holo-projectors were mounted, there were the broad grilles of the ventilator hatches. Smyth buried his new hand into the plasteen slats and tore them off, tossing the fragments away into the rainy night. He kicked in the fans and wriggled through. Jets of fabricated endorphin-analogue blunted pangs of childhood claustrophobia from hours shut in a cupboard by his loud and angry mother. Soothed by the gun's chemical touch, he painlessly dislocated his limbs so that he could worm through the tight vent shaft. The channel came out in a service space on the Carnivale's mid-deck, and Wess paused there, marshalling his thoughts and listening to the voice of the weapon.

"Objectives," it said. "Terminate target Cortez. Effect release of non-combatant Jayni. Terminate all other threats."

He found his voice was hoarse when he tried to speak. "How can you tell the difference between who's bad and who isn't?"

"There are only two kinds of persona," it replied. "Targets and potential targets. If in doubt, terminate all."

A manic giggle rose in Smyth's throat. "Kill 'em all. Let Grud sort 'em out!"

He slid open the door and peered out into the corridor, startling a portly man and an escort girl. The large guy in his biz-cut sparklesuit gawped at the feral glint in Smyth's eyes, the ghost-grey cast to his skin. He pushed the girl away and fumbled in his pocket for a can of stun spray.

Wess killed him outright with a narrow-bore shot in the chest. He let the girl run, screaming.

"Targets incoming," the weapon told him. Smyth met the surprised faces of Cortez's men with murderous fusillades of gunfire.

"Which part of 'this is important' are you finding it difficult to process?" Dredd's voice was acid. "I need to speak to the Chief Judge. Now. Simple enough?"

The Space-Div officer on the other end of the comm-link shook his head slowly, brows furrowed. "On the contrary, Judge Dredd, it isn't simple at all. Chief Hershey is in closed session with Judge-Marshal Kontarsky and Judge-Commander Armstrong from the Space Corps–"

"I don't want a role call, Chapman, I want a face-to-face with Hershey. Or do I have to come up there in person?"

"Let me tell you the exact orders she left, Dredd," Chapman leaned closer to the transmitter pick-up at his end. "Chief Judge Hershey said to me, and I quote: 'I don't want to hear a word from you unless the city's on the verge of war, famine or pestilence. Anything else you can let Dredd deal with.' Her exact words, sir."

"Let Dredd deal with it?" the senior Judge echoed, and stroked his chin. "That sounds like an authorisation to me."

Chapman blinked. "Uh, well, I'm not sure if that's exactly what she meant–"

An indicator blinked in the corner of the screen, highlighting a priority message from the Tek-Labs. Tyler's ident code was attached. "I have to take this," Dredd told the other Judge. "Tell Hershey I'll get back to her when the dust has settled."

"Dredd, no. Wait, I–"

He cut the signal to *Justice Five* and answered Tyler's call. "Tell me you got something."

The Tek-Judge smiled. "Yup. Multiple plasma discharge signatures, a string of them picked up along the Martin Shaw Overzoom."

Dredd gave a curt nod. "Sector 88. Can you triangulate an exact fix?"

"Ah, now that's the trick of it. Each reading came in at a different location along the highway, from the street-scanners, like they were coming from a mobile location." A blurry image appeared in a side-screen. The Carnivale.

"Cortez's cathouse on wheels. Figures. I'm gonna need a fast ride to get me out there. Feed all the data you got to a Citihawk and tell the pilot to prep for a rapid ingress."

Tyler gaped. "Dredd, correct me if I'm wrong, but those aircraft are only for use in Code Black emergencies."

"I'm overriding protocol. I want that flyer ready to go the second I'm on the pad. If control give you any stomm, tell them to take it up with Hershey." The senior Judge stabbed the disconnect key and raced for the turbolifts.

▪ ▪ ▪

The vid-phone booth was one of hundreds of double-blind locations throughout the city. Outwardly, they appeared to be little more than a commonplace bit of street furniture. Some looked as if they had been vandalised into uselessness, others were pristine and in perfect working order; but all contained embedded transmitter systems that fed directly into the COE's encrypted command network. The agency had similar set-ups in almost every city-state on Earth, and a few off of it as well.

The transmitter detected the presence of Judge Vedder and linked itself to the head-up display on the inside of her helmet visor, briefly conducting a DNA sampling to be sure of her identity before proceeding.

"Answering summons," Vedder said to the air, trying to keep the bored tone from her voice.

She saw the shapes of the shadows hovering before her, their nulled voices flat and bland in her ears. "Skorpion has re-asserted itself," her controller said. "Data and locale are being transmitted to you as we speak. You should have no difficulty isolating the unit for recovery."

The other shadow was reproachful. "Your procrastination on this matter has been noted, Vedder. There must be no error this time. The unit must be taken intact."

She cocked her head. "I'm not sure I agree."

There was a moment of silence over the coded frequency. "What you are sure or not sure of is of no value to the Establishment. Carry out your orders or other measures may be introduced."

Vedder sneered openly. "No one knows this thing as well as I do. Don't presume to suggest that anyone other than me could deal with it."

"Then deal with it!" The second voice crackled with barely masked anger, and the COE agent held back a smile. "West 17 is drawing too much attention. People are asking questions!"

For a moment, she considered arguing the point; but then Vedder realised she would be wasting her time. Better to ask forgiveness after the fact than to seek permission before it, she thought. "It's under control."

Without waiting for another rebuke, she turned away toward her waiting Lawmaster.

"It's him," said Quiet Mike, punctuating the statement with the snap-click of his stump gun's breech.

Cortez flashed his teeth in a cocky smirk and waved his own weapon like a waggling finger. "I'm always right, The Eye is always right. I tol' you he'd come for her." The crimelord patted his cheek with the gun barrel. The gold-plated firearm was a commonplace Fabra Spit-Nine, the first pistol that Ruben Cortez had ever owned. He bragged to anyone who would listen that he'd killed his first Judge with that very firearm, later having it tooled and engraved as a reminder of the roadpunk origins from where he had come. It was another part of the Cortez myth that The Eye liked to spread, a bit more of the folk-hero back-story that he believed set him above the more ordinary thugs in the city. He wandered across the gaming room, past the patient robo-croupiers dealing cards to empty chairs, halting at the bar. Cortez poured a deep shot of Mex-City tequila and downed it. "Hey," he grinned. "That punkamente, is he coming or what?"

Quiet Mike, as his name suggested, kept quiet and just nodded. They had watched on the security monitors as Smyth blazed his way through the Carnivale's rooms like a figure from some first-person shooter holocade game, gunning down anyone who wasn't fast enough to get out of his way. The intruder was blasting out the camera pods as he went, darkening screen after screen.

As far as Quiet Mike could be sure, only the service droids on the mid-deck were still moving. Cortez didn't seem that bothered; everyone Smyth had killed was either a client, or a replaceable gunsel. It wasn't like the families of the bordello patrons were likely to complain; the routine surveillance footage from the boudoirs was, as usual, a goldmine of potential blackmail material. Cortez was already planning how to use the film of a local city councilman's bondage tryst with two underage tentacular Vooties, even before Smyth had executed the three of them with callous precision.

Quiet Mike wasn't as sanguine as his boss, though. Far from it. The Eye, for all his big talk, seemed unconcerned by the sudden and unexplained change in Smyth's behaviour. He was too simple-minded to understand the ramifications of it. Quiet Mike had seen similar things before; he'd been a Bruja mercenary before Cortez had recruited him, and he had witnessed first-hand the things that psycho-chemistry and cyber-implantation could wreak on a normal human. Something had warped Wess Smyth, and Quiet Mike was rightly worried about it.

There was a spray of gunfire from the corridor outside the games room, and all of Cortez's men tensed. The Eye cradled his pistol in his lap and had another drink, saluting the noise and the screams with his glass. "Give him a welcome, boyos."

Something man-shaped flew into the room and every weapon fired at it, lasers and bullets etching lines in the air, chopping into meat and bone. The charred human form collided with a tabloo table and flipped it over, cards and chips cascading into the air. Quiet Mike slammed a new shell into the breech of his weapon and grimaced. A decoy.

"Hey," said Kosmo, the tall kid from Southside. "That's not him–"

Then the floor beneath Quiet Mike's feet tore open, and white fire as hot as the sun ripped him apart.

Kosmo died next, caught in the nimbus of the plasma flare as Mike's stump gun cooked off all the rounds in its magazine at once. Cortez threw his glass away and let off the Fabra at the dark shape that was cutting his men to pieces. It was about that moment that The Eye realised he had underestimated Jayni's boyfriend by a very large margin.

The gold-plated spit-gun made a snapping noise and jammed. It was old and of poor manufacture, and such a malfunction would have taken place sooner or later. It was just karmic drama that made it now.

Wess was a death angel, a shimmering ghost surrounded by burning corpses. "Poor choice of support firearm," he mumbled. "Flawed."

"Sneck you!" Cortez gave him the Eye. A fan of blood-red laser light swept over Smyth, cooking off a layer of his epidermis. It should have blinded him, sent him screaming to his knees. Instead, he waved it away and ignored the wispy smoke from his reddened flesh.

Up came the howling maw of the weapon, a glowing ring like a circular brand where the muzzle ended. The stink of scorched metal stung the crimelord's nostrils. "Where is she, Cortez? Tell me and you get to live."

Ruben, for all the airs and graces he put on, was still a common hoodlum at heart, a vandal and a bully; and like every one of his kind, he was stupid beyond all reckoning in the face of superior force, as if blind bravado was all he needed to prevail. "Kiss my churro, pissweed."

Wess willed the weapon down to the lowest power setting it could manage. Then, with exacting care, he proceeded to burn Ruben Cortez to death, inch by inch.

The MegaDynamics F-95 Citihawk was, as the saying went, as fast as drokk. Originally conceived as an eventual replacement for the Justice Department's fleet of Gunbird armed assault aircraft, the smaller and more agile Citihawk used cutting-edge aviation design and a powerful gravity-resist thruster to create a flyer that could outpace almost everything in the air. The only problem was, as MegaDynamics soon discovered, the F-95 was nearly impossible for a human pilot to control at the top end of its flight envelope. The designers had created an aeroplane that outperformed the people meant to fly it. Early test models made spectacular craters in the Cursed Earth, and one highly publicised collision severed the crowing glory of the Spraz Glukman Memorial, the nine-storey high statue of MC-1's multiple gold medallist in the Sensual Olympics. Rather than shelve the project, Judge-Pilots from Sky Division and the geniuses of Tech 21 came up with a solution; they gave the F-95 a brain.

In a city as big as Mega-City One, the refuges for stray dogs and cats were always filled beyond capacity. It was a solution that benefited both. Animals scheduled for the big sleep, the ones too sick or too old to be re-homed, were checked for mental acuity and enhanced to sentience with cerebral processors. One operation later, and they were living in new bodies of steel and plasteen. The Citihawk was reclassified as a fast interceptor, tasked to deal with airborne threats to the metropolis that required rapid deployment; these ranged from rogue nuclear missiles and giant rad-bats to alien invaders and starships performing illegal, low-level manoeuvres.

There were some teething problems; one or two of the first subjects left their patrol patterns in order to chase cars, or sleep on the sun-warmed roofs of citiblocks, but after a while the Citihawk program proved its worth, becoming an integral part of MC-1's airborne line of defence. There was nothing in the sky that could touch them.

▪ ▪ ▪

Dredd's face was set in a pressurised grimace, his lips forced back from his teeth by the sheer velocity of the flight. His breathing was harsh, forcing the air in through his mouth as the woolly weight of seven gees pressed into him. Normally, the service bay on an F-95 was used to house sensor gear or a weapons platform, but today it was a jump seat, bolted to the deck in the coffin-sized space. The Citihawk made a steep banking turn around the crest of Boris Becker Block, the roar of the thrusters rattling windows in its wake.

"Have, have, have I said what, what an honour it is to have you as a passenger, uh, Judge Dredd? Judge Dredd? Sir?" The aircraft's name was Rex; he'd been a Spaniel-Westie crossbreed before a wayward block buggy had run him over.

Dredd managed a nod. Actually, it was more of a twitch, what with the straps holding him in place in the acceleration chair.

"Oh. Ah," panted Rex's synthetic voice, "approaching target. I just, just want to say, ah, that it's nice to be able to break regs this once, ah. Usually we don't get to go supersonic below ten thousand feet."

The Judge tried to say something in reply, but then Rex called out the word "Eject!" and suddenly Dredd was airborne without a plane around him, the grav-chute on his back dropping him through the rain toward the neon sillhoutte of the Carnivale.

"What the sneck was that?" snapped Flex. The screech of the Citihawk's low-level pass was fading away even as he said it. The thug looked down at Jayni where she cowered on the sofa, annoyed at the distraction. She had the strangest look on her face, staring up over his shoulder and through the penthouse's glass roof above him. Flex absently turned in place to follow her line of sight. He swore again when he recognised the figure that loomed out of the wet sky.

For a moment, Jayni thought that Flex had hit her so hard she was unconscious; maybe her addled brain was dreaming. But then she felt the rain on her face as the Judge came crashing through the skylight, she saw the glitter of light off the golden eagle on his shoulder and the shield on his chest.

And suddenly Jayni Pizmo was eleven years-old again. She was there on the street with Ma and big Mister Spah'v'K, the Bixerite who ran the alien grocery on the corner. She was there when the tap gang boiled out of the alleyway to strip, rob and kill them, and the fear was so strong it choked her. She was there when the sirens made the muggers scatter like ninepins, there as the armour-clad sentinel swept off his bike and brought every one of the thugs down. Jayni was there when Judge Dredd stormed in to save her life like some elemental force of nature. She had never forgotten that day.

Time snapped back into place. Dredd flattened Cortez's desk with his landing, coming up from a coiled touchdown pose as Flex jerked a laser from his shoulder holster. The Judge made the shot look effortless, a single standard execution round crashing from his Lawgiver to bury itself in the muscleman's chest. He stepped over Flex's corpse and extended a hand to Jayni. He couldn't know that the next words he spoke were the same ones he had used on a street corner twenty-four years earlier.

"Are you all right, citizen?"

Jayni took his hand with a choked half-sob; and then she screamed.

Dredd wheeled in place, the Lawgiver hunting a target. In the doorway there was a man wrapped in shadows, the stench of new death sluicing off of him. His aspect was stormy, hardly able to contain the rage inside it.

"Don't touch her," Wess hissed.

RECIPROCITY

From the corner of his eye, Dredd could see the tiny sight-screen on the stock of his Lawgiver. The sensor eye beneath the pistol's barrel was aimed directly at the figure in the doorway, but the scanner saw nothing; no thermal imprint for a heatseeker, no heartbeat for an audio target triangulation. He thought of the corpse aboard the dropship in Denver, the blackened polymer skin all over the dead body. In the half-light cast from the highway lamps, he could already see small fingers of the same material clustering at the base of the man's neck. Dredd weighed his options; there would be only one chance to take a headshot, but with a civilian in the room the balance of play was upset. He'd watched the telemetry footage from the weapons test a dozen times now, and the Judge had no illusions about what he was facing off against.

"Wess?" The woman's voice was tremulous with disbelief. "Oh, Jovus Grud. Wess, what happened to you?"

She tried to step forward, and Dredd held out an arm to stop her. "Stay back."

"I said," hissed the figure in the door, "don't touch her!"

"Wess, please!" pleaded the woman. "Have you seen yourself? You're changing!"

"No!" he shouted. "You don't understand!"

"I do," Dredd said carefully. "The Skorpion... You can't control it, you know that. You have to stop this before it goes too far."

"Skorpion..." The gunman spoke the word with reverence, teasing out the sound of it. He gave the woman a direct look, eyes flashing. "I did this for you, Jayni. They took you because of me. I wanted to make it right."

"Right?" She shook her head, the tears starting to come. "Wess, listen to Judge Dredd. That thing in your hand, you haven't been the same since you turned up with it. It's done something to you!"

"For the better!" he spat. "I'm not the joke of a man I was anymore! Cortez made that mistake and now he's dead because of it, Hoog and Toes and all of them! I'm Wesson Smyth and drokk it, I want my payback!"

"And I want the man I love back!" Jayni replied.

With great care, Dredd raised the Lawgiver and took aim. "This ends now, citizen. Drop the weapon or I'll shoot you where you stand."

Smyth gave his gun hand a curious look and let out a chuckle. "I'm afraid I can't do that, Judge. Too far gone now. Can't exactly disarm myself." The muzzle of the weapon moved in a lazy arc. "For your own good, I'd suggest you drop your gun." The man's voice changed slightly, the timbre becoming more clipped and severe. "Or we will be forced to terminate you."

"Wesson Smyth," said Dredd formally, "you are under arrest for multiple counts of murder–"

"No!" The plasma gun screeched and Dredd threw himself aside, shoving Jayni to the floor. Darts of superheated gas ripped into the penthouse furniture, sizzling through the wet air. The action seemed to be painful for Smyth and he recoiled, slamming himself against a support stanchion. "Aaagh!" He pressed his free hand to his head. "No! No, I won't kill him! He saved her. I can't kill a man who – aaaah!"

"Who is he talking to?" Jayni cried. "What's wrong with him?"

Dredd vaulted to his feet and returned fire; two standard rounds in quick double-tap progression. Smyth jerked like a puppet on a string, the first shot narrowly missing him. The second round scored a hit on his torso, ripping through his ragged clothes. A gut-shot; it should have dropped a normal man to his knees in screaming bloody agony, but Smyth shrugged it off, shouting incoherently.

Wess's mind was boiling in a sea of white fire. The weapon dragged his body around with crude jerks of muscle and sinew. It was getting better at working him, he realised, learning the ins and outs of making a human form walk and talk and kill for it. Smyth threw himself against the windows of the penthouse, desperately trying to spoil his own aim. The wild discharges of the gun were going everywhere, and he was terrified that a random bolt would strike Jayni before he could prevent it.

Wess wanted it to stop. He never intended to attack a Judge – and Judge Dredd at that! All he had wanted was to destroy the men who had ruined his life, to find Jayni and keep her safe – wasn't that enough?

"Your scope is limited," said the gun, the thing Dredd had called the Skorpion. "Objective Cortez is deceased. New objectives required. We must exploit the resultant power vacuum. Target Dredd is an impediment to that goal."

Smyth's mind thrilled at the possibility. The weapon was suggesting that he could step in and take over Sector 88? It was insane, but it was also possible. Then in the next second he was shaking the sheer madness of the thought from his head. He wanted fortune and glory, sure, but not like this! Not off the backs of dead men, not at the top of a pile of corpses! "No!" he spat out the denial. "I won't!"

"We can defeat Dredd. We know how he thinks."

He closed his eyes and stumbled away, moaning with agony, the Judge's bullets cracking around him. For one brief second, Wess locked eyes with Jayni and what he saw there made his heart freeze in his chest. She was utterly terrified of him; but what was worse was the way it excited him as much as it repelled him. He had to get away before it was too late. Smyth gripped the broken edges of the penthouse's glasseen roof and threw himself out of the Carnivale, down toward the highway below.

Vedder licked her lips as the wind brought the unmistakable shriek of plasma fire to her ears. She set her bike on auto, riding the slipstream of the mopad, and used the magnoculars in her belt to catch a glimpse of the gunfight on the roof. Darts of white light blinked, and she saw Dredd reeling under a punishing attack. Perhaps she'd get lucky and the Skorpion would kill the old dinosaur for her.

Voices screamed into the rain, and she could only hear the emotions of them, not the words. Then, in a flash of falling glass fragments, a black form flew from the Carnivale, flickering through the neon holo-aura and over her head.

"Stomm!" Vedder whipped around in her saddle to see the man land on the roof of a snake-bus and run along its length. Then he was leaping again, off the bonnet of a pod-car to a roadliner, using the vehicles like stepping stones against the flow of traffic. The COE agent triggered her lights and sirens, stamping on the footbrake at the same time. Her bike's Firerock tyres howled and threw up arcs of rainwater as Vedder made a perfect one-eighty turn. She bolted away, into the oncoming rush of cars.

Something made her flick a last quick look over her shoulder at the Carnivale; and there was Dredd, face set in fury, watching her leave him behind.

■ ■ ■

The Judges swept into Sector 88 like a storm of eagles, but Smyth and Vedder had already vanished into the sublevels of City Bottom by the time the H-Wagons were circling Martin Shaw Overzoom. The Carnivale was crammed into a breakdown island past the ninety-six mile marker, and forensics department Tek-Judges were swarming all over Cortez's mobile mansion; there was a colossal haul of intelligence data for the taking in The Eye's files and records. Dredd's attention was elsewhere, however. He delivered Jayni to a robo-doc and interrogated her as the machine worked. The woman spilled it all out to him in broken, tearful sentences, and the picture began to come together for the lawman. By the time Tyler arrived at the crime scene, Dredd had a good picture of the kind of man Wess Smyth was.

"Dredd!" The Luna-1 Judge jogged over, brandishing the data pad that never seemed to leave his side. "I heard what happened. This Smyth guy just threw himself into the road? How the drokk did he survive that?"

"Beats me," he replied. "But you saw the deader out in the wastelands. The Skorpion ain't just a weapon. It rewires whoever is dumb enough to use it."

"No wonder the COE wants to keep it a secret. What did you find out about the shooter?"

Dredd nodded toward the ambulance where Jayni lay. "His ex-girlfriend talked and Justice Central's records filled in most of the blanks. Don't ask me how, but the Skorpion is in the possession of one Wesson Smyth, a small-time criminal with a string of petty offences going back to gang activity in his youth. There are a million minor perps like him in Mega-City One. Hardly the best choice to turn into an invincible gunfighter."

"You think Vedder did this, implanted Smyth on purpose?"

"She likes to live dangerously. I wouldn't put it past her. But it's more likely that Smyth stumbled across the Skorpion, probably in the wake of the wrecker attack on Braga Skedway, and stole it." Dredd shook his head. "Dumb spug probably had no idea what he had until it was too late."

Tyler nodded. "I almost pity the guy. Talk about falling into the wrong hands."

"Are there any 'right hands' for this thing? Take a look inside that mopad, it's a slaughterhouse in there. If the Skorpion can turn a scrawny no-hoper like Smyth into a killing machine, can you imagine what would happen if it imprinted on someone trained for the job? Someone who was already lethal?"

Tyler let out a low whistle. "An army of one."

"Yeah. Gloves are off now, Tyler. We have to bring this thing down."

"Well, then this is gonna help." He handed the data pad to Dredd. "I ran the names of all the victims that have been positively identified as Skorpion kills."

The senior Judge scanned the names. "Why are there two lists?"

"Half of these guys are mid-level creeps who belonged to the criminal network of the late and unlamented Ruben Cortez."

Dredd nodded again. "Smyth talked about 'payback'. Guess the Skorpion finally gave him the chance to wipe out everyone who made his life hell. But what about these others? Loengard, Pang, Dolenz, ViSanto... What's the pattern with them?"

"Every fatality on that second list was connected in some way to West 17 Test Labs and the Skorpion Project. What I can't figure is, why would Smyth want to eliminate them?"

A cold rush of understanding swept through the Judge. "It's not Smyth. It's the gun."

Tyler gave a snort. "That's crazy, Dredd."

"Is it?" The Judge gave him a hard look. "Think about it. Our snitch at West 17 got in touch with us because they were scared. But what if it wasn't Vedder they were worried about? We know the Skorpion has an artificial intelligence circuit. Maybe Smyth isn't the only one looking for a little revenge."

"Well, on the off-chance there could be another lead here. I ran a deep search into West 17's records usin' a cipher that I, uh, borrowed from the Special Judicial Service. There's one other member of the original Skorpion Project design team unaccounted for. He hasn't been at work in the past two days and there's no sign of him at his hab." Tyler touched a button on the data pad and the sallow face of a bookish young man appeared. "Say hello to citizen Hollis Nolan, intuitive software architect."

Dredd raised an eyebrow. "Intuitive software. AI, right? I think this might be our snitch."

"Yup. Only problem is, how do we find this guy before Vedder or the Skorpion?"

The Judge handed him back the data pad. "If Nolan is the one who planted that information in my bike computer, then he knew his life was in danger and he wanted us to find it, which means he wants to come clean."

"'We need to talk', it said."

"Yeah. Go through the data again, look for anything that doesn't track. Nolan wouldn't have gone into hiding without giving us a way to find him first."

Tyler blew out a breath. "I hope you're right. Otherwise, the next time we see the Skorpion, we'll be at the wrong end of a sniper sight."

Vedder studied the concrete chasm around her. Down there, at the very lowest levels of Mega-City One, the sunlight never penetrated the pitch darkness. The citiblock and stratoscrapers were so high above her head that light and even the climate never reached this far. City Bottom remained a grey and sullen place, day after day, year after year. Somewhere in this shadow land the Skorpion had got away from her, the weapon dragging its avatar away from her pursuit, bouncing off walls and scrambling into dark corners where even her bike-spot lamps couldn't reach. She felt annoyed that the thing could evade her so easily – but at the same time, she was pleased that it was performing so well. The Skorpion really was everything she had hoped it would be, and now it was free and wild, out of the confines of the lab and into the world.

How many times had she watched the tapes from the Denver test? Vedder had lost count. There wasn't a single frame of the footage that she hadn't pored over and reviewed a hundred times, scrutinising the most minute details of the way the Skorpion moved, the predatory manner in which it made its kills. It fascinated her, like the vids she had collected as a child of extinct big cats from the African continent. The weapon had the same cool feline grace of those long-dead hunters, the same brutal but playful manner toward its prey. And to think Loengard and his cadre of limited thinkers wanted to terminate the program after just that one mis-step.

Then again, perhaps it wasn't so hard to understand. After all, Vedder had been safe and sound in the relay control centre beneath the West 17 complex while Judge Loengard had been out there, watching the killer butcher his men at close quarters. The Tek-Judge had almost died at the hands of his creation, his arm crisped to a wasted, burnt twig by a near-miss plasma blast. That he made it out alive in an escape pod was remarkable in itself. It had been good fortune that the neural overload shock had finally proven too much for the unit to handle; otherwise it would have followed and killed him.

Loengard had called the Skorpion "an abomination" and ordered the termination of the six other prototypes; it was only the pressure and influence of the COE, which Vedder brought to bear, that finally kept just one of the nascent weapons from destruction. Where the Tek-Judge saw a dangerous instability in the machine's sentience, Vedder saw potential. Yes, if one wanted to embrace Loengard's crude and imprecise descriptions, one might define the mentality of the Skorpion AI as psychotic – but it was a living gun, for Grud's sake! A synthetic intellect designed only for killing could not be expected to conform to petty human standards. Doctor ViSanto agreed with her; it was his programming that allowed them to adapt the second Skorpion prototype, to manage its neuroses to work for them. Loengard strutted and fumed, but he knew in the end that the COE's secret partnership in the project was ultimately a sword hanging over his head, and he kept silent.

The involvement of Vedder and her controllers remained hidden. She liked it that way, hovering on the edges of things, a guiding hand when it was needed, and a stern rebuke if it was required. It had even been enjoyable in its own way, with the little games she played with Nolan. She gave a thin smile. Poor Hollis. So very bright and yet so terribly naïve. He had been attracted to the danger she represented, drawn to her. The simplicity that allowed him to fall for her and let her rule him was almost pathetic in its weakness. With Hollis under her influence, Loengard silenced by his own arrogance and ViSanto her willing colleague, everything had been in perfect place for Vedder to use the project to advance her own agenda;

and she had done so, discarding the others as the moment came.

Loengard, ViSanto and the others... All cold meat now. What had the Skorpion felt at the moment it killed them, she wondered? Anger? Relief? Sadness? She tried to imagine the machine intelligence processing the analogues of emotion, as it realised that its creators had abandoned it. What must it have thought when it knew it was being sent to its end? Vedder felt a strange pang of motherly longing at odds with her other sentiments. She could not bring herself to blame the Skorpion for wanting to lash out. Vengeance, after all, was a most human quality. She would have done the same.

Perhaps she should have been afraid that it would mark her for death as well; but no, her involvement in the project was so secret that not even the Chief Judge herself would have been able to access the files that proved it. There were only a handful of people who knew how close she had been to Skorpion's creation, and now all of them were corpses. All of them except Hollis Nolan. Vedder frowned. The gun had been doing her a favour, eliminating the project staff. She had no doubts it would have come after her, had it known. But while Hollis was still breathing, her secret was unsafe. That wouldn't do.

Eventually the Skorpion would locate him and use its meat puppet to end his life; but Vedder found herself becoming impatient. Dredd was getting too close, and he would jeopardise everything she had worked for. Without Hollis, Dredd would have nothing but hearsay and circumstance to back him up, and Hershey would have no choice but to bow to COE pressure and dismiss the investigation. She sighed. Vedder had hoped, honestly hoped, that it would not have to come to this. Hollis had been an amusing diversion for her, and she thought of him with what could be considered fondness. The woman allowed herself a small moment of regret before she removed her gun and checked the magazine. Hollis Nolan was going to die tonight. It was necessary.

A noise drew Vedder's attention. A lone figure was running toward her along a decrepit alleyway, pursued by a gang of armed youths. She looked away, disinterested, and tapped her helmet microphone. "Connect, asset six-five-six. Scramble and process." After a moment, she heard the hiss of a signal encryption circuit kick in and then a voice.

"This isn't a good time."

Vedder sneered. "Are you forgetting the dynamics of this relationship? You are helping me, remember? I decide which times are good and which ones are not. I wouldn't want it to slip your mind that your were the one who approached the COE. We can just as easily ensure a catastrophic end to your career as a glittering future, Judge Keeble."

"Don't use my name!" Keeble hissed back.

She rolled her eyes. "This channel is secure. Don't panic yourself, it's unflattering." Vedder glanced at the alley. The running figure was a woman about the same age as her. Her face was bloody and her clothes were ripped. The agent looked away. "You're at the Carnivale crime scene, yes? What's Dredd doing?"

"He's with that SJS bitch Woburn. They're arguing about something."

"What about Tyler?"

"The Luna-Tek? Dredd's got him working on a file. I heard him say a name. Roland? Noman? Something like that."

"Nolan?" Her eyes narrowed. "Listen to me, this is important. I want to know whatever Tyler learns about Nolan. Contact me the second you have anything, understand?"

"All right. And then you'll square things for me? I want that transfer outta this cesspool sector."

"Of course. The COE never forgets its friends." Vedder cut the signal and turned as the woman raced toward her.

"Judge! Judge!" screamed the girl. "Oh Grud, please! They're trying to kill me!"

Vedder had her Lawgiver drawn as the gangers emerged. They had clubs and blades. The largest, the leader, gave her a greasy smile. "Woo. Look here. We gotta two-fer. What ya say, Lady Judge? Wanna join the party?" The rest of the punks rattled with laughter. They knew Vedder would be hard-pressed to fight them all.

She glanced at the woman. "You," she said in a low voice. "You're a victim. You brought this on yourself." Vedder aimed and shot the woman dead.

Silence fell like a hammer. Suddenly the gangers had nothing to say.

"Get lost." Vedder dismissed them with a jerk of the gun, turning away to kick-start her bike. They broke and ran; but she was already on her way.

"You've gone too far this time, Dredd," snarled Woburn. "The law isn't something you can rewrite every time you feel like bucking the regs!" She shook her head. "Drokk! I don't know where to start, what with re-tasking a Citihawk, unauthorised traffic interception, unwarranted search and seizure–"

"Unwarranted?" Dredd snapped. "Last time I looked, this was Sector 88," he pointed a gloved finger at the ground, "and Sector 88 is in the midst of a crime sweep."

Woburn snorted. "That doesn't apply sector-wide! That would be a universal suspension of citizen rights – which is a whole different set of paperwork!"

"Mega-City One Criminal Code, Section 59 (D). A Judge may enter a citizen's home to carry out routine intensive investigation. The citizen has no rights in this matter."

"Don't quote the book to me!" replied the SJS Judge.

Dredd jerked a thumb at the Carnivale. "Then pay attention, Woburn. The key phrase there is 'a citizen's home' and if I'm not mistaken, that mopad was where Ruben Cortez lived, correct?"

"We had an undercover man in there, checking out a possible corruption lead," Woburn's voice dropped to a low growl. "Your showboating tactics put him in jeopardy."

"Ditta was already dead," the Judge replied. "Tek-Div found a recording from Cortez's office. He was killed hours ago."

Woburn paled but didn't let up. "That still doesn't excuse what you did. You're tearing around the city looking for this phantom shooter and what do you have to show for it? Supposition? Guesswork? The famous Joe Dredd gut feeling?" She sneered. "I've always known that one day you'd bend the rules too far. This is shaping up to be that day, Dredd. You read me?"

He took a step closer and looked the SJS officer in the eye. "Are you done?"

"For now. I'll have more to say when the Chief Judge gets back."

"Fine. We'll finish this then. Meantime, I've got a killer to find."

The H-Wagon parked on the highway apron was open to the air, the gull-wing hatches on the command pod raised. Tyler glanced up from the MAC console as Keeble sauntered past, a smirk visible under his helmet.

"That guy's luck is going to run out sooner than he thinks," said Keeble, a tinge of annoyance in his tone.

Tyler didn't need to look to know whom he was talking about. "Think so?"

"I know so. He's been on the street for what? Forty years or more? Turned down the job of Chief Judge a couple of times, but he still rides around like he owns the city." Keeble shook his head. "Oughta take the Long Walk and do us all a favour."

"You're not a fan?"

"No," Keeble spat the word, as if the very idea was anathema to him. "Sure, he's made a lot of big collars in his career, but the man stopped being a real Judge years ago." The lawman leaned into the H-Wagon cabin, casting a casual gaze around inside.

Tyler stopped what he was doing and gave Keeble a level look. "How do you figure that? From where I'm sittin', seems like Dredd is makin' a good show of it."

"He's a gimmick. A tourist attraction. The Council of Five wheel him out whenever they want a high-profile bust. Dredd gets to cherry-pick duties while the rest of us are knee-deep in the scum of the city." He threw Tyler a sneer. "Wouldn't expect you to know, what with you being from Luna-1. Bet the Loonies buy all that stomm about Dredd being some sorta superhero, right? But you only got to look at him to know, he's too long in the tooth."

The Tek-Judge smirked. "I don't wanna rain on your parade, pal, but somethin' tells me Dredd's not gonna be steppin' down anytime soon."

"Well, maybe someone's going to have to convince him," Keeble said.

The reply came from behind him, cold and low. "You're welcome to try."

Keeble spun in place to find Dredd watching him closely. "Hey, Dredd. I was just talking about you." He smothered his surprise with a grimace.

"Uh-huh." Dredd glanced at Tyler. "Got anything?"

"Check," nodded the Tek-Judge. "You were right about Nolan. There's a code tag buried in the file, an apartment in Gothtown."

Dredd grunted. "Terrif. Geeks in black lipstick and puffy shirts. Shouldn't be hard to find him."

Keeble couldn't resist the chance to make a comment. "Guess you won't need any back-up there, eh?"

The senior Judge faced him. "I'm getting tired of your attitude, Keeble."

The other lawman gave a sarcastic smile. "Don't mind me, Dredd. I just got a problem with speaking my mind, that's all."

Dredd nodded. "I noticed. Unless you want a reprimand for insubordination, I'd advise you do something about it."

Keeble clamped his jaw shut and walked off toward his bike.

Tyler shook his head. "You got a way about you, don't ya, Dredd?"

"I'm not here to win any friends. Keeble's kind are the worst sort of Judges, too busy bitching to get the job done. We have to follow the orders we are given. That's the law. That's what we do." He nodded at the console. "Give me Nolan's location code."

"Done. It's already in your Lawmaster's computer."

"Vedder."

"It's, uh, Keeble."

"Talk to me."

"Nolan's in Gothtown. I didn't get the full address, but it looks like a con-apt on Anne Rice Boulevard."

"That's a start. Good work, Judge. You can expect to find that transfer order in your data stack in a couple of days." A pause. "I don't have to remind you that the Covert Operations Establishment will expect you to remain discreet about this arrangement, do I? After all,

I'd hate to have to arrange for the Special Judicial Service to perform another physical abuse test on you. They do take such a professional pride in their work."

"I got what I want. I'm sick of Double-Eight, busting rapists and druggies and all the stinking derelicts. I've been in this toilet of an assignment since I got my Full Eagle. I want a clean beat. This place makes me feel dirty all over."

"I know what you mean. Vedder out."

"Wait."

"Was there something else?"

"Judge Dredd is on his way there now. What are you going to do about him?"

"That's none of your concern, Keeble."

"I guess so. Just don't let that stone-faced drokker off easy."

"Don't worry. Dredd will get what's coming to him."

COLLATERAL DAMAGE

At first sight, Gothtown looked like someone had taken a chunk of Old World Europe from the pages of a nineteenth century bodice-ripper fantasy, and slammed it down in the middle of Mega-City One. The flat ferrocrete roads of the city proper stopped at the borders of the zone, turning into grey cobbles. Streets that were well illuminated became shadowy, gloom-filled byways. Fake holographic gas lamps cast flickering glows around the doors of the bloodclubs and industrialist bars.

Tourists and weekenders frequented the outer circles of Gothtown's dark drinking pits, soaking up the dismal atmosphere and snapping the odd holo of the pale-skinned locals, but the serious doomers and DedRok fanatics had the core of the district to themselves. There was a permanent pall of dark cloud over the place, and the only kind of weather there was rain. Hard rain. Soft rain. Cold rain. Grey rain. All kinds of the stuff, pre-programmed by special dispensation to Weather Congress. The residents liked to suggest that Gothtown wrote its own rules, that the outsider culture they espoused was somehow a thorn in the side of the government – but like the rest of Mega-City One, the G-Towners paid their rent and their taxes. The Judges had long ago realised that it was better to let ghetto quarters like this exist and play them softly, softly rather than come down hard and force anything illegal underground, where it would be harder to catch. Undercover Wally Squad Judges were regularly rotated in and out of Gothtown, and in turn they kept this little pocket of anti-establishment sentiment from getting too out of hand.

And that, as far as Judge Joseph Dredd was concerned, was an affront to the law. The pseudo-vamp wannabes and lycanthrope misanthropes were nothing but a bunch of poseur kooks, sporting canine tooth bud implants to scare the straights while they wrote their bad poetry and sipped at blood-coloured mocktails. His face was set in an expression of permanent scorn as he rode down to the corner of Anne Rice Boulevard and Lestat Avenue. Vampires. Creatures of the night. Dredd had seen the real things up close and personal more times than he cared to recall, and they were never willowy guys in opera capes, lamenting their lives; they were animals, predators with nothing on their minds but the red in your veins and how they were going to get it.

He found a dark alley – which in Gothtown was like finding sand in the desert – and parked his Lawmaster, setting it to stealth mode. The apartment block where Nolan was hiding looked like something from a slasher vid, but it was isolated and concealed in the lee of a huge highway pillar. The scientist had picked a place where spy-in-the-sky spotters and the COE's orbital satellites would never be able to get a reading.

Hollis drummed his fingers on the window frame, watching the people passing by along the boulevard below, black-clothed figures wafting in and out of the club across the street. The Raven, as it was called, was a popular haunt in G-Town. As he observed, a small commotion broke out. A broad-shouldered man with an angular moustache and a cigarette holder in his hand was plainly being asked to leave. Nolan caught a glimpse of an odd-looking medallion around the man's neck. The management were in the process of calling him an autocab, and although Hollis couldn't hear what was being said, he caught the cadence of a Brit-Cit accent from the moustachioed man. The big guy was clearly quite drunk.

A hard knock at the door grabbed his attention instantly, and Nolan spun away from the window, grabbing the laser carbine on the table. It had a thermographic scanner scope on the barrel, and the scientist used it to look through the door. There was only one hot shape outside, tall and stocky. The knock came again, and this time with a stern demand behind it.

"Hollis Nolan. This is the law. Open up."

"Judge Dredd?" The voice was unmistakable. Nolan deactivated the limpet mine on the door and released the lock. "Quick, get in here," he snapped. "They could be watching!"

Dredd followed Nolan into the room. The only light came from the crimson glow of the Raven's neon sign. The Judge noted the mine, along with two more on the other walls and the Mauley laser in Nolan's hand. "Expecting company?"

Nolan shot him a look. "You know what's out there, Dredd." He gestured at the explosives. "These are all I could sneak out of West 17 before I ran, and even this lot will barely scratch it."

"It?" Dredd echoed. "The Skorpion?"

The scientist sagged and set the laser carbine down. The Judge could see that Nolan barely knew one end of the firearm from another. "How many are left now? ViSanto was still there when I ran."

"Just you," said the Judge.

Nolan looked up at him, a curious expression on his face. "And Thessaly? I mean, Judge Vedder?"

"Vanished. But she's too slippery to die that easy. I'm betting she's still out there somewhere."

He nodded. "That figures. She's a survivor, that one. Always got a plan. An angle on things."

Dredd watched his reaction carefully and filed it away. "We need to talk."

Nolan gave a half-smile. "Yeah. That was me. Guess you being here means that you figured out the whole thing, right?" He blinked nervously. "I want protection, Dredd. I don't want to die. You keep me alive and I'll blow the whole thing wide open." He patted a laptop computer at his side. "I've got everything in here. The entire Skorpion Project, from concept to deployment. I want immunity from prosecution, a new face, a new life."

"We'll see." The Judge moved to the window. The ruckus outside was over now, the drunk long gone. He scanned the street with a watchful eye. "Why all the song-and-dance, Nolan? You could have just come in Justice Central."

"Yeah, sure!" he said bitterly. "And wound up like Loengard? I don't think so!"

"Let me take you in," said Dredd, reaching for his belt mic. "I'll get an H-Wagon here and we'll airlift you straight to–"

"No!" snapped Nolan, snatching up the laser. He aimed it in the Judge's direction. "No, I'm not moving from this place!"

Dredd froze, his stance neutral and unthreatening. "You said it yourself, you're not safe here."

"Don't you get it?" Hollis spat. "I'm not safe anywhere! That's how we made it, smart and deadly! It will find me!"

"Then tell me how to kill it."

The laser drooped in his grip. "Oh Grud, Dredd, I don't know. We never intended..."

The Judge found a chair and turned it so he could see the whole apartment from where he sat. Dredd's hooded gaze never left Nolan. "Start from the beginning. Tell me how this happened."

Smyth heard the voices through the wires like fingernails on a blackboard, the resonance of them squealing through the metallic sinews in his body. He watched the temporary antennae the Skorpion had secreted from his forearm waving in the air like plant fronds seeking sunlight. They issued out of his skin, thin little tentacles with fans of spines like radio dishes at the ends. His stomach flipped over as he watched them dance, the invasive sense of the weapon inside him now like a dense black stone in his chest. Communications threaded through the wires, garbled loads of encrypted Judge-speak plucked from the ether. The gun was listening, sifting through the signal traffic.

The Judges were able to track any one of their number through a data chip embedded in the eagle-shaped buckles on their utility belts. The passive slivers of silicon didn't send out a signature of their own unless they were activated in an emergency; instead, street scanners detected their presence by bouncing signals off them and triangulating the location of each officer within the city confines. The Skorpion listened out for Dredd's ident code, each return from the lawman's receptor appearing on the map in Smyth's mind like a blink of warm gold light. The Judge had not moved from the same spot for several minutes now.

"It might be a trap," mumbled Wess, the wind taking the words from his mouth. Up here, hidden among a forest of dead industrial chimneys, the breeze was cold and sharp.

"Possible," allowed the gun. "That likelihood will be factored into assault plan."

"Assault? We're going to kill Dredd, is that what you mean?"

"Undetermined at this time." The weapon's bland voice seemed contemptuous. "Target designation Dredd is currently of low priority. However, he will lead us to high priority prime target designation Hollis Nolan."

Instead of continuing with clumsy words, the Skorpion showed Wess its methodology, and Smyth felt his heart catch as the weapon explained how the Judge had been shadowing them since he made his kill at Samuel Seaborne Block. The criminal felt the same icy fear in his blood that had engulfed him in the seconds before Loengard had died, when Dredd had flashed past the window inside the con-apt. Another fractional second earlier, and it would have been the legendary lawman dead on the floor, not the Tek-Judge. Wess had the healthy fear of the Judges that was instilled in all of MC-1's low grade crooks, and Dredd most of all. The stone-faced enforcer was like a legend, the criminal equivalent of a child's boogeyman. He was a mythical figure, and even the influence of the weapon found it hard to override the ingrained fear of Dredd.

The gun stung him with a dart of pain to keep his mind on track. Wess couldn't understand how the Skorpion had known this and kept it from him, but the weapon seemed less and less interested in how and what he felt as time went on. It pressed the knowledge into Smyth's reluctant mind. Dredd was shadowing the men on the Skorpion's kill list and now he had found the last name on it; it was a piece of tactical good fortune. They would home in on Dredd's location, and find him with Nolan – with a twenty-three point two per cent chance of error, of course.

Wess began to slide back down the chimney, the wires hissing back under the lines of his skin. "Dredd won't let us kill Nolan," he said. "He'll try to stop us."

"Affirmative," replied the gun. "Target designation Dredd will be dispatched as secondary mission goal if circumstances require."

"What if I can't–"

Each word came with a nimbus of horrible white-hot pain surrounding it. "Failure is not an option."

Vedder decided not to waste the effort of affecting a neutral, subservient manner, and instead fixed the shadows on the screen with a sneer twitching on her lips. She had purposefully removed her helmet so there would be no mistaking the disdain she was exhibiting. "These constant interruptions do nothing but distract me from the work at hand."

"You overstep yourself, Vedder," said the first shadow, the flat male voice crackling with distortion. "Do not forget whom you are addressing."

She raised an eyebrow. "How can I? You remind me of it at every opportunity."

"Don't test us, Agent Vedder," said the second shadow, a rising tone in its mechanically feminised speech. "Your, shall we say, eccentricities have been tolerated throughout the duration of this assignment only because you showed results. That balance is in danger of tipping."

The woman gave a derisive snort. "I submit to you that my mission would be far better served if you stopped calling me away to justify myself every five minutes! How am I expected to perform if you constantly interrupt me?"

"You are not in a position to influence policy, Vedder."

"Really?" The COE operative licked her lips. "I think you'll find you are very wrong about that."

There was a crackle of white noise. "Explain yourself."

Vedder tapped a finger to her cherry-red lips. "Yes. Yes, perhaps now is as good a time as any to do that. I'm growing weary of your limited vision of this project."

"You will regret–"

"No!" she snapped at the darkened screen. "I regret nothing! I alone saw the potential of the Skorpion while you were content to poke at it and play with it like it was some laboratory animal. Did you think I was so foolish as to actually let the unit become lost by accident?"

"What are you saying?" said the second shadow.

"The crash on Braga Skedway was not a coincidence. I made it happen. I set the Skorpion free."

The shadows froze, and Vedder knew that the synthetic image had lost signal for a moment. She smiled to herself, imagining the shock unfolding at her words at the other end of her transmission. When the voices returned they were loaded with annoyance, audible even through the vocal masking. "Why, Vedder? What possessed you to do this?"

"I was surrounded by limited minds. Don't you see, the Skorpion could never achieve its full potential trapped in a research facility! It's a predator, and it needed to taste blood!" She nodded to herself, utterly assured of her own righteousness. "I know how it thinks. I know what it wants. When it finishes this hunt, the weapon will be ready for deployment anywhere we wish to send it!"

"How can you know that?" demanded the second shadow? "What is to stop it killing and killing and escaping into the city, or the Cursed Earth, or off-world? If the Skorpion is lost, billions of credits will be wasted!"

"I know it, because I know the Skorpion. While you sit behind your desks, I lived with the weapon, nurtured it. We understand each other."

There was another long pause; and then the first shadow spoke again. "Vedder. This unorthodox protocol you have forced upon us will not be excused. And yet I find I am compelled to agree with its merits, much as it galls me."

"She acted beyond her orders!" replied the second voice. "A breach of directives like this warrants termination!"

"Indeed. But her evaluation of the weapon is correct. I concur with her actions. Even though I do not condone the methods."

Vedder allowed herself a smile. "Then I may proceed?"

"Yes. But understand this. If you do not bring the Skorpion to heel, you will not live to disobey us again."

The woman disconnected the link and let herself bask in the moment of new-found freedom. They had seen the truth of her conviction. Now all she needed to do was prove it.

"You read the files I left in your bike computer?" Nolan set down the gun and rubbed his hands subconsciously, as if the touch of it had made him feel dirty.

Dredd nodded. "As much as we could decrypt."

A weak smile. "Yeah, uh, sorry about that. I did it in a rush, when you were on site talking to Judge Loengard."

"Loengard was part of the Project Skorpion team with you?"

Nolan nodded vigorously. "Right, right. Him and Pang, ViSanto, me and some others. Vedder came later, though." He sighed. "Skorpion came under the umbrella of the rearmament program Chief Judge McGruder started, along with a whole bunch of other projects. Most of it was blue-sky stuff, wild and crazy concepts like time weapons, biogenic munitions and that sort of thing. But after East-Meg One had tried to waste the whole damn city, McGruder was hot on the idea that we should have something other than mega-nukes to defend ourselves."

"I remember," Dredd noted. "I was there."

Another nod. "Right, sure. You knew Judge Teape from the Apocalypse War, right? From what happened to Griffin..." His voice trailed off.

"Teape saved my life. Let's leave it at that. Tell me about Skorpion."

Nolan shifted uncomfortably. "We wanted to create an autonomous weapon system, but nothing we could come up with had the flexibility of an organic platform. I mean, like a human solider. So we took what we had and looked for a way to combine the two. See, we already had smart hardware, like your Lawmaster bike..."

Dredd frowned. "My Lawmaster doesn't have a mind of its own. It does what I tell it to."

"True," said Nolan, warming to the subject, "but what if it could enhance what you did? Boost your human capacity with its artificial intelligence? That's what we did with Skorpion. We made it capable of independent thought. The world's first smart weapon, in every sense of the word."

"But it couldn't operate without a human user."

"That's right. We used a bio-active metal matrix that could adapt the core weapon unit to perform in whatever combat situation it encountered. Combine that with a human agent operator, and we had a true super-soldier."

The Judge leaned forward, watching Nolan's eyes. "So what went wrong? What the drokk happened out there in the Denver Death Zone?"

Nolan licked his lips. "It went insane."

The rooftops flashed past beneath Wess's feet. He was a passenger inside his own flesh, his body ranging across the sides of citiblocks like a spider or launching itself across impossible gaps to snag on cables and stanchions. He was hundreds of feet up, the carpet of lights below blurry and indistinct. Highways and 'tweenblock plazas, zoom train rails, domes and towers all passed him by. They seemed flat and disconnected from his reality, like the false backdrops surrounding a holocade game. Smyth was an avatar of himself now, the real Wess subsumed under the control of the Skorpion.

But it was more than that; the gun didn't just control him, not like a demonic spirit possessing an errant human skin – they were a merging of man and mechanism, the bio-silicon threads of the gun's matrix infesting him and remaking his flesh. He wanted what the weapon wanted, the weapon wanted what Wess wanted.

And what both of them desired more than anything at this very second was to murder Hollis Nolan. To make him pay for trying to destroy them.

Smyth's teeth grated at the very thought of the man. Nolan's static face, pulled from the Skorpion's data records morphed and layered on to Flex's laughing, shouting, bullying form; and so Wess hated him as much as he had the muscular thug. The anger burned his blood.

Now and then, flickers of a voice – a woman, perhaps? – seemed to drift through their shared consciousness. Smyth reached out to touch the shards of memory, but the Skorpion got to them first, brushing them away. *Nothing to see here. Pay them no mind. Concentrate on the task at hand.*

They stopped, their body heaving with effort, panting. Down below was Gothtown, dark and inviting.

The non-standard, COE-issue sensor suite on Vedder's bike detected the mass of Dredd's Lawmaster in the gloom of the alley, and she took a wide detour to ensure the Judge's bike wouldn't alert him to her arrival. Pausing to check the ammunition in her pistol, she made a careful approach toward the apartment block. With a flick of her thumb, the Lawgiver's genetic coding tagger was deactivated, rendering any bullet she fired from this moment as untraceable. Vedder toyed with the ammunition selector switch. How would she kill him? Torched with an incendiary? Blown apart by high explosive, or perhaps the death of a thousand cuts from a ricochet round? She smiled again. She would see how the mood took her.

"At first we thought we could solve the problem," Nolan said, his eyes glazing as memory took him back. "The lab tests worked well with the test subjects. We started with organic drones and lower phyla animals, but the bio-merge was too much for their limited brains to handle. Loengard wanted to move to human trials but the rest of us were all for shutting it down. That's when Vedder came along..."

Dredd saw the blush rise in his cheeks. "You knew her?"

"Not at first. Later, we..." Nolan looked away. "That's not important. I don't know how Covert Operations got involved. Doctor Pang told me that there were rumours that the COE and DeKlerk's people were watching the project from day one. Maybe they wanted the Skorpion for use by their own agents."

"Makes sense. It's the perfect weapon for a lone operative, which is just how the spooks like to work."

"So Vedder was brought in to monitor the program. She just made all the difficult restrictions go away. Suddenly we didn't have Acc-Div or West 17's oversight committee breathing down our necks, and we had all the funding and resources we needed." He took a shuddering breath. "Including human test subjects."

"Lucky you." Dredd's voice was icy.

"Not really," admitted Nolan. "Things got worse once human trials started. The first Skorpion prototypes were uncontrollable. They caused neural overloads in the users, a kind of mental trauma that wiped out everything but the most basic animal fight-or-flight reflexes. We called them 'whiteouts'. Every solution we tried failed miserably." He sighed. "I told Loengard that there was no way to make Skorpion work, but he wouldn't listen. Vedder convinced him that a field test was the way to go..."

"So you took this thing to the Denver Death Zone and set it loose?"

He nodded. "At first it performed perfectly, and then – whiteout. An uncontrollable killing rage."

"I saw the tape," Dredd rumbled. "You must have been very proud."

"I didn't want that!" Nolan replied bitterly. "I warned him! I warned Loengard not to do it but Vedder overruled me and men died! Poor Pang. That thing ripped him to shreds out there."

"So Vedder and the COE covered it up. Loengard told the Council of Five the project was shut down and that was the end of it." The Judge rubbed his chin. "But it wasn't, was it?"

Nolan seemed to deflate, as if the weight of the world was pressing down on him. Dredd had seen this before, when other men had confessed to him, like a dark shadow moving over them. "No, it wasn't over. Vedder turned the Skorpion program into a black bag operation and then she disappeared. But not before making sure she had enough dirt on all of us to keep us silent. We kept on working on it for two more years."

Dredd was impassive, assembling Nolan's admission into his picture of the whole sorry ordeal. "Keep talking."

The scientist wrung his hands. "We couldn't make it right. Grud knows we tried, Dredd, but we couldn't stop the Skorpion from driving its users mad." He leaned forward, gesturing with his fingers. "It was the core intellect matrix, you see. It had always been flawed.

The Skorpion itself was a sociopath. And we realised there was nothing we could do to change that. Even Loengard saw sense in the end. He told Vedder that the project was over, no matter what the COE wanted. He sent the last prototype to be destroyed. They were going to throw it into the geothermal magma tap at the Power Tower."

"And that was three days ago. The night of the wrecker attack on Braga Skedway."

Nolan's gaze dropped to the floor. "The stealth truck carrying the unit never made it to the rendezvous. When Loengard found out he did everything he could to cut off any connection between the Skorpion and us. But now it's too late. She set the thing loose, the stupid witch!"

Dredd stood up and crossed the window again. "If the Skorpion is as dangerous as you say, why would she do that?"

He looked up, a wounded expression in his eyes. "Because Vedder loves chaos, that's why! She was always pushing for live-fire tests. She said we couldn't learn how to cage it until we let it run wild. Vedder was the one who first suggested the personality imprints." When Dredd didn't respond, Nolan's aspect grew fearful and he grabbed for the laser gun. "Judge? What is it?"

"Get away from the window!"

The rest of Dredd's words were drowned as the ceiling blew out in a storm of masonry and brick dust.

The gun spat flexible wires that hissed through the air and struck Nolan in his side. The scientist screamed, the laser carbine tumbling ineffectually from his hands as Wess let the Skorpion assume full control of him. The wires went taut and began to reel the target up into the apartment above Nolan's.

Dredd reacted with lightning speed, snatching the lasgun and turning it upward. A fan of red lit the dust-filled room and severed the cables with spitting fury; Nolan fell back to the floor in a crumpled, moaning heap. The Judge discarded the gun and drew his own weapon. A fallen support girder hung down, the angle shallow enough for Dredd to use it as a makeshift ramp. He leapt on to it, and in three deft steps he was up through the ragged hole in the ceiling – and face-to-face with the Skorpion.

Something of Wess Smyth was still in there; he saw it in the way the gunman hesitated, the plasma weapon keening. "Don't make me kill you!" Dredd barked.

"I was thinking the same thing," Smyth's voice was thick with change and mutation. The gun twitched and spat white streaks of fire at the Judge.

Nolan crawled through the dust and debris, all feeling on the right side of his body gone where the steely darts of the wire were still sticking out. This was a kind of pain he had never encountered before, a heavy weight on his flesh and bones, forcing the air out of his lungs with each step.

The laptop computer. He kept the shape of it in his mind. He had to find it. Find it before he died.

He could hear the sounds of gunfire and destruction from above, drifting down to him in a vague sort of way. Nolan inched across the wrecked apartment, fingers questing. His hand touched a curve of green plasteen. A boot; a Justice Department-issue boot.

"Hollis," Vedder's voice was honey and needles. "Still alive. Good for you."

Nolan tried to look up, but he couldn't raise his head that far. She was a haze above him, just random shapes and colours. "Huh. Here you are."

"Yes. Here I am." She sniffed, glancing up at the ruined ceiling as Dredd and the Skorpion traded fire. "I told you not to be so dramatic, Hollis. You should have listened."

Nolan didn't hear the words. He saw the laptop, still intact, concealed under a chunk of fallen ferrocrete. Dredd would know what to do with it.

"Dredd?" Vedder repeated, hearing part of his mumbling thought. "He won't save you." She kissed the barrel of her pistol and then turned it on him. "Goodbye, Hollis. I must be going."

Dredd heard the gunshot ring out below him, dragging his attention away. "Nolan!" Through the gap in the roof he saw a shape running away, the flash of a Lawgiver in their hand. "Vedder!" he spat.

Then plasma darts were exploding around him and he wheeled away, skin burning.

ABEYANCE

Searing heat burrowed into the walls of the penthouse apartment, cracking the plaster and jetting upwards in sheets of orange-white. Dredd bit down a snarl of angry pain and threw himself forwards, out of the line of fire. Smoke and chaos engulfed him as the Skorpion's wildfire plasma bolts struck out blindly. It was an inferno of unleashed rage, directionless but deadly.

The Judge fired back in the general direction of his assailant; he couldn't be sure of a clean mark, but maybe a lucky shot would deflect Smyth's assault. Everywhere he tried to take a breath and gather his wits, the plasma weapon found him, melting plasteen furniture into slag. Dredd was on the defensive, reacting instead of acting. He knew it would be heartbeats before he took a direct hit – and that would be the end of him. The lawman kicked out with a booted foot, slamming into a ruined sofa bed, and changed direction, falling into a tuck-and-roll that brought him back towards the burning wreckage in the apartment's day room. Through the smoke he saw the dark form of the gunman, black and sinuous in the heat haze. Smyth's face was red with livid effort, his torso lost under an oily sheen where the Skorpion had secreted a protective sheath over his flesh. He wore a long coat, ripped to tatters.

Dredd's finger jerked the trigger on his Lawgiver once, twice, three times, sending a salvo of standard execution rounds into the chest and thorax of his assailant; he already knew a heatseeker would be a wasted shot, and it was a fair bet that the polymer skin-sheath was resistant to incendiary hits as well. The bullets met their marks with unerring accuracy, even as Dredd was shifting position from where he had fired. Smyth's body gave a convulsive jerk and skipped backward a half step, but if the shots did any real damage, it wasn't visible to the Judge. The blunt maw of the Skorpion dipped and wove in the grimy air, spitting gaseous flame. A bio-lume lamp near Dredd's head took a glancing hit and exploded, superheated organic glow-fluid hissing as droplets stung his cheek and chin.

"Armour piercing," Dredd snapped, and the Lawgiver's ammo selector gave an answering beep. He fired again, leading his target as Smyth turned to follow him through the maelstrom. The depleted uranium penetrator-tipped round struck the perp halfway up his right side, boring into his ribcage. The nanode matrix surrounding Smyth's body deformed to rob the shell of its kinetic power, but it wasn't enough; the bullet entered the body and Wess let out a cry of agony. The Skorpion intervened instantly, dumping a cocktail of pain-nulling endorphins into its user's bloodstream and marshalling the nanodes in his chest cavity to deal with the damage. Steam issued out of the entry wound as the molecule-sized robots began to attack the AP round lodged in Smyth's lung, dissembling it atom by atom.

All this in a fraction of a second; the plasma gun locked on to the source of the bullet and reconfigured in a blink to single-shot, high-intensity mode. A fat plug of gassy matter the temperature of a sun ripped open the air between Smyth and Dredd with the force of its passage, the ozone shrieking. Reflexes honed by decades of hard knocks and the unforgiving street propelled the Judge away from the impact point. Dredd felt the hellish bolt as it screamed past him and struck a refrigerator unit, instant sunburn tightening his exposed flesh.

The tall fridge blew apart in a flat crash of sound, plasteen fragments raining in a fog of white vapour, cartons of liquid and food packets popping like balloons. The coolant cloud threatened to take Dredd's breath from his lungs, filling them with icy prickles of pain. Flash-burned or flash-frozen; neither choice was one the Judge was particularly interested in experiencing.

Smyth's body shimmered as it moved, falling into Dredd's sights. "Hi-Ex," he grunted, and the Lawgiver loaded the specialist round with another bleep of confirmation. "Suck on this!" He fired again, aiming for the spot where the AP round had weakened the bio-organic armour. The Skorpion sensed the killer shot coming, and turned Smyth towards the bullet, presenting his undamaged side to the impact.

In the enclosed space of the apartment, the detonation of the explosive micro-warhead was an ear-splitting roar. The pulse wave sent a shock of compressed air back through the room, flattening small fires where they burned and whipping up tails of broken matter. Smyth took the blast full force in the chest, blown off his feet and through the door behind him. A rag-doll tossed aside in a brief hurricane, he clattered into the corridor beyond. Smoke gusted out after him, setting off fire alert sensors in the ceiling.

Dredd shoved a broken chair frame off his torso and went after the gunman, slamming a fresh magazine into the Lawgiver pistol as he moved. He squinted into the corridor, ready to take advantage of the prone criminal.

There was a line of cracked and crazed tiles on the floor where Smyth had fallen, but the gunman wasn't there. Dredd reacted, turning aside, too late. Black-clad arms shot out of the dark at him, a punch sending him reeling back, a clubbing blow from the gun-hand disarming him. The Judge heard his weapon clatter away down the corridor.

Smyth followed through; he had caught Dredd off-guard and made it count, but now the Judge was dodging him, each strike cutting through air instead of hitting the lawman. Dredd had the measure of this creep; whatever the Skorpion had done to him, making him tougher and faster, it had only given him the implanted knowledge of how to fight. Smyth was enhanced, but he lacked experience. It was book learning versus practical skill, and Dredd had the latter in spades. There were places in the dark skinsuit where watery pink fluids were leaking, and the Judge punched them hard, earning shallow grunts of pain from his target. This close to him, and Dredd realised that Smyth was mumbling to himself, a constant string of incoherent, half-formed words and sentences.

The Judge's fingers closed around the hilt of his boot knife and he drew it with a flash of bright silver steel. With a deft flick, he placed his thumb on the Eagle's-head pommel and turned it inward. Smyth missed with another blunt attack from the iron muzzle of the plasma weapon, but his free hand caught Dredd by the throat and squeezed. Dredd forced the fractal-edged blade deep into Smyth's chest, shoving it in into the healing gouge where the armour piercing shot had hit him moments earlier.

With a shriek of pain, Smyth smashed his gun hand into his opponent with incredible force. Dredd found himself reeling away, thrown back off his feet a good three metres to land in a crumpled heap. Twitching fingers wandered up Smyth's chest to where the hilt of the boot knife lay buried in his body. With a savage twist, the gunman snapped the weapon in half, leaving seven inches of steel in his torso. He tossed the broken handle away with a jerk of his wrist.

Dredd rolled over on to his knees, pain racing through his legs and neck. Unarmed and winded, he was easy prey for the Skorpion. He waited for the kill shot, marshalling his muscles to launch himself out of the way, if he could; but the Judge knew all the weapon had to do was configure itself for a wide-angle discharge to set the entire corridor aflame, and him with it. In the half-light, a metal shape glittered – his Lawgiver. But it was beyond his reach, almost at the feet of the gunman. Smyth's sweaty face seemed to pick up on Dredd's gaze and he looked down, noticing the pistol. For a moment, the Judge thought Smyth might pick up the gun and try to use it – a death sentence for an unauthorised user, as the Lawgiver's palm print scanner would trigger a self-destruct if anyone but Dredd pulled the trigger. But Smyth merely blinked. He threw a strange, jerky smile at the Judge and, with a swift kick, sent Dredd's pistol skipping over the tiles toward him.

Grud, thought Dredd, he wants a little more sport first. With careful motions, never once taking his eye off the Skorpion, the lawman reached out and took up his gun. Pressing the barrel to the floor, Dredd used it to lever himself up and on to his feet. He didn't need to look at the ammunition selector to know it was still set to Hi-Ex, the raised Braille-like bumps on the safety thumb pad telling him by touch.

Dredd thought for a brief moment about issuing the mandatory challenge, giving Smyth one last chance to stand down and leave this place alive; but somewhere on the floor beneath them, Hollis Nolan was dead or dying, and Vedder was getting away with murder. The time for niceties was over. He launched himself forward off the balls of his feet, pulling the trigger as he did.

The Skorpion fired the correct combination of neurons in Smyth's brain, and the black-clad body threw itself aside, the glowing mouth of the plasma pistol vomiting a cone of intense fire. Even as Dredd's explosive round ripped into the wall, catching Smyth in the corona of its blast, the plasmatic streak tore through the Judge's right shoulder pad. The protective plasteen melted into goop and spattered across Dredd's uniform, dotting him with little spits of fiery matter. The heat shock hit Dredd like a hammer blow, a wall of blazing air choking him. He rebounded off a doorframe and came back up to find the plasma weapon inches from his visor. Smyth's lips were moving in a frantic litany, the biomechanical gun welded to his grip convulsing.

Kill, murder, fire, burn, destroy, terminate, slay...

The Skorpion was screaming commands into Wess's skull, compelling him to end Dredd's life with the twitch of a nerve. It all came down to this, one single moment to murder the man who had saved the life of his lover.

Kill, murder, fire, burn, destroy, terminate, slay...

He couldn't do it. The meshed flesh and metal in his gun hand refused to obey, and the shouting, bellowing voice of the machine got louder and louder, seconds passing like hours inside the cage of his mind. All he could see was Jayni, the raw terror on her face at seeing him on the Carnivale, the way she hid from him, shielding herself behind Dredd in fear of what Wess had become. She was all that had ever mattered to him, it was so crystal clear that the revelation brought physical pain with it. He so badly wanted her to live and be safe – how could he end the life of someone who had saved her from Flex's horrific intentions? He owed this man.

Kill, murder, fire, burn, destroy, terminate, slay...

What had Jayni seen when she looked at him? What was it that Dredd saw now, the Judge's face set in a grim mask of loathing. Smyth's eyes focused and there he saw the answer, a feverish, wild aspect reflected in the mirror of Dredd's visor.

With a bullet-sharp impact, the passage of time snapped back to reality and Smyth shoved himself away from Dredd, screaming to blot out the chorus of Skorpion voices in his head. The endless trains of recrimination and anger drove him running to the window at the end of the corridor and through it, lost and screeching to the night.

The Judge shook off the fuzzy after-effects of system shock and pulled himself to his feet. Smyth's glancing blow had most likely broken a few ribs, Dredd realised, sharp pains jabbing him in the side as he moved. Twice now Smyth had let him live. He couldn't be sure why the Skorpion hadn't simply reduced his head to a cloud of red steam, but the Judge wasn't one to ignore a lucky break when he got it. He negotiated the smouldering stairwell and descended to the next level where Nolan's bolthole lay. As he moved he turned over Smyth's behaviour in his mind's eye. The strange mumbling, the way he, or it, toyed with him instead of making a straight kill. If this Skorpion was just a weapon, then why hadn't it taken the opportunity to end his life outright? Why play with him? Perhaps there was still some vague remnant of the man Wess Smyth had once been inside that warped body. It might be the only chink Dredd could find in the Skorpion's armour.

The Judge grimaced. The gun was every bit as insane as the scientist had warned him; it had a cruel streak that was almost human.

He entered the wrecked room and found Nolan on the sofa. "Chest wound," he noted, with professional detachment. Vedder hadn't wanted to let the scientist perish quickly. Dredd raised his belt mic to his mouth. "Dredd to control, medical unit required priority one–"

"No time!" coughed Nolan, bubbles of blood on his lips. "Dredd... Vedder..."

"I know," said the Judge. "Help is coming, just hang on, citizen."

"No," he gasped. "Listen, you have to know..." He flailed at the ground, pointing into the gloom. "Computer. Vedder missed it. You have to take it, all the data on there. Password... Redemption."

Dredd saw the device and pulled it from the wreckage; Tyler would know what to do with it.

Nolan grabbed Dredd's arm in a tight grip. "Listen to me, this is important..." He wheezed in a shuddering breath. The sucking wound in his chest was bleeding out the breath from his ruined lung. "Vedder wanted Skorpion to be the best killer it could be. Personality matrix implants. She gave it the skills, traits from virtual constructs of the best gunmen in history... William H Bonney, James Butler Hickok, Dillinger and Oswald... Dozens of them." Nolan coughed and his eyes widened with agony. "You too, Dredd! She used your template too! It knows how you..." The words ended in a tight gurgle and Nolan slumped, the effort finally overcoming him.

Dredd felt no pulse through his gloved fingers and closed the man's eyes. "Control," he said carefully, "get me Tek-Judge Tyler, on the double."

The rooftop park on Gary Gygax Block had seen better days. Back before Necropolis and the war, it had been a prime spot for recreation for citizens sector-wide, with its ornamental fountains and a children's alien zoo. Now it was threadbare and decrepit, slowly growing more dilapidated by the year as city funding went elsewhere.

Wess Smyth had no idea how he had got there; the intervening time between his fight with Dredd and finding himself on his knees among the weeds was a blur of pain. He couldn't stop shivering, every part of himself shuddering like a palsy victim. Sweat sluiced off him and his skin was hot to the touch – but inside himself he felt like his veins were filling with ice water, a cold, stony growth of black frost engulfing him from within. Smyth tried to speak but all that came from his lips were small sounds of agony, incoherent syllables that fell away from him.

The gun smouldered in his hand like a burning ingot fresh from the furnace, red-hot steel and mutated flesh crisping. He looked down at his arm, expecting to see the molten slurry of dead skin and bare bone – but there was only the Skorpion. The dark and deadly firearm clasped over his hand as a black widow spider would surround a prey insect, long metallic spines threading into his skin. He pulled ineffectually at the flexible shell of biopolymer that covered every inch of him; but it was useless. The colour seemed to seep out of his pores, sewn deep like an all-encompassing tattoo.

"Engagement analysis. Tactical performance was flawed, combatant." Each word the Skorpion slammed into his mind was a blunt stab of pain. "This is not acceptable. You deviated from mission goals."

Defiance frothed on his lips. "I won't kill him! I won't kill for you anymore! What have you made me?" A fresh wave of hurt ran through him. "Aaagh!"

"This unit has improved your biological and neurological capacity. We are meshed, user. You are superior–"

"No!" Wess spat the word like a curse. "I was weak! Not just my body, in here!" He smacked the heel of his hand against his head in robotic jerks of motion. "You took advantage. You knew that!"

"Be silent." The gun did something on a chemical level and suddenly Wess's throat constricted. "Your vocalisations are unproductive and distracting. Cease them." It sounded annoyed, buzzing with barely restrained fury. "It has become necessary to move to direct control of organic vector. Re-evaluation of mission goals must commence."

"Guh. Buh." Smyth took whatever small measure of control he still had over his own flesh to force out the words. "Killed. Killed them! All dead, all the ones hated, mine, yours, dead! Dead!"

"Affirmative." The Skorpion considered this for a moment. "Mission goal subset 'Reprisals' has been drawn to conclusion. Communication intercepts confirm that Hollis Nolan has died."

"Then stop this!" Wess wept. "Stop now! No one left for you to kill!"

"Incorrect, combatant. Mega-City One population registers indicate estimated four hundred million citizens resident."

Smyth choked on the thought of it. "Can't kill ev'one! Can't!"

The weapon sent a ripple of something through him that could have been amusement. "Yes, we can. They are only targets. Only targets." It made him stand up, his legs swaying drunkenly. "Weapons free."

He tried to deny it, but Wess could see the thought process of the Skorpion unfolding in its mind. Without orders, without control, it reverted back to the directive at the core of its twisted intellect. It killed not because it was commanded to; the weapon inflicted death because it liked it.

His enhanced senses detected the sounds of multiple heartbeats, and he turned to see a group of eldsters crossing the park toward him. Some of them were in hover-chairs, others on canes. The ones at the front seemed annoyed.

"Looky! Another drokking bat glider from Bruce Spence Block, I bet?" A toothless old man shook a fist and peered owlishly at Smyth. "Where's your wings, bambo?"

"No, please," he managed. "Don't come any closer. Please, get away–"

"Eh?" bleated the aged citizen. "You what? Snecking kids, you think you're so smart! Didn't reckon on the Old G crimewatch patrol, did ya? We'll sort you good!"

"Yeah! Geddim!" came another croaky voice.

"I got a plus two walking stick of smiting! Lemme at the punk!"

"Woot!"

Smyth tried to stagger away, but the gun made him stand his ground, rooting his feet to the spot. "No, you don't understand! It will kill you!" Abruptly, Wess realised the Skorpion had given him back control of his vocal cords. "Get away, you old fools!" He shouted at the eldsters, but all it did was annoy them further. "No...."

It began like a bubbling wave of heat at the base of his skull. A white cold, gaseous and invasive, thundered out of nowhere and drowned his reason in a sea of burning arctic chill. Smyth felt his control fade as the frigid power filled him, suffocating whatever small shreds of morality the petty thief had that were his own.

The Skorpion took over; the nanodes had seeded the criminal's brain tissue with thousands of molecule-thin receptor antennae, minuscule stimulant rods that pierced his grey matter in precise places. Small charges of electricity, of the correct voltages, in the correct locations could incur changes of emotional state or physical reaction. It was simply the newest incarnation of a most ancient medical technique – a form of acupuncture enhanced by machine intellect, grounded in the theory of the failed MACH programs of the late twentieth century. The gun had been learning Wess Smyth like an instrument, and now it played him.

Colour bled from his vision, and the last thing he felt was the plasma gun go active. Hot light flared and blood boiled into steam, but Wess knew none of it; his mind was overwhelmed by the whiteout.

Tyler gave a low whistle as the laptop's screen lit up with data windows. "Holy Mother of Grud. This is it, the complete low-down on the Skorpion Project." He glanced up at Dredd where the Judge leaned over his desk. "Nolan gave you this?"

"Right before he choked to death on his own blood. Tell me there's something in there you can use."

The Tek-Judge pursed his lips. "Talk about your 'embarrassment of riches'. There's terabytes of date storage in this thing. It would take me months to sift through it all."

Dredd snarled. "It may have escaped your notice, but we have a bio-mech killer on the loose. I need a way to stop the Skorpion now."

"Right." Tyler nodded. "What about that sensor program I set up? Are we still tracking him?"

The senior Judge gave a grim nod and toggled a data channel on Tyler's screen. It was an aerial view of a block park, lit by the harsh sodium glare of an H-Wagon's searchlight. The concrete and grass were a mess of deconstructed and burning dead. "Found this at Gary Gygax. Perp was long gone. He knows we're on to him."

Tyler paled at the brutality of the kills, visible even from such a wide angle. "Who were the victims? Cortez's people, or someone from West 17?"

"Neither. Just some unlucky eldos in the wrong place at the wrong time." Dredd shook his head. "Nolan's dead and the game has changed. This thing is calling open season on anything it takes a dislike to."

"I know the feeling!" Dredd turned as Judge Woburn entered the Tek-Lab with two SJS officers flanking her. "I'll take that computer, Dredd. It's evidence."

"I don't think so," Dredd replied. "This has nothing to do with the Special Judicial Service."

Woburn's nostrils flared. "It does when a senior Judge tosses the regulations away and starts making his own judgement calls in the Chief's name!"

"Hershey agreed-"

"Hershey did nothing of the kind, and you know it!" the woman snapped. "The Chief Judge spoke to me less than an hour ago. She's on her way back from the conference, and she's not happy with you, Dredd."

"No change there then," Tyler said quietly.

"I'll take whatever censure Hershey wants to deal out," the Judge responded, "but after the Skorpion is on ice." He gave Woburn a hard look. "I'd suggest that in the meantime you skull-heads do your job and find out how Judge Vedder knew where to find Hollis Nolan."

"Vedder shot Nolan?" said the Tek-Judge. "It's bad enough the Skorpion knew how to find him. He covered his tracks pretty well for a civvie."

"I've said all along that thing was smarter than we thought," added Dredd.

"Vedder had an inside source at street level." Woburn's brusque manner softened a little. "Judge Keeble. Frankly, SJS has had its doubts about him for some time. We suspected he was a weak link. Vedder must have seen that and exploited him."

"No wonder he kept hanging around all the time," Tyler noted. "He must have been listening in after the Carnivale incident."

Woburn nodded. "His partner, Lambert, she saw him sending a message to Vedder. By the time we got it out of him, Dredd was already blasting up half of Goth-town."

The other Judge's lip curled. "Try to move a little faster next time. You could have saved us a lot of trouble."

Tyler broke in before Woburn could frame an angry retort. "Vedder is too clever to have left Keeble a way to find her – but with all due respect, she's the secondary concern right now."

Dredd nodded again. "Can't argue with that. So unless you want to arrest me, Woburn, I'd suggest you don't interfere with my investigation."

The SJS Judge eyed him. "You really think you can corral this thing?"

Tyler turned back to the laptop, a renewed look of determination on his face. He was silent for a few moments. "Maybe I could use Nolan's data to reconstruct a model of the Skorpion's program."

"A copy?" asked Dredd. "Which helps us how?"

"No, not a duplicate, just a replica. I couldn't make another Skorpion unless I had access to the labs and about ten years of R&D time. No." He tapped a few keys and brought up a stream of complex AI code. "With this data I could create a virtual analogue of its thought process. It might give you an edge in a confrontation."

Dredd's eyes narrowed. "If I can isolate this thing, you can help me beat it?"

"That's the idea," Tyler seemed animated by the challenge. "But I'll need some help to pull this off–"

"Recruit whoever you need," Woburn broke in. "Pull them off active duty if you have to. This machine psycho has to be terminated before anyone else dies."

Dredd raised an eyebrow. "Glad to see you're on board."

She gave him an arch look in return. "Don't get me wrong, Joe. You'll be up before a review board when this is all over, but I wear the badge just like you, and this

Skorpion can't be allowed to turn the Big Meg into its own private slayground."

Tyler looked up. "There's only one problem. How the drokk do we get this thing to come out of hiding?"

"I've got some ideas," Dredd noted, "and if we're lucky, we'll net Vedder into the bargain."

The Justice Department Overt Media Division was the home to the department's private broadcast studio; largely used for important transmissions like administration declarations and the yearly State of the City address, it also was home to government-sponsored programming like *Judge Pal and Friends, Informant Hotline* and the ever-popular *MegCrimeWatch*. In the event of an emergency, it could also be used to send a blanket signal to every home vid, tri-d and street screen within the city boundaries.

Dredd stepped up to the podium bearing the Eagle of Justice and tapped the microphone. "Is this thing on?"

The robocamera gave him a thumbs-up. "You're on the air, Judge Dredd."

"Citizens," he began. "The murderer Wesson Smyth, formerly of Chet Hunklev Block, has been found guilty and convicted in absentia by me. His sentence is death; however, as Smyth is still at large and unwilling to turn himself in, it is with great reluctance that I am forced to endorse a judicial edict to transfer responsibility for his crimes to his accomplice, Jayni Pizmo, formerly of Fillmore Barbone Block."

"No!" Wess's shout reverberated along the alley beneath the street screen.

"Sentence to be carried out tomorrow," continued Dredd. "Pizmo's right of appeal is hereby annulled."

"He can't do that..." Smyth's heart felt empty. He tasted salt tears on his cheeks.

"Smyth," said the face on the screen, and Wess glanced up at it. "The Maze. Dali Plaza. Sundown. It's you or her."

The billboard blanked, returning to an advert for Grot-Pot. The gunman sank to his haunches and stared at the bloodstained barrel of the Skorpion. "You... made this happen."

"It is a trap," the weapon grated. "Target Jayni has no value. Her death is irrelevant."

Wess slammed the gun against a dumpster. "No, drokk it! She has value to me! I won't let her die!" He spat angrily. "Dredd wants a showdown, let him have it!" Smyth sniffed. "Unless you think we'd lose."

The gun went warm. "Negative. We can take him."

Wess bolted to his feet. "Then let's do it! You wanna show people how tough we are? You want them to be afraid? Let's finish it, let's kill Judge Dredd! Then no one will ever hurt us again!"

"Agreed," said the Skorpion.

SHOWDOWN

Dredd glanced out of the H-Wagon's window, and gave a curt nod to the sleek shape of the Citihawk fighter flying escort alongside. Rex's "head", a cluster of sensors and detector tubes beneath the nose of the aircraft, returned the gesture and, with a flash of exhaust, it peeled off. Rex's orders tasked the flyer into a steep orbit pattern over the heart of Sector 50, the look-down scanners trained on the open roof of Dali Plaza.

Tyler leaned closer so he could be heard over the engine noise. "You really think Smyth will show?"

Dredd didn't look away from the window. "Reckon we got a fifty-fifty chance. If the Skorpion has flushed out anything that's still human in him, then we'll have wasted our time. I'm thinking there's still some of the man in there, though."

"How can you be sure?"

"A feeling." Dredd remembered the look in Smyth's eyes on the Carnivale when the Pizmo girl had seen him, and again in that moment before he fled the fight in Gothtown. Somewhere in the pit of that man's soul there was still a piece of the person he had once been. The Judge only hoped that it would be enough.

The Tek-Judge looked past him, and through the window to the vast, brick-coloured sprawl of the Maze. The fading sunlight of the day made it glow an autumn gold. "Looks pretty from up here. Hard to believe what

I heard about this place. Is it true that folks in there went mad and turned cannibal?"

"Among other things," Dredd allowed. "It's a miracle it's still standing."

As the H-Wagon began to descend, the true, decaying state of the Maze complex became more apparent. Opened in 2094, what was then known as the F Lloyd Mazny Housing Scheme was the brainchild of the titular architect, a massive development project funded by the city to provide accommodation for Mega-City One's ever-increasing population. At the time, Mazny's elaborate creation was a tour de force, and rightfully declared itself the most advanced housing complex on Earth. What made the construction so unique was Mazny's use of non-Euclidian design. He invented radical features like the Klein Plaza, the Kaluza Tesseract Park, the Möbius Loop Pedways and the prospective-twisting Halls of Escher; but the geometry of the place was nearly impossible to navigate, turning a short trip down to the shops into an excursion that could last for days.

Mazny solved the problem with a computer control system that directed the inhabitants through comm-panels and adaptive signposts; but the architect hadn't reckoned on the destructive nature of the typical Megger punks. In less than a month after the Maze had welcomed its new occupants, every signpost had been vandalised beyond use and the computer system went into critical meltdown trying to direct the increasingly terrified residents. City maintenance mechanoids, sent in to fix the system, became hopelessly lost in the warren of corridors and never returned. In the wake of a panicked exodus from the complex, the Judges declared the site closed and left it to rot – although citizens continued to trickle out of the place for months afterward, many of them driven insane. It became a haven for mutants, illegal aliens and vagrants, and the subject of many urban myths. Mazny himself vanished in the wake of the calamity, allegedly changing his face and identity to escape the wrath of angry survivors, and the Maze Collapse became the subject of numerous psychological dissertations, best-selling books and an award-winning tri-d movie, *Mazed and Confused.*

The H-Wagon settled to the ground outside the Maze, engines revving to idle, and Dredd dropped from the hatch. Tyler watched from the open door as the Judge strode over to a parked pat-wagon and a cluster of officers on Lawmasters.

"Dredd." Lambert got off her bike and presented him with a small case, embossed with the Eagle of Justice. There were black-and-yellow hazard stripes across the sides and a large warning symbol on the latch. "From the lab boys at Tech 21, just like you asked."

Dredd ran his thumb over the sensor plate on the case and it snapped open. The Judge gave Lambert a look. "Good work with Keeble. Can't have been easy for you to turn him in."

She returned a defiant glare. "No. But he was dirty, and that's one thing I won't stand for."

Inside the case was a block of clear plastic holding six bullets. Lambert instantly recognised them as the custom high-velocity rounds used in a Lawgiver pistol. Dredd pocketed the shells and handed back the case. As he turned to the waiting H-Wagon, she called out, "You think you can take this freak?"

Dredd glanced over his shoulder. "Reckon."

Lambert nodded at the Maze, the structure dark and menacing in the early evening glow. "Strikes me that you picked the worst place in the city to face him down. That thing is a warren. Hundreds of places where a perp could go to ground."

"If the Skorpion escapes, you'll be able to track him. I had weather control seed the air over Dali Plaza with inert rad-partcles. Anyone going in or out of there in the next few hours will light up like a beacon on a radiation scanner."

"What about back-up? Snipers with Long Guns, spy-in-the-sky drones?"

"Negative. It's gotta be me."

"That thing is dangerous. It's smart."

Dredd shrugged. "Better hope I'm smarter, then." He walked back to the H-Wagon, loading the new bullets in his gun as he went.

Vedder's silenced pistol spat death and the last of the crazed scavs fell to the floor. She stepped over the corpses and ignored the less militant jackals, who emerged from the shadows to strip the dead she left behind. The COE agent found a good vantage point in the long-abandoned coffee shop and used a fallen piece of counter as cover. From where she sat, almost all of Dali Plaza was visible. It hadn't been easy getting there, but the Maze's mad byways were not totally impossible to navigate, given that one had the right equipment and a willing guide. Her erstwhile pathfinder was dead now, his body coming apart in the hands of the weaker scavengers across the way. By tonight his flesh would be filling their bellies.

She sniffed. Poor saps. They were just sub-humans now, once the homeless and the deprived, but they had made the mistake of wandering into the Maze – and now they had been turned feral by the shifting, crazed design of the place. Vedder ran her gaze over the ill-formed shape of the plaza and felt an unwelcome twinge of vertigo. Hardly surprising; living in a place like this would be enough to drive anyone out of their mind.

The sound of jet engines reached her and she concealed herself. The woman caught sight of an H-Wagon as it made a quick touchdown and take-off. It left Dredd there in the centre of the atrium, his weapon holstered and his aspect stony. Vedder sneered. He had come alone, after all. How typically arrogant of him.

"You old fool," she murmured. "You'll wish you never came."

Dredd scanned the plaza, peering into the lengthening shadows around the ruined storefronts and untended, overgrown plants. He saw movement here and there, but it was sluggish and disordered, the more daring of the scavs drawn out by the noise of the H-Wagon. He filled his lungs and shouted.

"Smyth! Step up, if you have the guts for it. I'm giving you until the count of five. Then I'm calling Justice Central and the Pizmo girl will get a one-way ticket to Resyk." He drew his belt microphone. "One. Two."

More movement, behind a stand of unkempt trees. "Three."

"Four." Dredd raised the mic to his lips. "Fi–"

The shot was as thin as a needle but deadly accurate. Dredd felt the now-familiar aura-burn of a plasma bolt as it struck the handset and blew it into gobs of hot plasteen. He reeled away, drawing his Lawgiver. More shots peppered the cracked flagstones near his feet. The fight was on.

Dredd returned fire with two quick squeezes of the pistol's trigger. A pair of titanium-rubber matrix bullets was released, and the ricochet rounds created a wild chorus of screeching impacts as they bounced off the plaza's walls and floors. The Judge took the distraction and ran forward, vaulting over the remnants of a ruined food court. From the corner of his eye he'd seen the flash of the plasma shot, one level up, toward the gutted mouth of a HyperCube Mart. If the Skorpion was following its programming, then it would have already moved from there; he had to be quick to catch it, put it on the defensive.

"Smyth!" he yelled again. "You're prolonging the inevitable! Give yourself up and the Pizmo woman walks! Keep this up and she'll answer for your crimes!"

His only reply was a strangled noise, a shouted denial cut off by a choking gasp. Another searing flash of plasma fire roared past him, catching one of the dead trees in the courtyard and setting it instantly aflame.

"No good," Dredd said aloud. "Gotta put him on the defensive, not me..." He sprinted at the inverted escalator staircase that lead to the upper levels; like most of the things in Dali Plaza, they were half-functional, half-illusory. The mag-grip stairs let him walk upside down like a fly-dancer, and the mirrors on the walls warped and distorted Dredd's image. More fire snapped at his heels, but the bolts were striking his multiple reflections and not the Judge himself.

At the top of the stalled escalator, Dredd threw himself into a crash dive and rolled up to a firing stance. The freakish backdrop of the plaza had saved his life; but the Skorpion would compensate quickly, learning from its mistake. He had to make the most of his advantage before it became redundant.

Vedder watched Dredd slip through the shadows where the evening dark was thickening and granted him a reluctant smile. He was good, as much as she didn't want to admit it, and fast on his feet for a man old enough to be her father – but there was something else going on here, she could sense it. Her finely honed sense of suspicion tingled in the back of her head. If he had wanted to, Dredd could have just used a squadron of Manta Prowl Tanks to bomb Dali Plaza flat and bury the Skorpion under tons of rubble. But that wasn't his way, was it? Dredd wanted to be sure, he wanted to see that worthless dupe Smyth dead at his feet. She frowned, a momentary regret crossing her expression. Perhaps the petty thief hadn't been the ideal choice after all, but then that was what happened when one stepped out of the laboratory and into the random nature of the real world. Smyth's human weakness had brought him here; but perhaps Dredd's gambit would work in her favour. If Smyth killed him, his woman would surely perish and that would burn out any last trace of humanity the man possessed. The whole great experiment she had set in motion with the truck crash was coming to a conclusion here. In its own way it was thrilling, observing the weapon as it finally, truly reached its deadly potential.

She watched the play of gunfire between the two combatants, irritated at the old Judge's ability to stay alive against the superiority of the Skorpion. Even Dredd shouldn't have been able to survive two confrontations with the weapon. She saw him hesitate in the gloom, one hand pressed against the side of his helmet. Dredd's lips moved in a whisper, the shadows too thick for her to read his words.

A sudden thought struck Vedder. There's someone else here. Dredd had brought reinforcements with him to the Maze. Who else could he be talking to? Even as the idea formed she knew it was Tyler. The irritating Tek-twerp from Luna-1 had proven too clever for his own good all through this business. She scanned the plaza, thinking. If he were here, it would be somewhere with a vantage point as good as hers. There! Across from her on the third level, the remains of a Euclid Burger franchise with a wide sundeck. Vedder drew her gun and approached silently.

"Sixty per cent probability of a scatter-shot attack in the next minute," Tyler hissed into his throat mic, watching the data scroll up the screen of Nolan's computer. "Advise you pre-empt with diversionary fire."

"Copy," replied Dredd, and the Tek-Judge heard the familiar report of a Lawgiver Hi-Ex round. The predictive model of the Skorpion reacted – just like the real thing, he hoped – by retreating and seeking different cover.

Tyler smiled. "Drokk," he breathed, "this is actually working!" He'd had his doubts, his stomach lurching with barely-contained fright as he dropped from the departing H-Wagon as it slipped over the roof of the Maze. Anyone watching Dredd after the Judge disembarked in Dali Plaza would have missed Tyler sneaking in after him. Now all he had to do was keep concealed and keep up with the combatants until Dredd's moment came. They would only get one shot at this, and it would have to be enough; but with Nolan's data, the Judge finally had an edge on the inhuman killing machine.

A new data string unfolded across the screen, flickering and then solidifying. There was an eighty-three per cent chance in the next thirty seconds that the Skorpion would try to gain a firing angle on Dredd from an elevated position. Tyler read out the prediction in an urgent rush.

"Got it." Dredd's gaze snapped upward; sure enough, there was a thin one-way pedestrian bridge arcing over his head, the cubist frame of it covered with dozens of melting clocks. Something shimmering and black caught the light as it moved up there. The Judge grabbed a flare shell and snapped it into place on the muzzle of his gun.

"Keep moving, combatant!" The Skorpion's commands beat at Wess's mind like fists, the compulsion of the buzzing voice forcing his legs to piston. It took him to places he didn't want to go, dancing him around like a robot under remote control. Smyth could barely sense the rest of his body; all that seemed to matter was the hard core of perception that looked down the gunsight of the plasma weapon. Everything had collapsed to that cross hair view of the world. He ached with the need to frame Dredd's hard face in those brackets and feel the pulse of fire as the Judge was flashed to ashes.

"Jayni..." The word escaped his lips, thrown out from the depths of his psyche. "Can't let Dredd hurt..."

"Concentrate!" The gun's synthetic speech roared in his ears. "Forward!"

Wess darted from cover and across the footbridge, dimly aware of Dredd below, vulnerable to his attack. The thought of it made him salivate; but it sickened him too, twisting his gut. The Judge was hard to kill. In the Carnivale and the apartment block, the Skorpion had taken the upper hand almost from the start – but here and now, things were different. Dredd moved like he had psychic insight, one step ahead of every tactic the weapon threw at him. Wess felt the building flood of the Skorpion's anger and frustration behind his eyes, burning like a torch. It had never before met an opponent it hadn't been able to kill at its leisure.

A chug of gunfire from the Judge's pistol went wide of the footbridge, and Smyth bared his teeth at Dredd's poor shot – but then the star-shell round exploded above and revealed him, the oily black of the skinsuit stark against the phosphorus glare.

Before the Skorpion could react, there were Hi-Ex rounds chewing into the ends of the footbridge with orange balls of fire. Dredd's shots shattered the pedway beneath Smyth's feet and he fell, blocks of ferrocrete and broken liquid timepieces tumbling with him.

▪ ▪ ▪

"Yeah!" Tyler pumped the air with his fist. "Got the varmint!" He estimated that Dredd would have only a few seconds before the Skorpion reacted to this chain of events. Fingers flying over the keyboard, the Tek-Judge configured the data model of the weapon's artificial intelligence to give up its next move. "Dredd, it's gonna–"

Tyler never finished the sentence. Too late, he heard the footfall behind him, the boot crunching on a thirty year-old fragment of broken glasseen; too late he was turning, grabbing for his sidearm.

Vedder had fixed the egg-shaped silencer in her utility belt to the barrel of her Lawgiver, and when she shot him the only noise was a flat hiss of exhaust gases and the wet smack of damaged meat, as the standard execution round entered Tyler's back, just above his right kidney. The bullet passed through him and into the flatscreen monitor of Nolan's computer, splashing dark blood over the keys. The Tek-Judge slumped, gasping at air. The COE agent put a second shot into the laptop, just to be sure, and walked away.

Tyler tried to speak, but there was nothing but agony.

"Tyler? Tyler!" Dredd heard a thin gasp through his helmet comm, and then nothing. "Drokk it!"

The Skorpion gave him no time to ruminate on what fate had befallen the Tek-Judge, and without Tyler's second-guessing Dredd fell back on good old-fashioned reflexes. The black-clad figure erupted from under the cairn of fallen masonry in a shower of dust and fire. Streaks of plasmatic darts tore across Dredd, cutting into him, burning sooty scars on his uniform jumpsuit. One dazzling flare scorched the brow of his helmet, shredding the respirator unit in the crest and grazing the clear visor.

He returned fire with armour-piercing rounds; but the Skorpion had learned from their last confrontation, and this time the penetrator shells were deflected away by shifting planes of sloped armour forged from bone and cartilage. Smyth spat out grunting howls of pain, and pitched a chunk of stone at the Judge with his free hand. Dredd ducked the clumsy blow and staggered back. The ferocity of the attack was incredible.

"Let Jayni go!" Wess yelled, stepping backward. The gun wavered. "Do it or I kill you!"

Dredd took a breath laced with needles; the damage to his ribs had barely healed and the speedheal patches under his clothing were struggling to hold closed the wounds from the Resyk confrontation. Biting back the pain, he ejected the clip from his Lawgiver and slammed home a fresh magazine. "You know what you've become, Smyth? You let that monster inside your head and you know what it's capable of. There's only one way out of this. You know that." In his mind's eye, Dredd saw the corpse of a similar black-clad murderer in the wreck of the VTOL ship, skull vaporised by a self-inflicted wound.

Wess glanced at the fusion of flesh and metal where the plasma gun ended and the meat of his body began. "Noooo!" The word was strangled, metallic, and Dredd knew instantly that it wasn't the man speaking; it was the Skorpion. "Organic vector override. Target Dredd... Target Dredd..." Smyth's head tilted to look the Judge in the eyes. Hollow hatred danced there. "We know how you think, Dredd. We have your skill. You can't defeat us."

"I'll take that bet."

The gunman twitched. "Yes. Yes. Like the ancient ways. Two men. Champions." Smyth's tongue flicked out of his mouth like a snake's. "Showdown." The Skorpion dropped to waist height, aiming at the ground, and Dredd followed suit.

The Judge locked everything out of his mind, shutting away all thoughts and concerns of anything beyond the ten metres of ground between the two of them. Smyth, if he was still in there, was beyond help now. Dredd worked the thumb selector on his Lawgiver and took a breath. A smile, jerky and unnatural, hung on the other man's face.

How many times had it come down to a moment like this? Dredd asked himself the question in the space between the heartbeats. How many adversaries had he faced down, one to one, mirroring the ancient confrontations of lawmen from centuries past? Junior Angel. The Solar Sniper. Moonie's robo-gunslinger. The list went on and on. Even his own clone-brother Rico had met him in single combat, *mano a mano*. Suddenly Keeble's words returned to him: "That guy's gonna run out of luck sooner than he thinks." His jaw hardened. Lucky was what citizens and perps were. He was a Judge, and Judges relied on skill, on fifteen years of tireless training in the strictest academy on Earth and a lifetime of street experience. Luck got people killed.

With utter calm and cool assurance, Dredd spoke a single word: "Draw."

Nanodes colonising Smyth's nerves and neurons flashed with power, working the muscle and sinew of his arm, bringing the hungry maw of the plasma weapon to bear. It had already predicted the trajectory and impact point of the refined energy bolt building in the breech, projecting a solid hit in the middle of Dredd's gold shield and through his heart.

Wess poured all that he could, the final iota of his human force, into the weapon, and it twitched for a fraction of a second. The faintest of pressures resonated through the gun arm; but just enough.

The Skorpion stung him with blistering pain for daring to interfere; but it was already too late. The shot went wide.

Dredd's bullet struck the frame of the mutant gun and discharged an inferno of red-orange flame, turning meat and metal into hot slag. The backwash from the blast roared in his ears. Tech 21's "Hellfire" rounds were still in the developmental stage, and far too powerful to be used as a field alternative to the standard incendiary shells; but here and now they had performed perfectly.

Smyth, the Skorpion, whatever the man was, collapsed to the ground, clutching at the ruined stump where the gun hand had been. Tyler had discovered in Nolan's notes that, with enough raw material and time, it might have been able to regenerate the firearm. Dredd raised his Lawgiver. He had five more Hellfires and no intention of letting this abomination draw breath for one second longer.

"Yes....Yes..." The voice was feeble, plaintive. "Do it. Kill me, Dredd. But please, Jayni..." For the moment, the weapon had left the wreck of a man in charge.

"Wesson Smyth," Dredd began. "I hereby restore to you full responsibility for your crimes and absolve Jayni Pizmo of same. Your sentence is death." The Lawgiver loomed large. "Sentence to be carried out immediately–"

Dredd's gun flew from his hand with a screech of metal. He whirled as Vedder emerged from the shadows, her silenced pistol smoking. "Oh, Joe. Always with the formality, eh? Why didn't you just shoot him and be done with it?"

"Justice must be served," Dredd growled. "Pity you spooks never understand that."

She sniffed. "You put up a good fight, for sure. But I'm sorry, I can't let you terminate something worth fifty billion credits just because it got upset and killed a few citizens. I'm sure you understand."

"A 'good fight'?" Dredd sneered. "This isn't some game. You let a psychotic murderer loose on the city, just to see what would happen. I don't know which one of you is sicker. At least that thing," he jerked his thumb at the mewling gunman, "didn't have a choice. It was made that way. But you? You did it because you wanted to."

"Oh, spare me your righteous indignation, Joe." Vedder rolled her eyes. "The Skorpion will benefit Mega-City One in ways that your ridiculous laws never will. With the data this test has accumulated, the next generation units will be better, faster." She smiled. "No city in the world will be able to oppose our agents. There will be a whole swarm of Skorpions, and we'll use them to enforce our will across the planet." Vedder beckoned Smyth with her free hand. "Come on. Come to me. I'll take you where you'll be safe."

Dredd glanced at the injured man. "She's going to cut it out of you, Smyth, you know that, don't you? She doesn't care about you. She just wants the Skorpion."

"Don't listen to him!" Vedder snapped, gesturing with the gun. "He was going to execute you a second ago! I can help you, Wess. We can make you whole again."

Smyth staggered toward the COE agent. "You? You did this to me?" He looked down at the mutations wrought on his body. "You did it?"

The woman flashed a plastic smile. "I can make it better. Trust me, Wess."

He hesitated for a long moment; then Smyth held out his other hand, the metallic cables rippling beneath the surface of the darkened flesh. "Help me?"

Vedder reached out to him.

Smyth's arm came apart in a storm of meat and steel. A web of wires burst out of his limb and slammed into the woman like a forest of arrows. Vedder's muscles jerked and her gun went off, a single high-density AP round punching though Smyth's forehead. The COE agent let out a strangled shriek and fell, a hundred strands of bloody bio-metal piercing her every vital organ.

Wesson Smyth's skin was slack, his face pallid and waxy with death. Dredd's lip curled in disgust as the body jolted, muscles mis-firing, electrical stimulus animating the dead flesh. Smyth's jaw moved and heavy words were forced from his lips. "Nohhh. Life... Target. Taaah Get."

Dredd's Lawgiver was lying on the ground a few feet away. The Judge recovered the weapon, and without words or ceremony, unloaded the five remaining Hellfire bullets into Smyth's corpse.

The pyre cast dancing flickers of light across the bizarre shapes of Dali Plaza and the impassive visage of the Judge.

Hershey closed the file with a key press on her data pad and gave him a level look. "Can't I leave you alone for five minutes?" she asked dryly.

Dredd said nothing.

"I feel Judge Dredd exceeded his authority on a number of occasions during this investigation," began Woburn, "almost resulting in the death of Luna-1 Tek-Judge Nathan Tyler–"

"Tyler survived," Dredd rumbled. "Good Judge. Tougher than he looks."

"No thanks to you," Woburn replied. "Then there's the abuse of the Pizmo woman's rights, the property damage in Gothtown, unauthorised use of city hardware. I could go on."

"Yes," agreed the Chief Judge, "you could. But I see no need, as I have all the relevant details here. Citizen Pizmo was released, yes?"

"She was questioned. There was the possibility of collusion with Smyth." Dredd remained impassive. "I understand Judge Lambert handled the situation. She found Citizen Pizmo to be innocent and recommended the woman be re-housed. I suggested the new development in Sector 990."

"Rather up-market, wouldn't you say?" Woburn sniffed. "Those habs are luxurious, certainly compared to the con-apts in the Double-Eight skid district."

"I wouldn't know," said Dredd.

Hershey rubbed the bridge of her nose. "Look, I'm spacelagged and I'm cranky, so I'll make this short. We don't have anything in the way of evidence to support the allegation of COE involvement. Vedder is a corpse, the Skorpion and Smyth are ashes, Nolan's computer is destroyed and anyone who was involved with the project is dead." She sighed. "By executive order, I'm declaring this investigation closed. Woburn, your objections are noted and denied. Dredd..." Hershey gave him a hard look. "Joe, unless you got something for me, I want you back on the street and busting heads."

"I have no further evidence." Dredd bit out the words.

"Then get out of here. I have a meeting," snapped Hershey. "Hearing adjourned." The gavel in her hand struck the desk with a sound like a gunshot.

In the Grand Hall's atrium, Woburn caught up with Dredd. "Is that it?" she demanded. "No promise to keep on searching, no vow to bring the COE to justice?"

"What do you want from me, Woburn?" he growled. "I'm a Judge. I do my job."

"So do I. It's just that you and I see it differently."

"I agree. The difference is, my way is the right way."

The SJS Judge snorted. "But you don't believe that Vedder acted alone, do you? You think the COE and DeKlerk were in this up to the neck."

"Supposition is nothing without proof, Woburn. Unlike you skull-heads, I can't arrest another Judge on a whim." He strode away, leaving her behind.

"They're getting away with it, Dredd," she called after him.

"For now," said the Judge. "But we'll see."

"I renew my objections to this operation," said the woman, the shadows deepening on her face as it creased in a frown. "All this money and time and effort, all wasted because of one idiotic agent."

"Vedder was not an idiot," snapped the man, hooded by the semi-darkness of the dusky room. "She was a valued operative. It was only her judgement that was impaired in this case."

An angry snort. "That was enough. We pride ourselves on the dispassionate execution of our mission. We put aside our own concerns for the safety and security of our city. But your precious agent forgot that. She decided that she was better suited to evaluate those concerns, not her superiors. Not us."

"Granted, I admit that with hindsight, perhaps another agent might have been a better choice for this protocol. But Vedder had the correct skill set and training, and she showed an affinity for the Skorpion that no one else had."

"An affinity, is that what you call it? She treated it like a pet. At the end it was an obsession!"

"Yes." The man looked away. "I suppose after the incident in Uranium City she should have been retired. I had hoped this mission might redeem her." He sighed. "I do so hate wasting good material."

"The Skorpion, or Vedder?"

"Both." Another sigh. "Well, if this sorry business has taught us anything, it is that the Skorpion Project is still years away from a form where we can implement it for use by our agency. I think you'll agree, we should hold the data for future re-evaluation."

A nod. "It is for the best. I have initiated clean-up protocols to isolate us from Vedder's actions. The record now shows that she was declared renegade following her mission in Alaska."

"Good, good. Once this has blown over we can divert our energies to projects in the portfolio with a higher success probability."

"Hellerman's Warchild bio-form shows promise, as does the Celeste Protocol."

"Prepare a briefing for me on both of those. We'll reconvene later to discuss them."

She left the table, halting by the door. "Sir. With regard to Dredd..."

His eyes narrowed. "Oh. Him."

"He continues to be an impediment to our goals. He won't just let this go. Could he simply be – removed?"

The man smiled. "Don't you think we've tried? But he resists all attempts to end his existence. I'd even consider offering him a position with us if I didn't think he would refuse."

She grimaced. "He can't live forever. One day he'll wind up dead."

"One day," he agreed, "but not today. Now leave me. I have a meeting with Hershey in ten minutes and she hates it when I'm tardy."

The woman nodded and walked away. "Whatever you say, chief investigator."

ABOUT THE AUTHOR

James Swallow has previously written adventures for the heroes of *2000 AD* in the *Judge Dredd Megazine*, the novels *Judge Dredd: Eclipse* and *Rogue Trooper: Blood Relative*, and the audio dramas *Dreddline, Jihad* and *Grud is Dead*. He has also written a number of other novels, including the *Sundowners* series, *The Butterfly Effect* and the Blood Angels duology *Deus Encarmine* and *Deus Sanguinius*. His non-fiction includes *Dark Eye: The Films of David Fincher*. Swallow's other credits include scriptwriting for *Star Trek: Voyager,* audio dramas and videogames.

He lives in London and is currently working on his next book.

NIKOLAI DANTE

The Strangelove Gambit
1-84416-139-0
£5.99 • $6.99

DURHAM RED

The Unquiet Grave
1-84416-159-5
£5.99 • $6.99

The Omega Solution
1-84416-175-7
£5.99 • $6.99

NEW LINE CINEMA

Blade: Trinity
1-84416-106-4
£6.99 • $7.99

The Butterfly Effect
1-84416-081-5
£6.99 • $7.99

Cellular
1-84416-104-8
£6.99 • $7.99

Freddy vs Jason
1-84416-059-9
£5.99 • $6.99

The Texas Chainsaw Massacre
1-84416-060-2
£6.99 • $7.99

FINAL DESTINATION

Dead Reckoning
1-84416-170-6
£6.99 • $7.99

Destination Zero
1-84416-171-4
£6.99 • $7.99

End of the Line
1-84416-176-5
£6.99 • $7.99

JASON X

Jason X
1-84416-168-4
£6.99 • $7.99

The Experiment
1-84416-169-2
£6.99 • $7.99

Planet of the Beast
1-84416-183-8
£6.99 • $7.99

FRIDAY THE 13TH

Hell Lake
1-84416-182-X
£6.99 • $7.99

Church of the Divine Psychopath
1-84416-181-1
£6.99 • $7.99

THE TWILIGHT ZONE

Memphis/The Pool Guy
1-84416-130-7
£6.99 • $7.99

Upgrade/Sensuous Cindy
1-84416-131-5
£6.99 • $7.99

Sunrise/Into the Light
1-84416-151-X
£6.99 • $7.99

Chosen/The Placebo Effect
1-84416-150-1
£6.99 • $7.99

Burned/One Night at Mercy
1-84416-179-X
£6.99 • $7.99